PUFFIN BOOKS

THE RUNAWAY SHOES

A Puffin Bedtime Story Chest

The Runaway Shoes is a true lucky dip of bedtime stories for all ages.

There are modern stories, such as 'Trouble in the Supermarket' and 'The Old Woman Who Lived in a Coca-Cola Can', alongside more classic tales of princes and princesses; there are stories of hedgehogs, goats and mice as well as tales of dragons and monsters; familiar figures such as *My Naughty Little Sister* appear alongside those not so familiar such as *The Harum-Scarum Boys*.

Contributors to this delightful collection include such well-known children's writers as Beverly Cleary, E. Nesbit, Arthur Ransome, Mary Norton, Dorothy Edwards and Leila Berg.

Delightfully illustrated by Glenys Ambrus and Caroline Sharpe, this book will provide hours of fun and amusement whether read alone or out loud.

The Runaway Shoes is a sequel to *Never Meddle With Magic*, also selected by Barbara Ireson and published in Puffin. Barbara Ireson is a story writer herself and is highly acclaimed for her many anthologies of stories and poetry, including the classic *Young Puffin Book of Verse*.

D1637802

Other collections from Barbara Ireson

HAUNTING TALES
THE YOUNG PUFFIN BOOK OF VERSE
IN A CLASS OF THEIR OWN

A PUFFIN BEDTIME STORY CHEST

THE
RUNAWAY SHOES

Chosen by Barbara Ireson

Illustrated by Glenys Ambrus
and Caroline Sharpe

PUFFIN BOOKS

PUFFIN BOOKS

Published by the Penguin Group
27 Wrights Lane, London W8 5TZ, England
Viking Penguin Inc., 40 West 23rd Street, New York, New York 10010, USA
Penguin Books Australia Ltd, Ringwood, Victoria, Australia
Penguin Books Canada Ltd, 2801 John Street, Markham, Ontario, Canada L3R 1B4
Penguin Books (NZ) Ltd, 182–190 Wairau Road, Auckland 10, New Zealand

Penguin Books Ltd, Registered Offices: Harmondsworth, Middlesex, England

First published as *Story Chest: 100 Bedtime Stories* by Viking Kestrel, 1986
Published in Puffin Books (containing the last 50 stories), 1989
1 3 5 7 9 10 8 6 4 2

Made and printed in Great Britain by
Richard Clay Ltd, Bungay, Suffolk

Contents

CONTENTS

CONTENTS

LOUISE

I wasn't too pleased when Mum told me one of her friends was coming to tea and bringing her little girl. I don't like girls. They're soppy, they only play at dolls and going shopping, and they're always crying. Well, I suppose I sometimes cry myself, but only for something serious like when the sitting-room vase got broken and Dad told me off and it wasn't fair because I didn't do it on purpose and anyway it was an ugly vase and I know Dad doesn't like me to play football in the house but it was raining outside.

'You must be nice to Louise,' said Mum. 'She's a dear little girl, and I want you to show her what good manners you have.'

When Mum wants me to show what good manners I have she makes me wear a blue suit and a white shirt and I look a proper Charlie. I told Mum I'd rather go to the pictures with our gang and see the western they were showing, but Mum gave me that look of hers which means she's not standing for any nonsense.

'And you are not to be rough with little Louise, or you'll have me to deal with, understand?' Mum told me. So at four o'clock Mum's friend arrived with her little girl. Mum's friend hugged me and said oh, what a big boy I was, like people always do, and then said, 'This is Louise.' Louise and I took a look at each other. Louise had yellow hair in pigtails, blue eyes, and her nose and dress were red. We shook hands, very quickly

Then it was tea-time, and that was O.K., because when people come to tea there's chocolate cake and you can come back for another slice. During tea Louise and I didn't say anything much, just ate without looking at each other.

When we'd all finished Mum said, 'Well, children, run along and play. Take Louise up to your room and show her your nice toys, Nicholas.' Mum had a big smile all over her face, but she was still giving me that look which means she's standing no nonsense.

Louise and I went up to my room, and I didn't know what to say to her. Louise started it, she said, 'You're all got up like a monkey!' That annoyed me, so I said, 'Well, you're only a soppy

7

girl!' so then she thumped me. I felt like crying, but I didn't because Mum wanted me to show what good manners I have, so I pulled one of Louise's pigtails instead and she hacked my shin. I couldn't help letting out a yell then because it hurt.

I was going to thump Louise back when she changed the subject. 'How about these toys of yours?' she asked. 'Are you going to show me?' I was about to tell her they were boys' toys when she spotted my teddy bear, the one I shaved half the fur off with Dad's razor. I only got half of it shaved because the razor gave out. 'Gosh, do you play with dolls?' said Louise, and she began laughing. I was just going to pull one of her pigtails again and she was just going to hit me, when the door opened and both our Mums came in.

'Well, having a nice time, children?' asked Mum. 'Ooh, yes!' said Louise, opening her eyes wide and fluttering her eyelashes. Mum hugged her and said, 'She really is adorable! Such a dear little chicken!' and Louise put in some more work with her eyelashes. 'Show Louise your nice books!' said my Mum, and the other Mum said we were *both* dear little chickens, and they went out.

I took my books out of the cupboard and gave them to Louise, but she didn't look at them, just dropped them on the floor, even the one about Indians which is terrific. 'I don't like silly old books,' said Louise, 'haven't you got anything that's more fun?' And then she looked in the cupboard and she found my red plane, the good one with an elastic band which makes it fly. 'Leave that alone,' I said, 'that isn't a girl's toy, that's my plane!' and I tried to get it back. But Louise dodged me. 'I'm the guest,' she said, 'I've got the right to play with all your toys and if you say I can't I shall fetch my Mum and then we'll see!'

I didn't know just what to do, I didn't want her to break my plane but I didn't want her fetching her Mum either because that would mean trouble. So while I was thinking, Louise was turning the propeller to wind up the elastic, and then she let go of the plane and it flew out of the window. 'Now look what you've done!' I said. 'You've lost my plane!' And I started to cry. 'Don't be daft, your plane isn't lost!' said Louise. 'Look, it came down in the garden. We'd better go and get it.'

We went down into the sitting-room and I asked Mum if we

could go out to play in the garden, and Mum said it was too cold, but Louise did her eyelash trick again and said she did so want to see the pretty flowers. So then Mum said what a dear little chicken she was and told us to wrap up well before we went out. I'll have to learn that eyelash trick, it seems to work wonders!

Out in the garden I picked up my plane, luckily it was all right, and then Louise said, 'What shall we do now?' 'No idea,' I said, 'you wanted to see the pretty flowers, didn't you? Well, go ahead, look at them, there are masses over there.' But Louise said she couldn't care less about our flowers and they were a rotten lot of flowers. I wanted to punch Louise's nose, but I didn't, because the sitting-room window looks out on the garden and both our Mums were in the sitting-room.

'Well, I haven't got any toys down here,' I said, 'only my football in the garage.' Louise thought that was a good idea. We went to get the football, and I felt very embarrassed. I was dead scared some of my friends might see me playing with a girl. 'You stand in between those trees,' said Louise, 'and I'll shoot at goal and you try to keep it out.' That really made me laugh, and then Louise took this great long run and wham! It was a great shot, right into goal! I couldn't begin to stop it, and the ball broke the garage window.

Our Mums came running out of the house, and my Mum saw the garage window and she grasped the situation in a flash. 'Nicholas!' she said, 'you ought to look after your guests and not play rough games with them, especially when they're as nice as Louise!' I looked at Louise. She was strolling round the garden smelling the begonias.

I didn't get any pudding at supper-time, but I didn't mind. Louise is great! We'll get married when we're grown up.

She kicks a really fantastic goal!

RENÉ GOSCINNY

THE LIMP LITTLE
DONKEY

Peter's donkey was a limp little donkey, a saggy, thin little donkey, a floppy old donkey. He was knitted from grey wool, with red and green stripes round his middle, and little brown feet. He no longer had enough stuffing to make him stand up, or sit up, or even lift up his head!

Peter liked to have the limp little donkey in bed at night, but when morning came, Peter would be off to play. Mother would find the donkey under the blankets when she came to make the bed.

She would try to prop him up, and *try* to prop him up, but he couldn't stand, or sit, or even lift up his head. He could only lie with his legs going all ways. In the end, Mother would leave him on his back on top of the cupboard, and there he'd have to stay.

One day, someone gave Peter a new, golden teddy bear. That night Peter took *him* to bed and forgot his limp little donkey.

The donkey was left lying on top of the cupboard. 'I wish I were a big strong toy! I wish someone would play with me. I wish I could stand up, or sit up, or even lift up my head to see what is going on,' he said to himself.

Nothing changed. Weeks and weeks went by, and no one played with the limp little donkey. He stayed on top of the cupboard, a dusty, forgotten little donkey.

Then Peter's brother brought home a puppet he had made at school – such a funny fellow, dressed like a clown. He was very limp too, with dangling wooden arms and dangling wooden legs. He had pieces of string tied to each ankle and wrist, and whenever the strings were pulled, he danced.

'We're going to have a puppet show,' said Peter's brother. 'We'll get all the toys and dolls and put strings on them too.'

Peter's brother made a stage out of boxes and old curtains, and he hid behind it and made the clown dance. He tried to make the dolls and the teddy bear dance too.

11

'It's no use,' he said. 'They're too stiff. Where's that limp little donkey?'

So the limp little donkey came down from the top of the cupboard. Strings made from black cotton thread were tied to his four legs and to his neck too. Then he was put on the stage where everyone could see him. Peter's brother pulled the black cotton strings, and oh – oh –

Up came the donkey's head! It nodded from side to side.

Up came his legs. They kicked this way and that.

'Look at me! Look at me!' he cried to the other toys. 'I can stand, I can sit, I can even lift up my head – and *I can dance*! Dance, dance, *dance*!'

Peter laughed and clapped his hands. The limp little donkey was the best puppet of all!

When the puppet show was over and Peter was going to bed, he said, 'Come along, little donkey. Where have you been all this time?'

The limp little donkey, the saggy, thin little donkey, the floppy old donkey cuddled up happily between Peter and the golden teddy bear, and was soon fast asleep.

JUDY BOND

THE HARE

This story is about a hare who got a bit above himself. It all started when the old lion, King of the beasts, died, and his son succeeded him. The old King had been wise and good but his son was foolish

12

and mean. He got into the habit of killing other animals just for fun, even when he wasn't hungry and didn't need to kill for food.

But after a while the lion got tired of hunting, even for amusement, and decided it would be much easier if the food came to him. So he issued an order saying that every day a different animal, or several animals if they were small, should report to his cave to be eaten as his dinner.

There was nothing the animals could do but agree. At least this way the lion stayed fairly quiet and killed just a few animals each day. So the animals drew up their lists and each group took it in turn to provide the lion's dinner; bears one day, deer the next, rabbits the next and so on. And so things went on for some time, until it was the hares' turn to provide the lion's food. About twenty young hares were chosen – surely this should be enough to satisfy the lion for one day.

After the usual sad farewells, the hares set off through the forest to the lion's den. Their mouths were dry with fear and they stopped at a well to have a last drink. While they were drinking, they looked at their reflections in the clear water and this gave one of them an idea.

This young hare had always been particularly bright and pleased with himself, and when he said confidently to the others, 'You lot go back home. I know how to deal with this lion and I can do it on my own,' they were quite sure he meant what he said, and did go home.

Once the young hare was alone, he took his time getting to the lion's den, and in fact it wasn't until evening that he got near the place, and then he slowed down his walk to a limp and pretended to be very tired. His ears drooped, and he looked altogether exhausted.

The lion was pacing up and down outside his den, swishing his tail angrily.

'And where have you been?' he roared. 'You were supposed to be here this morning. I've been waiting for food all day, my stomach's making the most awful noises, and it's your fault. Where have you been?'

The hare drooped even more and said in a sad, gasping voice, 'Oh sir! I am one of the twenty hares chosen to come here today. We all set out in good time, but on the way we met another lion

who asked where we were going. Well, we said we were coming here to the King of the beasts, and were honoured to be chosen as your dinner. But the other lion only laughed at us.

'"*I'm* the King of the beasts," he said, "there's no other King but me, and as you're supposed to be the King's dinner, I shall eat you."

'And then he attacked us. All my friends were eaten, but luckily I managed to escape and came here to you as fast as I could manage.'

When the lion heard this, he was furious and quite forgot how hungry he was. All he cared about now was finding and punishing this other lion who was challenging him.

'Take me to this thief,' he roared to the hare. 'I'll make him pay for his cheek.'

So the hare, still limping and with his ears still drooping, led the way through the forest until they came to the well where the hare and his friends had drunk that morning. Then the hare pointed to the well and said, 'The other lion's down there. That's where he goes to sleep after a big meal.'

The King lion nodded and stole towards the well, and peered over the top down into the water; and there below him was a lion with a terrible shaggy mane, snarling teeth and flashing eyes.

'A big fellow,' thought the lion, 'but not too big for me,' and he roared again to show he wasn't afraid. At the same moment the lion in the well roared, even louder. The King lion snarled and stretched out his paw, flashing out his claws, and the other lion did the same. Everything the King lion did, the lion in the well did too, until the King lion was so furious that he dived head first into the well, through his own reflection, and was drowned.

The hare had watched all this from a safe distance, and when it was over, he went bouncing home very pleased with himself. Naturally, he became the local hero. Everyone wanted to congratulate him and give him presents and say flattering things about him.

This was all very well, until the hare really began to believe the things his admirers said. He became very spoiled and full of himself, and began to act as if he too were King of the beasts. He growled and tore at turnips savagely with his teeth, half-closed his eyes and turned his head from side to side as if he were swishing a great hairy mane. He thought of himself as a lion, but to all the other animals he looked a fool, and they started to make fun of him.

One day the hare had visitors – the tortoise and the hedgehog – who were modest animals and didn't care for boasters.

'My lord,' said the tortoise. (You had to call the hare 'Sir', or 'My lord', otherwise he wouldn't listen.) 'My lord, you think of yourself as a great King, greater than the lion, but we think you're no more than an ordinary quick-footed hare. In fact we're not sure you're even as good as an ordinary hare, for we are both sure that we can run faster than you and beat you over any distance.'

The hare tried to smile in a snarly, lion-like way and said, 'You are both very stupid, and to show you how stupid you are, I shall accept your challenge. I will race and beat both of you separately and still have enough breath left to tell you what I think of you!'

The tortoise and hedgehog agreed and left the hare before he could see the smiles on their faces.

Next morning, the three animals met and arranged that the

hare and the tortoise would race first, and then they decided on a course.

'On your marks,' said the hedgehog, 'get set!' He whistled through his front teeth, and off they went: the hare bounding in front, ears straight, kicking up his legs and turning somersaults. The tortoise followed behind, tramping along slowly and heavily. Soon the hare was well ahead. When he looked back he couldn't see the tortoise anywhere, so he decided he'd already won the race, the tortoise couldn't possibly catch up now. The hare didn't even bother to carry on towards the winning post. He played for a while, and then lay down in a shady spot under a willow tree and went to sleep.

But along the path leading to the winning post came the tortoise, his eyes screwed up against the sun, tramping along slowly and heavily, but never stopping. On and on he went, past the tree where the hare lay asleep, and on until he reached the winning post.

By that time it was dark and a little chilly. The hare woke up and decided to go home, quite forgetting he was in the middle of a race. When he got back he found the tortoise and the hedgehog waiting for him.

'Well,' said the hedgehog. 'I was the referee and I say the tortoise won that race by about four hours.'

The hare was cross with himself, and decided that when he raced the hedgehog the next day, he'd win by so much, no one would remember the tortoise had beaten him.

But the hedgehog had a different idea. He and his wife looked very much alike, so alike that only another hedgehog would know the difference between them. Early next morning, the hedgehog told his wife what to do during the race.

'You stay here on the far side of the field and I'll be at the start with the hare,' he said. 'When the race begins, the hare will soon get in front of me, and then I'll turn and go back to the start. When he gets here and sees you, you must behave as if you've been here for ages, and then he'll think that you're me and that somehow I managed to get ahead of him.'

And that's exactly what happened. The hare was very business-like and determined to win. When the tortoise started the race, the hare ran as fast as he could, straight for the winning post, leaving the hedgehog far behind. But when he arrived at the winning post, the hare met the hedgehog's wife, looking very fresh and rested.

'I seem to have won, don't I?' she said.

The hare didn't understand at all, and was very cross with himself. Surely he could beat a hedgehog!

'Let's try again,' he said. 'Back to the start.'

'Very well,' said the hedgehog's wife, and off they went. Exactly the same thing happened again. The hedgehog's wife turned back after a few yards and her husband was waiting, fresh and rested, at the winning post.

By now the hare was desperate. He refused to give in. He went on racing up and down all day, and every time the hedgehog and his wife played the same trick. Until, at last, when it was getting dark, the hare flung himself on the ground, panting: 'I give up!'

That was what they were waiting for. The hare, who thought he was greater than the lion, the King of beasts, couldn't even beat a hedgehog and a tortoise in a running race.

After that, the hare was a much quieter and more sensible creature – and so he is today.

RONALD EYRE

THE HARUM-SCARUM BOYS

Charlie Cadwallader lived with his Mum and Dad at the bottom of West Street. He hadn't any brothers or sisters, but he had a lot of friends. Most of them were big boys who went to school.

'Please, Charlie,' said his Mum one day, 'will you go to the shop for me, and get three doughnuts for our tea? Be sure to go to the baker's at the *top* of the street; they have the jammiest doughnuts

17

in town. Here is some money, and you can keep the change to buy yourself some jelly babies; but don't dilly-dally on the way, and don't stop to hob-nob with any of your harum-scarum friends. I want you home by five o'clock.'

Charlie hurried up West Street. It was a steep, steep street. There were some interesting shop-windows on the way, so a little dilly-dallying would have been very pleasant; but Charlie remembered what his Mum had told him, and kept on walking till he came to the baker's at the very top of the hill.

There was a great pile of doughnuts in the window: round, golden-coloured, crispy-soft, jammy doughnuts, shiny with sugar.

Charlie went inside and handed his money to the lady.

'Three jammy doughnuts, please,' he said.

The lady put three fat doughnuts in a paper bag, and gave them to Charlie, with some change. Then they both said 'Thank you,' and Charlie walked out of the shop with the change in his trouser pocket. There wasn't much change because the doughnuts were rather expensive.

The sweet-shop was next door to the baker's. Charlie went in for his jelly babies. The friendly sweet-shop lady knew Charlie very well.

'Hello, Charlie!' she said. 'Do you want some of the usual?'

'Yes, please,' said Charlie, and he showed her how much change there was to spend.

She put two of each sort in a little paper bag for him. Two red ones, two green ones, two yellow ones, two orange ones, two black ones, and two whitey ones; and then an extra red one.

When Charlie Cadwallader came out of the sweet-shop, there were all his harum-scarum friends waiting for him outside. There was Oliver Ollerenshaw, Freddy Fotheringay, Cliff Christopherson, Willie Wilberforce and little Gilbert Gilhooley, all hob-nobbing together on the pavement.

Charlie forgot that his Mum had told him to be back at five o'clock. He passed his jelly babies round twice. Nobody said 'No, thank you,' so there was only one left. It was the extra red one. Charlie took it out of its little bag and popped it inside the doughnut bag, to remind himself to have it after tea. Then he put the little bag in the litter basket.

18

When there wasn't anything much left to hob-nob about, Oliver Ollerenshaw said, 'I'm going to play hopscotch. Got any chalk?' But nobody had any chalk. They had all sorts of other useful things in their pockets, but not chalk. So Oliver began playing a harum-scarum sort of hopscotch by himself on the lines and spaces of the big paving-stones. Soon all the others joined in, and nobody waited for turns, so there was a good deal of bumping.

Charlie found it difficult to hop properly while he was carrying the bag of doughnuts; there was no room in his trouser pocket for them.

'I'll put them up inside my jersey,' he said to himself, 'and carry them that way.'

But before he had time to put them there, 'Crash!' Oliver Ollerenshaw collided with him so suddenly that the bag was knocked right out of his hand!

Out came the three jammy doughnuts and the red jelly baby, and away they rolled down West Street.

Pell mell

Tappy lappy

Helter skelter

Roly poly down the hill!

And away ran Charlie Cadwallader after them.

Pell mell

Tappy lappy

Helter skelter down the hill!

And away ran Oliver Ollerenshaw, Freddy Fotheringay, Cliff Christopherson, Willie Wilberforce, and little Gilbert Gilhooley.

Pell mell

Tappy lappy

Helter skelter down the hill after Charlie Cadwallader!

So what do you think happened to all that lot when they reached the bottom? You remember, don't you, that Charlie's Dad and Mum lived at the bottom of West Street? Well now, the Cadwalladers' house had a doorstep that stuck right out on to the pavement, making a fine full STOP! Up bounced the red jelly baby and the three jammy doughnuts and landed plop! on the Cadwalladers' doorstep!

Roly poly came Charlie Cadwallader and landed topsy-turvy

on top of the red jelly baby and the three jammy doughnuts! And roly poly, topsy-turvy came Oliver Ollerenshaw, Freddy Fotheringay, Cliff Christopherson, Willie Wilberforce and little Gilbert Gilhooley on top of Charlie Cadwallader. What a heap of boys it was!

Mrs Cadwallader poked her head out of a window when she heard all the hurly-burly outside. And when she saw all that hugger-mugger of harum-scarum boys on her front doorstep, she thought she had better do something about it. So she opened the front door, and picked the boys off the heap one by one, starting with little Gilbert Gilhooley.

She shook them all gently, dusted them down, straightened their jerseys, and stood them on their feet in the passage. They were more surprised than hurt.

'Well, well! If this isn't our Charlie!' she said as she set to work on the last boy, who had been at the bottom of all the others, next to the doughnuts.

'Yes, it's me, Mum,' said Charlie. 'Is it five o'clock yet?'

'There's the church clock just striking five now,' said Mrs Cadwallader, 'so you've managed to get home in time for your tea.'

'I'm glad,' said Charlie, 'because I did hurry home; but I don't think the doughnuts look as nice now as they did in the shop.'

'I'm sure they don't,' said his Mum. 'They look a proper mishmash! More like pancakes than doughnuts. Never mind, I've got a very big tin of biscuits in the kitchen, that I keep for unexpected friends; we've got the unexpected friends, so now we can have biscuits for tea instead. Go on right inside, boys!'

So Charlie Cadwallader, Oliver Ollerenshaw, Freddy Fotheringay, Cliff Christopherson, Willie Wilberforce and little Gilbert Gilhooley thumped into the kitchen where Charlie's Dad was just sitting down to his tea. He was a bit surprised to see them all, but he managed to find chairs for nearly everybody. Charlie and little Gilbert sat on the floor.

There were enough cups or beakers for everyone to have tea or milk or orange juice; and there was some bread and jam and that very big tin of biscuits. The boys generally remembered to say 'Please' and 'Thank you,' and when they forgot somebody nudged them, and then they remembered.

When the biscuits had all gone Charlie's Mum said, 'I hope you boys have all had enough to eat.' The boys just smiled and nodded their heads because they did not want to speak with their mouths full. All of them, except Charlie, had had tea at home before they came out.

When Oliver Ollerenshaw's mouth was quite empty he said, 'We'd better be off now. Thank you very much for the tea, Mrs Cadwallader.' So that reminded Freddy Fotheringay, Cliff Christopherson, Willie Wilberforce and little Gilbert Gilhooley to say, 'Thank you very much for the tea, Mrs Cadwallader.'

When they had all gone Mrs Cadwallader set to and scraped the mish-mash off the doorstep and put it on the bird-table in the yard; she swept up the crumbs and washed up the tea things. Charlie and his Dad helped.

'Well!' she said when everything was tidy again. 'Harum-scarum they may be, but what *nice* boys they all are! I'm glad you've got such good friends, Charlie. Tomorrow you can help me bake some more biscuits, ready for the next time they come.'

KATHLEEN HERSOM

THE OLD WOMAN WHO LIVED IN A COLA CAN

Not all that long ago, and not so far away, there was an old woman who lived in a cola can. 'All right,' you'd hear her say, 'the place *is* small, definitely chilly in December and scorching hot in July – but the floor never needs a coat of polish, and there's no dark corners where a spider can lurk.' The old woman reckoned it wasn't at all a bad place for a home, especially seeing there wasn't a penny to pay in rent.

One day, though, she went in for a telly, and she suddenly saw all sorts of things she'd never seen before. She saw all the adverts and loads of films – but instead of making her happy, all the new things only made her mad. She shouted and swore and shook her fist at the programmes.

'Rotten shame! Rotten shame! T'ain't fair – it ain't fair!' she created. 'Why should I make do in this tinny little place when there's some lucky devils got nice flats in brand new tower blocks, with lifts to take them up and chutes to send the rubbish

down? What's wrong with *me*, I'd like to know? Why can't I have a chance to be choosy?'

She went on like that for ages, banging and clanging inside her can – till one day, by a stroke of luck just before her voice gave out, someone special heard her from the road: a flash young man who had won the pools and was looking for ways to get rid of his money.

He couldn't get across the grass to her quickly enough.

'Gordon Bennett, darlin', what a noise, what a *girls an' boys*! But I heard what you was shoutin', and I've got to say I do feel sorry. I do. I feel choked, *prodded an' poked*. But say no more, girl, an' just you keep your pecker up. Give us a couple o' days for some wheelin' an' dealin', watch out for the motor – an' we'll see what we're gonna see!'

So the old woman said no more. She switched off her telly, kept her eyes glued to the road, and before the milkman had been round three times, the flash young man was back, sitting on his motor and calling out across the grass:

'Come on, love, get out of the can! Jump in the car, the old *jam jar*, and come along o' me. I'll soon sort you out.'

She didn't need telling twice. She jumped in his car, just as she was, and before you could say knife, there she was in the town, in a nice little flat in a brand new block, with a lift to take her up and a chute to send the rubbish down.

And she was over the moon with delight. But she clean forgot to say thank you to the flash young man. And anyway, he'd shot off to get on with his spending. He'd gone to the races, and smart sunny places, to Catterick, Corfu and Crete. But after a while, when his mouth ached with smiling, he thought he'd go back to see how the old woman was getting on.

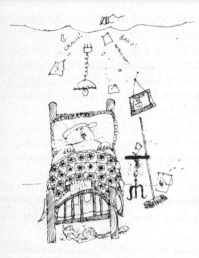

And what did he hear when he got there? The tinkle of friendly tea-cups, a few contented sighs like the summer wind in net curtains?

Not a bit of it. Just the slamming of doors and shouts enough to wake the caretaker.

'Rotten shame! Rotten shame! T'ain't fair – it ain't fair! I'm just about up to *here*, miles off the ground in this poky little flat – when there's some folks in the know got houses in streets, and their own front gates, with cars out the front and patios round the back. What's wrong with *me*, I'd like to know? Why don't I get the chance to be superior?'

The flash young man listened to every word she said. He kept dead quiet till he'd heard everything: then he put his eye to the spy-hole and he shouted through the door:

'Cheer up, doll,' he pleaded, 'no need for all that. Say no more, girl, and keep your pecker up. Give us a couple o' days for some wheelin' an' dealin', watch out for the motor – an' we'll see what we're gonna see!'

So the old woman said no more. She stopped banging doors, kept her eyes on the parking bays, and before the kids had ruined the lifts three more times, the flash young man was back, leaning on his bonnet and calling up at her balcony.

24

'Come on, love, get down them stairs! Jump in the motor, the old *haddock an' bloater*, and come along o' me. I'll soon sort you out.'

She didn't need telling twice. She ran down the stairs, jumped in the back, and before she could say Jack Robinson, there she was in a neat town house in a proper little street, with a car out front and a patio round the back.

And she was over the moon with delight. But she clean forgot to say thank you to the flash young man. And, anyway, he'd shot off to get on with his spending. He'd gone to casinos and sporting club beanos, to Monte, Majorca and Maine. But after a while, when his hand hurt with winning, he thought he'd go back to see how the old woman was getting on.

And what did he hear when he got there? The contented creak of an old cane chair, the sound of soft singing to Radio Two?

Not a bit of it. Just the slam of a swing-bin being attacked and shouts which ran to the end of the road.

'Rotten shame! Rotten shame! T'ain't fair – it ain't fair! Here am I shunted off in this common little house – when there's some people live it up in tree-lined cul-de-sacs, with nicely spoken neighbours and a man to do the grass. What's wrong with *me*, I'd like to know? When do I get a chance to be posh?'

The flash young man heard everything she said, then he rang upon her chimes.

'Heaven help us, love, what a state! What a Terrible *two-an'-eight*! We can't have this, noan' dealin', watch out for the motor – an' we'll see what we're gonna see!'

So the old woman said no more. She stopped kicking-in the kitchen and packed her bags instead. And before she'd carried the dustbin through three times the flash young man was back, elbow on the dashboard and tooting at the door.

'Come on, love, leg it over that gate! Jump in the Bentley, the old *gently-gently*, and come along o' me. I'll soon sort you out.'

She didn't need telling twice. She slammed herself into the car with her hat in her hand, and before she could say one o'clock, there she was in a double-fronted house in a cul-de-sac, with nicely spoken neighbours and a man to do her grass.

And she was over the moon with delight. But she clean forgot to say thank you to the flash young man. And anyway, he'd shot off to get on with his spending. He bought up some pubs and three football clubs, United, Juventus and York. But after a while, when he got fed up with watching other people run around, he thought he'd go back and see how the old woman was getting on.

And what did he hear when he got there? The plop of fresh coffee being poured for the vicar, the rinsing of hands to get spoon polish off?

Not a bit of it. Just the rip of a radiator off a wall and shouts loud enough to divert the traffic.

'Rotten shame! Rotten shame! T'ain't fair – it ain't fair. Here am I, overlooked in this middle-class place, when Lords and Ladies have mansions in big country parks, and servants to send off to Harrods. What's wrong with *me*, I'd like to know? When do I get the chance to be Upper Crust?'

The flash young man caught every word she said, then made his way round the back.

'Hold your horses! Half time!' he called through the tradesmen's entrance. 'You'll make yourself sick, *Uncle Dick*! Say no more, girl, and keep your pecker up. Give us a couple of days for some wheelin' an' dealin', watch out for the motor – and we'll see what we're gonna see!'

So the old woman said no more. She put a few favourite bits into a suitcase – and by the time she'd turned three collecting tins away from her door, the flash young man was back, purring into the driveway and breaking the beam on her burglar alarm.

'Come on, love, let's move it. Jump in the Jag, the old *boast an' brag*, and come along o' me. I'll soon sort you out.'

26

She didn't need telling twice. She shot in as fast as the speed of greased lightning, and before she could say hell for leather there she was in a mansion, a duchess no less, with servants to send off to Harrods and a tiara to put on her head.

And she was over the moon with delight. But she clean forgot to say thank you to the flash young man. And, anyway, he'd shot off to get on with his spending. He bought up an airway to make a cheap fare-way for tourists on trips to the States. But after a while, when he got fed up with being pointed at, he thought he'd go back and see how the old woman was getting on.

And what did he hear when he got there? The click of a croquet ball sent through a hoop, the flow of a pool being filled?

Not a bit of it. Just the sound of a summer house being destroyed, and shouts loud enough for three counties to hear.

'Rotten shame! Rotten shame! T'ain't fair – it ain't fair. Here am I, just a two-bob old duchess down here, when there's SOMEONE WE KNOW with a crown on her head! What's wrong with *me*, I'd like to know? When do I get the chance to be Royal?'

The flash young man took note of what the old woman said, then he made an appointment to see her.

'Your Grace, what a row! What a *bull and a cow*! You are comin' on strong. But I know what you mean, so you don't need to say another word. Give us a couple o' days for some wheelin' an' dealin', watch out for the motor – and we'll see what we're gonna see!'

So the old woman said no more. She threw her tiara into the pool, kept her eyes peeled for the car with no number, and before she had time to sack three of her maids, the flash young man was back, gliding up towards her in his silver Rolls Royce.

'Come on, ma'am,' he invited. 'Jump into the Roller, the *top hat an' bowler*, and come along o' me. I'll soon sort you out.'

She didn't need telling twice. She got into the back, cocked her head on one side, one side, and started waving away out of this window and that. And before she could say, 'It gives me great pleasure,' she was there.

Back in her home in the cola can: where, yell as she liked, she lived for the rest of her life.

But she never saved up for a telly again – and she wouldn't have said thank you if you'd given her one.

A modern telling of a traditional tale by
BERNARD ASHLEY

SALLY'S CHRISTMAS EVE

It was Christmas Eve at Sally's house and everyone's house.

Sally had eaten her lunch and already she had hung her stocking from the mantelshelf in the sitting-room. There the stocking hung ... long and thin and empty ... and waiting ... waiting for Santa Claus to come and fill it with surprises for Sally.

On one foot and then on the other foot Sally hopped about the sitting-room looking at her empty stocking. Everywhere Sally hopped was the exact place her Mummy wanted to push the vacuum-cleaner brush.

Very soon Mummy said, 'Please, Sally, hop out of the way of

the cleaner. I must hurry if the house is to be as neat as a new pin for Christmas Day tomorrow.'

On one foot and then the other foot Sally hopped right through the house to the laundry. She was a very good hopper but with each hop her hair ribbon flopped about and slid about until it was hanging loosely from Sally's hair. Another hop and it would fall off surely.

But Sally stopped hopping and leaned against the end of the ironing board to watch Nan.

Nan at once stopped ironing to say, 'Please, Sally, don't stand so close to the iron. This is your best dress I'm ironing and there mustn't be a crease left in it. You must look your prettiest for Christmas Day.'

Then Nan tied Sally's hair ribbon into a new firm bow and she said, 'You always look your best when your hair is neat and tidy.'

Sally's hair ribbons were always slipping off. At least four times each day someone tied a new bow for Sally so that her hair didn't untidy itself about her eyes. Perhaps Sally hopped too much. She handn't learned to hop properly for so very long and now she was tired of it, so she skipped ... one leg, then the other leg ... all the way to the dining room.

The door was shut. Her big sister, Margaret, was in there. By stretching Sally could just reach the door handle but she couldn't turn it to open the door. She banged on it and called through the keyhole, 'Let me in! Let me in, Margaret.'

'You can't come in, Sal,' Margaret shouted. 'I'm wrapping Christmas presents for *everyone*. Go away, Sally. You can't come in.'

So Sally just had to skip away, right out of the house to the house next door. She would play with her friend, Peter.

The front door of Peter's house was closed, and so were the windows. Peter's bike lay sideways on the path.

'Pete! Peter!' called Sally as she ran along the path to the back of Peter's house. The back door was closed too and Peter didn't answer Sally. Then Sally remembered. Peter had gone with his family to do the last of the Christmas shopping.

For a while Sally rode Peter's bicycle along the path, but it wasn't much fun when Peter wasn't there to say, 'My turn now.'

Soon Sally left the bike *right way up* on the path and climbed on Pete's gate. She looked for him to come down the street.

Peter didn't come.

Christmas Eve was a long, long day, thought Sally. She sighed. Everyone was so busy.

She went on swinging, backwards and forwards on Pete's gate, until she heard Mummy calling.

At last! Now Sally would be as busy as everyone else.

She sped inside her house. On the kitchen table was a tin of biscuits. Every Christmas Eve Sally picked from that tin the nicest biscuits for Santa Claus to eat when he called at her house during the night. Sally ate a biscuit with a red cherry on top. It looked pretty and it tasted nice so Sally put three cherry biscuits on a plate. She carried it to the sitting-room. Sally left the plate beside her stocking.

Now she was ready to find a bottle of drink for Santa Claus in the box of drinks which was under the kitchen table. Sally was a long time making up her mind. The green drink looked pretty, so did the red one, but orange drink was Sally's favourite. In the end she took the bottle of orange drink to the sitting-room and put it beside the plate of biscuits. Santa's supper was ready for him.

All the time that Sally was busy she talked to Mummy about Santa. 'Do you think his reindeer would like some biscuits too?' she asked.

'Reindeer eat grass, Sal,' her Mummy answered. 'I don't think that Santa would give them biscuits.'

Sally went straight out to the lawn and soon filled both the pockets of her dress with little blades of grass. She piled the grass in little heaps on each step leading to the front door. The reindeer were sure to find the grass there, ready and waiting for them. Mummy thought so too. Just before Sally went to bed that evening she looked out to see if the grass was still where the reindeer could find it.

The next morning was Christmas.

Before Sally opened one parcel poking from her stocking she looked to see if Santa Claus had eaten his supper. He had! Only a few crumbs were left on the plate. The orange drink was gone too.

Sally ran to the front door, standing on her toes to open it. Did the reindeer find the grass? It was gone! Gone! Not a wisp was left on the steps. And on the top step was the tiniest of parcels. That was the first parcel opened by Sally on Christmas morning. A red ribbon, as red as Santa's own coat, tumbled out. Lovely! A beautiful ribbon. Sally wore it to church, tied in a big bow on top of her head. The ribbon was still there when she found a silver button in her slice of Christmas pudding, and at tea-time the ribbon was under the purple crown of paper that Sally had found inside her bon-bon. Not once, not once all Christmas Day did Sally's ribbon come undone. And it was still in place when Sally went to bed that night. But then, it was a very special ribbon. It was a present for Sally who had thought to be kind to Santa's reindeer.

JEAN CHAPMAN

31

BENNY TRIES THE
MAGIC

The lady from across the road called to Benny. 'Will you look after baby, Benny love, so I can get on with my washing?'

She fastened the baby into a battered pram with a cracked hood. The baby was fat. He had the sort of face that is generally laughing and covered with jam, but just now it was like a stormy sky, split by thunder and lightning.

'What a terrible noise!' said the baby's mother. 'Here's Benny going to look after you – such a good boy! – and this is what you show him. Shame on you! Give Benny a nice smile, lovey.'

But lovey wouldn't. He howled, he screamed, and he went stiff in his pram and wouldn't bend at the middle when his mother wanted to make him sit.

'Push him down the road a bit, chuck,' she said to Benny. 'When you push the pram, he stops crying.'

Benny unfastened his red balloon from the door knocker, brought it back over the road, and took hold of the pram. A dusty little breeze tugged at the string and almost took the balloon away because Benny couldn't see how to hold the balloon and the pram handle at the same time.

'Tie it to the pram, chucky,' said the baby's mother. And she did it for him. Suddenly Benny noticed that the baby – whose name, he remembered, was Joey Moss – had stopped crying. He was staring at the balloon. But when he saw Benny looking at him, he quickly crumpled up his lip again and gave one or two sobs in his chest, because he could tell Benny was thinking of *not* pushing the pram.

Benny hastily took hold of the handle again and started off down the hill. The balloon, which he had got from the rag man, bobbed gently up and down, and the baby kept opening and closing his hand doubtfully, as if he wasn't quite sure whether the balloon was right next to him or up in the sky with the sun and moon.

The hill was very steep. Sitting in a soap-box cart, you could go right down to the bottom of Fern Street, without pushing with your feet at all.

Now they came to the little door in the high wall. Benny clenched his fingers round the pram handle. Would it open and someone come out? Every time he was near the door, he wondered this.

He was sure it was not an ordinary door. First of all, it was such a tiny door, a wooden door painted green, and the wall was so big and strong and grey. The door was so tiny it must surely not be made for an ordinary grown-up person.

And as if the tininess and the oddness of the little wooden door weren't enough, Benny had once seen the door standing open, and inside, instead of a yard as you would expect, there was grass! There was *country* inside that little wooden door, in the middle of all the dust and the dirt and the rubber-smells and the dye-smells of Fern Street. And if that wasn't magic, Benny would like to know what was.

He stopped, with one hand on the pram, and screwing up his other eye, tried to peer through the crack in the door. He could see greenness. He wondered where you would get to, if you went through the door. To Boggart Hole Clough perhaps, where the peacocks lived, or to the railway poster places – to a farm with yellow fields and green hills and cows that munched and stared – or even to the sea.

He didn't look very long with his one eye, because he was always afraid an eye on the other side would be staring into his. So he came away from the greenness and started pushing the pram down the hill again.

Now he was at Davidson's, the toffee-shop. He stopped and looked at the beautiful window. Sherbet bags, dabs and suckers, sticks of spanish, liquorice laces, fairy whispers, jelly babies, gob stoppers that changed from white to pink, and pink to purple and blue and yellow while you sucked them, and lucky bags, and trays of Davidson's special Devon Cream toffee.

When I grow up and can choose what to do, thought Benny with his nose on the pane, I won't be a tailor or a doctor or a teacher. I'll sell Devon Cream toffee. I'll have enormous slabs of it, like Mr Davidson does, as big as the counter, and when someone comes to buy some, I'll take a weight and I'll knock the Devon

Cream toffee – *knock-knock, knock-knock* – till it breaks into little pieces.

Benny began to imitate the way Mr Davidson knocked the Devon Cream toffee, and the lovely flat clickety noise it made, first in the tray on the counter, then in the palm of Mr Davidson's hand as the pieces got smaller and smaller. *Knock-knock, knock-knock.*

At last he took his nose off the pane and moved dreamily down the hill again. And it was quite some seconds before he remembered. The pram! Where was it? It couldn't just have vanished! It couldn't have! Perhaps he had never had a pram! A pram couldn't just turn into nothing. A baby couldn't just disappear. What would the baby's mother do? What would his own mammy say? He went on and on down the hill, too frightened to stop walking or to do anything except pretend to himself that everything was perfectly ordinary.

And in a little while, in the most perfectly ordinary way in the world, a man came up the hill towards him, pulling a pram from the hood side. It had a fat baby in it, and a red balloon that was bobbing up and down. The man took off his hat politely to Benny as if Benny was a lady, and said: 'I think this is your pram.'

Benny clutched hold of the handle again without saying a word. And the man went straight past him up the hill again, without speaking or looking back, or showing in any way that he thought anything frightful or terrifying had happened. The baby looked just the same everyday baby as before. The pram was just the same battered everyday pram with the cracked hood, and the balloon was the same plain red balloon.

So Benny went a bit further down the hill to make himself understand that everything was perfectly ordinary and there was no reason for him to feel clenched-up inside or to do anything different from what he had meant to all the time. And then he turned the pram round, and came up the hill again, his legs well behind him, his head down between his arms, pushing as hard as he could against the steep hill.

When he got back to the baby's house, Mrs Moss was just hanging out the washing in the yard. She gave Benny a big smile and wiped her frothy hands on her apron so that she could tickle the baby's tummy. It made the baby give a funny happy noise, rather like the rag man's donkey, though when the ragman's donkey made the same noise it was a sad one.

Then Benny started to undo his balloon. Immediately the baby went quite stiff and unbendable again. Benny didn't know at first that it was to do with his balloon. He went on untying it, not taking much notice of the way the baby was behaving. But the baby's mother said: 'What is it, lovey? Is it Benny's balloon?' So Benny stopped untying it and wondered what to do.

'He does like the balloon so much, Benny,' said Mrs Moss. 'Do you think you might like to have something else instead?'

When she said that, Benny remembered the ragman. The ragman had said to Evvie Fineman: 'Just keep on giving. And one day you'll get the thing you want.'

Perhaps that was a secret sign to Benny. Perhaps it was magic. And he had to do what the magic told him.

'I'll see if you've got anything I'd like,' he said politely to Mrs Moss. And they left the pram, with the baby in it cheerfully blowing bubbles, and the red balloon still fastened to the handle. They went into the scullery, where the copper had filled the air with steam, and into the kitchen which was damp and cool.

'Let's have a look,' said Mrs Moss. And she poked about on the dresser shelves, and started opening cupboards. Mostly she looked inside cracked cups and jugs without handles, because that was where treasure was always kept.

There were lots of different buttons, little pearly ones and dull black trouser buttons, and there were two or three big screws and a hook or two, and some Jewish National Fund stamps for helping to plant trees in Palestine, and a very small bit of pencil, and some flat white tailor's chalk.

Benny was just going to say he would have the chalk, thank you, when Mrs Moss suddenly held out a tiny bottle. Benny had never seen one so tiny. It was tiny for a bottle the way the green door in the wall was tiny for a door. And it was a funny shape. It was flat, like tailor's chalk – but flat and round, like a penny. And it had a real gold top. Mrs Moss took off the top and put the bottle under Benny's nose. 'Smell, chucky,' she said.

Benny smelt it. It was a wonderful smell, wonderful. Benny had never smelt it before. It had nothing to do with dust or cabbage leaves or rubber or the thick black River Irwell. He took deep breaths of it.

'It's Ashes of Roses,' said Mrs Moss. 'Would you like it?'

'Oh yes, please,' said Benny. He took the special bottle that was empty of everything except beautiful smell, and he corked the smell up again with the gold stopper so that it couldn't fly away. He held it in his hand, and as he went home he stopped every few steps to undo the stopper just a tiny bit, screwing it up again very quickly so that the smell would be caught again.

LEILA BERG

Young Hedgehog Has
A Good Friend

Young Hedgehog and his friend Rabbit and their friend Mole lived in the daisy field.

One day, Young Hedgehog and Rabbit were sitting by the hedge doing nothing, just sitting. It was that sort of a day. It was warm, with just the littlest breeze fanning the leaves at the tops of the trees. The birds were singing, not noisily like they do first thing in the morning but now and again, sweetly and prettily, chirping and cheeping. Young Hedgehog and Rabbit watched Squirrel scramble down the trunk of his tree, pick up a nut and nibble it, holding it with his two little hands. Field Mouse was climbing up and down the stalks and scuttling through her little passages in the grass. Butterflies were fluttering among the meadowsweet flowers in the ditch. It was a lovely day.

'Everybody is enjoying this beautiful day!' said Young Hedgehog.

'Everybody except Mole!' Rabbit said.

'Ah, yes!' nodded Young Hedgehog. 'Everybody except Mole. What a shame! He's down there under the ground digging all those tunnels of his. It can't do him any good, you know, he only comes up once in a blue moon for a drink. We must have a talk with him for his own good.'

'Yes,' said Rabbit, 'but where is he?'

'Over there,' Young Hedgehog said, 'by that clump of bracken. See those two brown heaps of soil? They weren't there yesterday, so that's where he's digging. Come on, let's call him.'

Young Hedgehog and Rabbit crossed over the daisy field till they came to the two heaps of soil. Rabbit shouted and Young Hedgehog shouted.

'Mole! Mole! Come up this minute!'

'What's all the commotion about?' cried Mole, popping out of the ground like a jack-in-the-box.

'We want to talk to you,' said Young Hedgehog.

'What about?' asked Mole. 'I haven't an awful lot of time you know. I'm just about to start a new tunnel.'

'That's what we want to talk to you about,' said Young Hedgehog. 'We decided that you shouldn't spend so much time under the ground digging those endless tunnels of yours. It would do you much more good up here. See what a lovely day it is?'

'Yes,' said Mole.

'Can you smell the meadowsweet?' Young Hedgehog asked.

'Yes,' said Mole.

'And look at those daisies, lovely, aren't they?' said Rabbit.

'Yes,' said Mole.

'There are other things in life besides digging tunnels you know,' Young Hedgehog said.

'Are there?' said Mole.

'Yes,' said Young Hedgehog. 'so how about staying up here for a while and enjoying yourself for a change?'

Mole looked doubtful.

'I'd rather not,' he said.

'Oh come on,' coaxed Young Hedgehog. 'After a while you will like it so much you won't want to go back under the ground.'

'I don't think so,' Mole said, shaking his head.

'Just try it for a little while,' said Young Hedgehog.

'Just for a little while then,' Mole agreed. And he stood there beside them, shuffling his feet and blinking his eyes and looking bored.

'Stop fidgeting!' said Young Hedgehog.

'I can't,' Mole said. 'I'm thinking of that tunnel I should be working on.'

'Forget the tunnel,' advised Young Hedgehog.

Then Mole began to get angry.

'I can't forget it, and I won't, so there!' he cried.

Young Hedgehog suddenly lost his patience.

'Oh go and dig your tunnel, for goodness sake!' Young Hedgehog cried. And in a few seconds Mole had disappeared under the ground.

'That's what you get for doing somebody a good turn!' said Rabbit.

'It seems to me,' Young Hedgehog said, 'that everybody is happiest doing what they want to do.'

'Yes,' said Rabbit, 'I suppose you're right. Now I'm going to find myself some dandelion leaves and sit in the sun and eat them.'

'And I'm going for a trot round the field,' said Young Hedgehog. 'I'll enjoy that. I might even go as far as the wood.' And he did. On the way back he rustled through the ferns that lay by the hedge and the sound frightened Mrs Thrush who was sitting on her nest in the hawthorn bush. She rose up with a great flutter of wings.

'It's all right, it's only me!' called Young Hedgehog.

'Oh dear,' chirped Mrs Thrush. 'I get so nervous when I'm minding my eggs.' Then she settled down again on her nest.

Young Hedgehog was feeling peckish so he began to root about in the grass to find something to eat, when his nose came bang up against something hard. It was Hereford Cow's right foot at the front.

'My!' cried Young Hedgehog. 'You're so big I can see only a bit of you at once! I'm too near to see all of you.' So Young Hedgehog trotted backwards a little way till he could see all of Hereford Cow.

'Goodness me!' Young Hedgehog cried. 'You make me feel so small!'

'So you are!' said Hereford Cow. 'Now do you mind leaving me in peace?'

So Young Hedgehog trotted off, feeling very small and not very important. Suddenly, looking up, he saw Shire Horse looming in front of him.

'Good gracious!' cried Young Hedgehog. 'You're so big it makes me dizzy to look up at you!'

'Then don't look!' snapped Shire Horse who was feeling very tired and tetchy after a hard day's work pulling a heavy cart.

'Sorry!' said Young Hedgehog, feeling smaller than ever, and he trotted off to find his friend Rabbit. On his way he saw the back of Large White Pig so he trotted down along the side of him to get to the front.

'You're so big,' said Young Hedgehog, 'it's a long way from one end of you to the other.'

'What do you want, little one?' grunted Large White Pig.

'Have you seen Rabbit?' asked Young Hedgehog.

'No,' said Large White Pig. 'I'm too busy eating to see anybody unless they push themselves under my nose as you have done.'

'I beg your pardon,' said Young Hedgehog, 'but I'm a bit upset.'

'What are you upset about?' asked Large White Pig. 'Talking of upsetting, you've got your foot on the edge of my dish!'

'Sorry,' Young Hedgehog said. 'You see, I'm upset because everybody is so big and I am so small.'

'You *are* small,' Large White Pig grunted. 'Now leave me in peace and let me finish my dinner.'

So Young Hedgehog trotted off again. He saw Rabbit at the end of the daisy field where the Ragged Robin flowers were growing. Just then, Big Badger ambled by.

'Out of my way, Tiny!' Badger gruffled.

'He called me Tiny!' Young Hedgehog cried, when he caught up with Rabbit.

'Well,' Rabbit said, 'I suppose he thinks you are.'

'Oh dear!' sighed Young Hedgehog. 'I've been made to feel very small today.'

'But you're big, really,' said Rabbit.

'Me!' Young Hedgehog cried. 'I'm not big!'

'Beetle thinks you are,' said Rabbit.

Young Hedgehog looked down at Beetle who was scurrying about under his feet.

'Hm,' said Young Hedgehog, 'now you come to mention it, I

suppose Beetle does think I'm big.' And suddenly Young Hedgehog began to feel a lot better.

'And look at those ants down there,' said Rabbit. 'They must think you're a giant!'

Young Hedgehog looked down at the tiny ants scuttling about.

'You're right,' he said. 'They *must* think I'm a giant!' And suddenly Young Hedgehog began to feel quite big and important. 'Now I'm going hunting for some food. Are you coming?'

'Not now,' said Rabbit. 'I'm just going to sit here in the sun and listen to the bees humming.'

'Very well,' Young Hedgehog said. 'I won't be long.' And off he went, mooching along by the hawthorn hedge, stopping now and then when he saw something interesting. He hadn't got far when he met Weasel. Young Hedgehog didn't like Weasel. Nobody liked Weasel. But when Weasel said 'Good morning,' Young Hedgehog's good manners told him to say 'Good morning' too.

'You're not with your friend Rabbit today,' said Weasel.

'No,' said Young Hedgehog, 'he just wanted to sit in the sunshine and listen to the bees humming.' And Young Hedgehog began to walk away, but Weasel said,

'Wait a minute, I haven't finished speaking.'

Young Hedgehog stopped.

'I was thinking,' said Weasel, 'about that Rabbit friend of yours.'

'What about him?' asked Young Hedgehog.

'Well,' Weasel began, 'he isn't very brave, is he?'

'No,' said Young Hedgehog, 'but he's a jolly good friend.'

'Hmm,' Weasel said. 'That Rabbit, he's not very clever either, is he?'

'No,' said Young Hedgehog, 'but he's a jolly good friend.'

'Hmm,' Weasel said. 'This Rabbit friend of yours isn't very strong, is he?'

'No,' said Young Hedgehog, 'but he's a jolly good friend.'

'Hmm,' said Weasel. 'This Rabbit isn't very fast either.'

'No,' Young Hedgehog said. 'But he's a jolly good friend.' And then Young Hedgehog felt he liked Weasel even less, so he walked down along the hedge and half-way across the daisy field, and all the time he couldn't help thinking of what Weasel had said. It was quite true. Rabbit wasn't very brave, and he wasn't very clever, and he wasn't very strong, and he wasn't very fast. Come to think of it, Rabbit wasn't very good at anything. Young Hedgehog just couldn't think why Rabbit had become his best friend ... How much better it would have been to have had a very brave friend like Badger, or a very strong friend like Hereford Bull, or a very clever friend like Red Fox, or a very fast friend like Horse. Young Hedgehog made up his mind to do something about it, so he trotted into the wood to find Badger, who he knew was very brave. Badger was changing his bed, throwing out all the old grass he used for bedding.

'Hello,' said Young Hedgehog. 'I was wondering if you would like to be my friend.'

'Oh, don't bother me,' growled Badger. 'Can't you see I'm busy!'

So Young Hedgehog trotted off to find Hereford Bull, who he knew was very strong. Hereford Bull was in a bad mood.

'Hello,' said Young Hedgehog. 'Would you like to be my friend?'

Hereford Bull snorted and stamped his hooves.

'Who wants to be a friend of a little thing like you!' Hereford Bull bellowed. 'Don't annoy me, I'm in a bad mood already!'

So Young Hedgehog trotted off to find Horse, who he knew was very fast.

'Hello, Horse!' said Young Hedgehog. 'Would you like to be my friend?'

Horse had a bunch of grass hanging out of his mouth. Chewing away with his large teeth he looked down at Young Hedgehog, but he didn't speak until he had swallowed all the grass he had in his mouth. Then he said,

'How would you like a friend as small as one of your feet?'

Young Hedgehog looked down at his own feet.

'No,' he said. 'I wouldn't like a friend as small as one of my feet. I'd be afraid of losing him.'

'Right,' said Horse. 'You are just as small as one of my feet! Now be off with you!' And Horse tugged up another mouthful of grass and began to chew.

So Young Hedgehog trotted off to find Red Fox, who he knew was very clever. He saw Red Fox padding along by the hedge.

'Hello,' said Young Hedgehog. 'Would you like to be my friend?'

'I'm nobody's friend!' growled Red Fox. 'Especially not a friend of a prickly little thing like you!' And off he trotted.

Suddenly, Young Hedgehog began to get very angry with himself.

'What on earth am I doing going about asking all those animals to be my friend when I have a good friend already!' And off he went to find Rabbit.

There was Rabbit, waiting for him by the hawthorn hedge, sitting among the daisies and buttercups.

'Hello, Rabbit!' Young Hedgehog said. 'It's nice having a good friend like you.' And Young Hedgehog and Rabbit sat by the hedge chatting and listening to the humming of the bees and smelling the meadowsweet flowers.

VERA RUSHBROOKE

THE FLYING RABBIT

One day, Small Rabbit was out in the meadow, as usual. He looked up at the birds in the sky. He thought to himself, 'I'm tired of walking about on the ground all the time. I'm going to fly, like the birds.'

He climbed a tree. It wasn't easy, because his front legs were too short and his back legs were too long.

When he was half way up, he looked down. The ground was a long way off. 'All right,' he thought. 'Now's the time to fly!'

He spread his front legs out like wings, and gave a great big rabbit-jump off his branch.

But he was lucky, for just underneath his flying-branch was the nest of the Crow family. He landed in it with a bump.

'Ow!' said the two little crows. 'Watch where you're falling!'

Small Rabbit didn't answer. He was wondering why he hadn't been able to fly. 'Can you fly?' he asked the little crows.

'Not yet,' they answered. 'But we will one day, if we try hard enough.'

'So will I,' said Small Rabbit. 'I'll stay here with you until then.'

Small Rabbit stayed in the Crows' nest all day. It was a bit of a squeeze, especially when Mr and Mrs Crow came back. They weren't pleased to find a new rabbit baby in their nest.

As it began to get dark, Mrs Rabbit noticed that Small was missing. She went out to the edge of the field to look for him. 'Small?' she called. 'Sma-all! Where are you?'

'Up here,' said Small, poking his head over the side of the Crows' nest.

'Good gracious! Whatever are you doing up there?' asked Mrs Rabbit.

'Learning to fly.'

'Come down, you silly child. Rabbits don't fly.'

'I won't come down.'

His mother went back to the burrow and fetched Mr Rabbit. He came and sat beside her under the tree. 'Be careful, Small,' he said. 'It's a long way down.'

All the nine little rabbits came too. They all sat in a row under the tree, looking up at Small.

No one knew what to do. Mr and Mrs Crow began to get cross. 'Look,' they said to Small. 'You can't stay here all night. There isn't room.'

'It won't take all night,' answered Small. 'As soon as I can fly, I'll go.'

'But rabbits can't fly,' shouted the Crows.

'In that case, I'll make history,' answered Small.

The Crows got angrier and angrier. The two baby crows were squashed under Small's furry tail. The big crows had to sit hanging over the edge of the nest. They looked like umbrellas that hadn't been folded up properly.

At last Mr Crow lost his temper. 'You stay here,' he said to Mrs Crow. 'I'm going out.' And off he flew.

So there they all sat, eleven rabbits in the field under the tree, and one rabbit and three crows in the nest. The biggest crow was hanging over the edge. The shadows of night began to creep across the field.

44

Mr Crow was away a long time. At last, just as the sun was beginning to disappear behind the hills, he came flying back. He landed on the side of the nest, and nearly fell off again, there was so little room.

'It's all right,' he said. 'I've been to see Owl and he's told me what to do.'

'What did he say?' asked Mrs Crow.

'Come up here and I'll tell you,' answered Mr Crow.

Mr and Mrs Crow flew to a branch higher up the tree, and he whispered into her ear behind his wing. No one else said anything. The eleven rabbits in the field, and the one rabbit and two crows in the nest, sat still and waited.

At last Mr and Mrs Crow came back. 'Come on, little crows,' said Mr Crow. 'Time to be going.'

'Going? Going where?' said the little crows.

'To the rabbit warren, of course. If rabbits are going to start flying, crows will have to start living in holes in the ground. Down we go!'

He picked up one of the little crows in his beak, and flew off. Mrs Crow elbowed Small out of the way with her wing, and flew off with the other little crow. They circled round and down, towards the rabbit burrow on the other side of the field.

Small watched them go. All at once he began to feel lonely. The sun had almost gone. He was getting cold, all on his own in the nest. He looked down. The eleven rabbits from his family were still sitting on the ground watching him.

'I . . . I think I'd better come down,' he said.

'All right,' said Mr Rabbit. 'Are you going to fly?'

'Not today. I don't feel much like flying any more. Rabbits ought to stay on the ground, and leave flying to the birds.'

'How will you get down then?'

'I'll have to jump,' said Small nervously. 'Will you catch me?'

'You can't jump,' his mother said. 'You'll hurt yourself.'

'I know!' said Mr Rabbit suddenly. He whispered to the other rabbits. Then he and Mrs Rabbit lay down, and Large climbed on to their backs. When he was ready the Medium Twins climbed up and balanced on top of his head. Then the bravest of the Triplets climbed up and stood on their heads. Soon there was a ladder of

rabbits, reaching all the way up to the Crows' nest. The baby rabbits were too small to climb, but they stood by ready to catch anyone who fell.

'Come on, Small,' said Mr Rabbit in a squashed sort of voice. 'Be quick, before we all fall over.'

As soon as Small was down, the rabbit ladder unsorted itself.

'Thank goodness for that,' said Mr Rabbit. 'It was flat work being at the bottom.'

'Don't ever do a thing like that again,' said Mrs Rabbit crossly to Small. 'Look what's happened now. We've got a family of Crows moved into our burrow. How are we going to get rid of them?'

But there was no need. As soon as the Crow family saw that their nest was empty, they flew back and put the baby crows safely inside it. 'We'll move into a new one tomorrow. As high as we can go,' said Mr Crow.

That's why, if you go and look, you'll find that all crows live in nests right at the top of very high trees. And rabbits stay on the ground.

KENNETH MCLEISH

TROUBLE IN THE
SUPERMARKET

One day when he was in a very joking mood Mr Delmonico offended a word witch. He did it by being a bit too clever. (Too much cleverness is often offensive to witches.)

Mr Delmonico, with his twins, Francis and Sarah, was shopping at the supermarket. The witch was there too, pushing a shopping trolley and talking to herself as word witches do ... they need a lot of words going on around them all the time.

'I'll have some peanut butter,' she said.

'You'd butter not,' cried Mr Delmonico, laughing at his own joke. The word witch took no notice, just went on talking to herself.

'And then perhaps I'll have a loaf of wholemeal bread,' she went on.

Mr Delmonico winked at the twins. 'How can you make a meal out of a hole?' he asked. 'It doesn't sound very nice.'

Francis and Sarah were horrified to hear their father speaking so carelessly to a word witch. But the witch ignored him. She was trying hard to behave well in a public place.

'I'll get some beans,' she muttered.

Mr Delmonico looked at the beans. He couldn't resist another joke. 'They look more like "might-have beans," ' he remarked with a smile.

Now the witch turned on him, glaring with her small red eyes. 'I've had quite enough of you,' she cried. 'You shall suffer from whirling words and see how you like it.'

Mr Delmonico was suddenly serious as the word witch scuttled away.

Whirling words sounded as if they might be painful.

'I'm afraid I might have got us into a bit of a jam,' he said to the twins.

'Daddy, be careful!' cried Sarah, but it was too late. They were up to their ankles in several kinds of jam. Francis was mainly mixed up with strawberry, Sarah with plum and apple, while Mr

Delmonico himself had melon and ginger jam up over the turn-ups of his trousers. The manager of the supermarket came hurrying up.

'What's going on here?' he cried.

'Nothing really,' Mr Delmonico said, trying to sound casual. 'Just some jam that was lying around.'

'There's something fishy about this,' declared the manager and then gasped, for a large flapping fish appeared out of nowhere and struck him on the right ear. Sarah and Francis realized that anyone near Mr Delmonico was going to suffer from whirling words too.

'You are to blame for all this mess,' said the manager, 'and you'll have to pay for it.'

'Oh, will I!' replied Mr Delmonico, trying hard to keep calm. 'Wait till I ring my lawyer.'

An elegant gold ring with an enormous diamond in it appeared in his hand. Mr Delmonico looked guilty and tried to hide it behind the bottles of vinegar.

'You can do what you like, you'll have to pay,' said the manager.

'*Me? Pay?* Look at my trousers all over jam! I shall lose my temper in a moment. You're just egging me on.'

Eggs began to fall out of the air. A few of them hit the super-market manager, but most of them broke on Mr Delmonico. He was jam to the knees and egg to the ears.

'Stop it!' cried the manager. 'And you talk of lawyers – why, you haven't got a leg to stand on.'

Mr Delmonico sat down suddenly in the jam.

'We must get out of this before the balloon goes up,' whispered Francis to Sarah, and he found himself rising out of the jam, Sarah beside him. To their delight a beautiful air balloon was carrying them gently away.

'Quick!' said Francis. 'Grab Dad.'

Catching Mr Delmonico by the collar and by the belt of his trousers his clever twins hoisted him into the air.

The manager waved his fist at them and shouted: 'You haven't heard the last of this.'

The balloon swooped through the supermarket door and skimmed over the roofs of the town.

'Home!' ordered Mr Delmonico. 'I'm not going to *that* shop again. They have a very funny way of displaying fish and jam.'

Francis shook his head. 'You shouldn't have teased the word witch, Dad.'

'Oh, these word witches need to be teased,' Mr Delmonico replied grandly. 'Wispy creatures with their heads in the clouds – whereas I am a pretty down-to-earth fellow.'

At that moment Mr Delmonico's collar and trouser belt gave way and he fell to earth – fortunately into his very own garden which he had dug and raked that morning until it was as soft as velvet.

'We're home,' said Francis, 'but the whirling words are still with us. What will we do about that?'

MARGARET MAHY

THE CITY BOY AND THE COUNTRY HORSE

Once a little boy named Johnny went with his mother and father to live on a farm.

Johnny felt very lonely. He had never been on a farm before. Everything was strange and new to him, and there was no one to play with. But the first morning, he woke up and the sun was shining and the birds were singing, and when he went outdoors in the clean, sweet air, he felt very happy.

Johnny saw a little baby horse grazing in the grass. His brown coat gleamed in the sun. When the little baby horse saw the little boy, he looked at him with such deep brown eyes that the little boy felt that he and the horse should be friends.

So Johnny went up to the white wooden fence and called to the horse, 'Hey there!'

The baby horse, being a horse, thought the little boy had some hay for him. Over he ran – gallop, gallop, gallop – up to the fence. He put his head over the fence and waited for his hay.

But Johnny did not have any hay for the baby horse.

The little horse thought, 'This little boy has tricked me.' He hung his handsome horse head and walked slowly away.

And when the little horse walked away and left Johnny standing alone on the other side of the fence, the little boy thought, 'This little horse doesn't like me.' He hung his little-boy head and walked away too, feeling lonelier than before.

The next day Johnny woke up bright and early, and the air smelled clean and good. His mother gave him a delicious hot breakfast, and the sun and the blue sky made the world look so beautiful that he was sure he could make friends with the baby horse.

'I'll try again today,' Johnny thought.

So he went out to the pasture and called to the horse, 'Hey there!'

The little horse thought, 'He looks like such a fine little boy, I'm sure he won't trick me again.' So he went running over to the fence on his slender legs – gallop, gallop, gallop.

But, of course, the little boy had no hay.

The little horse hung his head and walked away, swishing his tail from side to side in disappointment.

'That little boy tricked me,' the little horse thought. 'I can't be his friend.'

When Johnny saw the baby horse walking away he hung his little-boy head and tears came to his eyes.

'That little horse still doesn't like me,' he thought.

And more than anything, Johnny wanted to be friends with the little horse.

So the next morning, while he was eating his breakfast, he asked his mother a question.

'How do you make someone like you who doesn't know you?'

His mother asked him a question.

'How *can* you make someone like you if he doesn't know you?'

The little boy started to think.

'Then how can I make the little horse know me?' he wondered.

'What do little baby horses eat?' he asked.

His mother smiled.

'Horses eat carrots and oats and hay,' she said. 'There's lots of hay behind the barn.'

Johnny swallowed his last bit of cereal and gulped down his last swallow of milk, and ran out of the house. He filled his arms with the hay he found behind the barn. Then he ran to the pasture as fast as he could.

'Little horse!' he called.

When the little horse heard him, he lifted up his head and thought, 'Today he doesn't call and pretend he has some hay. Today we *might* make friends.' And he came running over on his long spindly legs – gallop, gallop, gallop.

And there was the little boy with an armful of hay.

The little horse ate it gratefully. He munched each wisp, shaking his head with every mouthful. Then he nuzzled the little boy with his velvety nose and licked the little boy's hand with his rough wet tongue.

Since the little horse couldn't talk, Johnny never knew why they had not been friends right from the start. He put his arms around the horse's head and rubbed his face back and forth against the short, stiff horse fur. He and the baby horse were friends at last.

They grew up together and they had many good times. Johnny never again thought that someone who didn't know him didn't like him.

CHARLOTTE BROOKMAN

THOMAS AND THE MONSTER

Thomas put on his wellies and his lucky woollen hat and walked up the garden path.

'I see you've got your lucky hat on,' remarked Snoodles the tortoise, who was just waking up from a nap on the grass. 'Are you going somewhere special?'

'Just looking for Monsters,' said Thomas. 'There might be one at the bottom, where the stream is.'

'Well, don't shout for me if you find one,' said Snoodles sleepily. 'I'm just going to have another little sleep in the rhubarb patch.'

Thomas walked on under the cherry trees until he came to the little summer-house by the stream. It was very quiet down here. The stream was half dried up and only made a soft murmur as it ran and the birds only twittered now and then because they were resting in green branches away from the hot sun.

He walked round the summer-house and looked in through its small dusty window. He couldn't see very well because the dust was quite thick, so he rubbed the glass with his lucky woollen hat.

Then he looked again. Inside was a wooden table with two chairs. On the table lay a heap of red cherries. And sitting on one of the chairs was a Monster.

Thomas knew he was a Monster because his hair was green and very short, like fur, and he had two horns sticking out – one above each ear.

Thomas put on his lucky hat again and opened the door.

'Hello,' he said, 'are you a Monster?'

The Monster looked rather frightened. 'I hope you don't mind me being here,' he said nervously in a kind of choky voice, as though he had a sore throat. 'I couldn't find anywhere else to sleep. And I had a few cherries.'

Thomas sat down on the other chair. 'I don't mind at all,' he said. And he gave the Monster a handful of cherries and took some himself.

'I was on my way back to the mountains,' the Monster explained, putting some cherry-stones neatly in a row, 'when somehow I took a wrong turning. I got mixed up with motorways and railway stations and yards full of buses. Nobody saw me because I'm rather good at dodging underneath things. In the end I found myself in your garden. I am quite worn out. So I had a drink of stream-water and a few cherries, and came in here.'

'You can stay as long as you want,' said Thomas kindly. 'Which mountains are you going to?'

'This year,' said the Monster, 'I'm going to Wales. My uncle told me of a nice dry cave by a lake that will just suit me.'

'I think my Dad's got a map of England and Wales,' said Thomas, looking excited. 'Wait here for me.' And he ran up the path into the house. Thomas went into the kitchen and asked Mum if he could borrow the map for a little while. Mum got it out of the bureau drawer for him.

'Be careful with it,' said Mum, 'and put it back in the drawer when you've finished.'

Thomas carried the map down to the garden and spread it out on the table so that the Monster could see it properly. After a little while he said happily, 'Now I see where I went wrong! Do you mind if I take a few cherries in my pocket? Thank you very much. I'll be on my way now. And if ever you come to that lake in North Wales I showed you, be sure to look me up. My relations will all be very pleased to meet you. I suppose,' he added, blinking his rather beautiful green eyes, 'I suppose you wouldn't let me try your hat on before I go?'

Thomas was a little doubtful if it would fit him, as he had a couple of horns to manage; but when Thomas passed it over he put it on his head quite easily, letting the horns poke through on each side.

'It *does* feel nice and warm,' said the Monster, giving a sort of sigh. And he was just going to take it off when Thomas said suddenly, 'No, you keep it. It's a lucky hat, so I'm sure you'll get to Wales all right.'

The Monster beamed. 'I'll be off, then. Goodbye!'

And he hurried through the door and disappeared among the bushes.

Thomas folded the map up carefully. Then he looked at the Monster's cherry-stones lying in a neat row.

'I'll keep them,' said Thomas to himself. 'Then nobody can say I haven't really seen a Monster.'

When he got back to the kitchen Mum said, 'Where's your lucky hat?'

'I've lent it to a Monster,' said Thomas.

'Well,' said Mum, 'it was time you had a new one, anyway.'

And that very evening she started to knit him a new one.

MARJORIE STANNARD

IRRITATING IRMA

Irma was very good at climbing. Her parents were calm people, who, if they saw Irma clamber up a church steeple or the outside of a lighthouse, would just murmur admiringly, 'Lovely, darling.' So when they took a holiday cottage near some steep cliffs and

56

Irma told them she was going looking for eagles, they just said, 'Lovely, darling.'

Irma began to climb the cliffs and half-way up she found a little door. The door belonged to a dragon who was having a very nice long sleep, and he wasn't a bit pleased to be woken up. He stared at Irma's teeth braces and glasses and he wasn't very impressed. He rumbled like a forge.

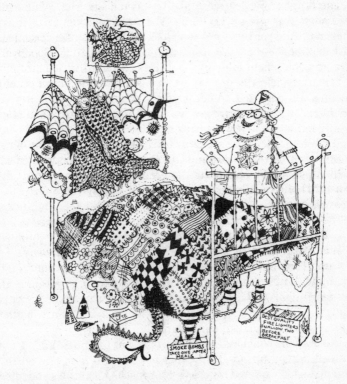

'What a cute green lizard!' said Irma.

The dragon, insulted, uttered a huge echoey roar which splintered granite flakes from his cave.

'That's a nasty cough you've got,' said Irma.

The dragon eyed her Spiderman T-shirt and torn jeans and the cap that she had got free from a service station. He remembered clearly that maidens usually wore dear little gold crowns and embroidered slippers, and they always squealed when they met him and looked ill at ease. He glared at Irma and spurted forth a long, smoky orange flame.

'No wonder you've got a cough,' Irma said. 'Smoking's a nasty habit and bad for your health. And this cave certainly is musty and it needs airing.'

The dragon made a noise like bacon rashers frying but Irma was busy inspecting everything. 'You need a broom for a start,' she said. 'And maybe a cuckoo clock up there by the door. Tch! Just look at the dust over everything! Tomorrow I'll bring some cleaning equipment and anything else I can think of.'

When she left, the dragon set to work, only he didn't do any dusting. He collected boulders and filled up the cave entrance. Bouldered up, and fortressed up, and buttressed up, he smiled grimly to himself and went back to sleep.

Some hours later he woke to a whirring headachy rumbling. Granite chips rattled around his ears, and Irma scrambled in, carrying a bright pneumatic power drill. 'Good morning,' she called. 'There must have been a landslide during the night. But I cleaned it up.'

The dragon's scales rattled. Angry little flames flickered in his jaw. He made a noise like a hundred barbecues and he squinted ferociously at Irma.

'Don't frown like that,' she ordered, tying on an apron. 'You'll end up with ugly worry lines. There's a lot of work to get through this morning. First I'll sweep this gritty sand away, and you could really do with a nice carpet in here, or maybe tiles would be better. If there's one thing I just can't stand, it's disorder.'

The dragon sizzled fretfully, but worse was to come. When Irma finished tidying up, she turned her attention to him. She bossily trimmed and lacquered his claws. She polished his scales and lifted up his wings and dusted under them with talcum powder. The dragon blushed but Irma didn't take any notice, because she was busy tying a blue ribbon around his tail. 'I've got to be going now,' she said. 'But I'll be back tomorrow.'

The dragon watched her climb down the cliff. 'There's only one way to get any peace,' he thought. 'I'll just have to eat her.

Tomorrow. Freckles will taste nasty, and so will ginger hair, but maybe if I shut my eyes and gulp, it won't be so bad.' He groaned. Parents, he knew from past experience, usually came looking for devoured maidens, waving lances and acting very unfriendly.

When Irma arrived next morning, he opened his jaws, without much enthusiasm, ready to eat her, but Irma said, 'Look what I brought you!'

She shoved a plate under his nose. On it was a layer cake with strawberry cream filling, iced with chocolate icing and whipped cream, sprinkled with hundreds and thousands, lollies and meringues. The dragon shuddered weakly and felt ill.

'You look as though you're coming down with the flu,' said Irma. She took his temperature and spread a blanket over him. The blanket was fluffily pink and edged with satin binding, and the dragon thought it was very babyish. Irma wrapped it around him and fastened it with a kitten brooch. 'I'll leave you to get some rest now, you poor old thing,' she said.

'You will?' thought the dragon hopefully.

'But I'll drop by first thing tomorrow,' said Irma. 'It's lucky for you I still have three weeks of my holiday left.'

And for three weeks, every day, she came, and the dragon suffered. She decorated his cave with pot plants and cushions, a beanbag chair, posters, a bookcase, calendars, and a dart board, and she brought along a toothbrush and bullied him into cleaning his teeth.

But at last, one morning, she said, 'I've got to go back to school tomorrow. You'll just have to look after yourself till next summer holidays.'

When Irma left, the dragon purred and capered about the cave. 'Hooray!' he thought. 'Good riddance! No more boring chatter and no more being organized, and best of all, undisturbed sleep!' He curled up and shut his eyes.

But his dreams were fretful, and he got up at daybreak feeling tetchy and cross. He paced his cave and wondered why the silence seemed weary, and the hours bleak and long. He brooded and nibbled at a claw, and crouched in his doorway staring down at the beach, but it was empty, because all the holiday people had gone. Irma had gone.

'Hooray!' he roared. 'And she won't be back for many glorious months!'

But why, he wondered glumly, were tears rolling down his cheeks?

Everywhere he looked in his cave he saw things Irma had lugged up the cliff to decorate his cave without permission. 'Yuk,' said the dragon morosely, and he kicked a pot plant over the cliff. A wave snatched at it, and the dragon gave a roar of anger and slithered down the cliff and grabbed it back. He carried it crossly back to his cave and plonked it down on Irma's bookcase.

'Even when she's not here, she's irritating,' he thought. 'I should have eaten her and got it over with. And the very next time I see her, irritating Irma will be my next meal! Freckles and all! Just wait!'

And he waited, but all his little flames flickered out one by one,

and his scales lost their sparkle, and his ribboned tail drooped listlessly. Winter howled though his cave, and he brooded, and led a horrid, bad-tempered life.

But at last gay umbrellas began to blossom like flowers along the beach, and it was summer. The dragon sharpened his teeth against the rocks and tried to work up an appetite. And the day came when Irma bounced in through his door, and the indignant dragon opened his massive jaws wide.

'Hello!' cried Irma. 'I meant to write, but I forgot your address, but just look what I brought you! Suntan lotion, and a yo-yo with a long string so it will reach down to the bottom of the cliff, and a kite with a picture of you on it, and now tell me, did you miss me? I certainly missed *you*!'

The dragon blinked in despair at her tangly plaits and glasses and teeth braces. 'She's talkative and tedious and her manners are terrible!' he reminded himself fiercely.

('And yet,' he thought, 'it's strange, but I rather like her face.')

'Nonsense!' he roared to himself. 'She's annoying and bossy and

61

an utter little nuisance, and no one invited her here; she just walks in as though she owns the whole cliff!'

('And yet,' he thought, 'of all the maidens all forlorn, I rather like her best.')

'Didn't you miss me?' demanded Irma.

The dragon began to shake his head indignantly, but try as he could to prevent it, the headshake turned into a nod.

'Then we'll celebrate,' said Irma. 'What would you like for lunch?'

'Plain scones, please, Irma,' said the dragon.

ROBIN KLEIN

THE FISH ANGEL

Noreen Callahan was convinced that her father's fish store on Second Avenue was, without a doubt, the ugliest fish store on the East Side. The sawdust on the floor was always slimy with fish drippings; the fish were piled in random heaps on the ice; the paint on the walls was peeling off in layers; even the cat sleeping in the window was filthy. Mr Callahan's apron was always dirty, and he wore an old battered hat that was in worse shape than the cat, if such a thing were possible. Often, fish heads would drop on the floor right under the customers' feet, and Mr Callahan wouldn't bother to sweep them up. And as time passed, most of his customers went elsewhere for their fish.

Mr Callahan had never wanted to sell fish in a fish store. He wanted to be an actor, to do great, heroic, marvellous things on the stage. He tried, but was unsuccessful, and had to come back to work in his father's fish store, the store which was now his. But he took no pride in it; for what beauty was possible, what marvellous, heroic things could be done in a fish store?

Noreen's mother helped in the store most of the week, but Saturday was Noreen's day to help while her mother cleaned the house. To Noreen, it was the worst day of the week. She was ashamed to be seen in the store by any of her friends and class-mates, ashamed of the smells, ashamed of the fish heads and fish tails, ashamed of the scruffy cat, and of her father's dirty apron. To Noreen, the fish store seemed a scar across her face, a scar she'd been born with.

And like a scar, Noreen carried the fish store with her every-where, even into the schoolroom. *Fish Girl! Fish Girl! Dirty Fish Girl!* some of the girls would call her. When they did, Noreen wished she could run into the dark clothes closet at the back of the room and cry. And once or twice, she did.

But pleasant things also happened to Noreen. A few weeks before Christmas, Noreen was chosen to play an angel in the church pageant, an angel who would hover high, high up on a platform above everyone's head. And best of all, she would get to wear a beautiful, beautiful angel's gown. As beautiful as her mother could make it.

Mrs Callahan worked on the angel's gown every night, sewing on silver spangles that would shine a thousand different ways in the light. And to go with the gown, she made a sparkling crown, a tiara, out of cloth and cardboard and gold paint and bits of clear glass.

On the day of the pageant, Noreen shone almost like a real angel, and she felt so happy and light that with just a little effort she might have flown like a real angel, too. And after the pageant, Noreen's mother and father had a little party for her in their living room. Mr Callahan had borrowed a camera to take pictures of Noreen in her angel's gown. 'To last me at least a year of looking,' he said.

For though Mr Callahan hated his fish store, he loved Noreen with a gigantic love. He often told Noreen that some children were the apple of their father's eye, but she was not only the apple of his eye, but the peach, pear, plum and apricot, too.

And Noreen would ask, 'And strawberry?'

'Yes, b'God,' her father would say. 'You're the fruit salad of m' eye, that's what you are. Smothered in whipped cream.'

And so he took picture after picture with the big old camera that slid in and out on a wooden frame. Noreen had a wonderful time posing with her friend Cathy, who had also been an angel in the pageant. But the party came to an end as all parties must, and it was time to take off the angel's gown and the tiara, and become Noreen Callahan again. How heavy Noreen felt after so much lightness and shining. Into the drawer, neatly folded, went the heavenly angel. 'Perhaps next year,' her mother said, 'we'll have it out again.'

That night, Noreen dreamed that she was dancing at a splendid ball in her dress of silver and her crown of gold. Round and round the ballroom she went, as silver spangles fluttered down like snow, turning everything into a shimmering fairy's web of light. And then she was up on her toes in a graceful pirouette. Everyone watched; everyone applauded. As she whirled, her dress opened out like a great white flower around her and ... suddenly she felt herself sliding and skidding helplessly. She looked down; the silver spangles had changed to fish scales. The floor was covered with fish heads and fish tails and slimy, slippery sawdust. And everyone was calling: *Fish Girl! Fish Girl! Fish Girl!*

Noreen awoke, not knowing quite where she was for a moment. Then she turned over in the bed and cried and cried, till she finally fell asleep again.

The next week passed in a blur of rain and snow that instantly turned to slush. Every day, when she came home from school, Noreen looked at the dress lying in the drawer. *Wear me, wear me,* it seemed to say. But Noreen just sighed and shut the drawer, only to open it and look again an hour later.

And then, all too soon, it was Saturday. The day Noreen dreaded. Fish store day. How she wished she could turn into a real angel and just fly away.

Suddenly Noreen sat down on her bed. She knew it was decided before she could actually think. The angel gown! How could anyone wait a year to have it out again? She would wear it now. Now! In her father's store. And then people would know that she had nothing to do with that dirty apron and filthy floor. And perhaps those children would stop calling her Fish Girl. She would be a Fish Angel now.

Mrs Callahan saw the gown under Noreen's coat, as Noreen was about to leave the house. She rarely scolded Noreen, but this was too much! It was completely daft! That gown would be ruined; her father would be very angry. Everyone would laugh at her; everyone would think she was crazy! But Mrs Callahan saw that nothing, absolutely nothing, could stop Noreen. And she finally gave in, but not before warning Noreen that next year she would have to make her own dress. An angel's gown in a fish store! Why it was almost a sin!

When Noreen arrived at the fish store and took off her coat, Mr Callahan was busy filleting a flounder. But when he saw Noreen he gasped and nicked himself with the knife.

'*Aggh!*' he called out, and it was a cry of surprise at the gown, and anger at Noreen, and pain from the cut, all in one. He nursed his finger, not knowing what to say to Noreen in front of all those customers.

'What a lovely gown,' said a woman.

'What happened?' asked another. 'Is it a special occasion?'

'His daughter,' whispered a third. 'His daughter. Isn't she gorgeous?'

And Mr Callahan simply couldn't be angry any more. As the customers complimented him on how absolutely beautiful his daughter looked, he felt something he hadn't felt for a long, long time. He felt a flush of pride. Perhaps marvellous things, even heroic things *could* be done in a fish store.

Mr Callahan watched Noreen as she weighed and wrapped the fish, very, very carefully so as not to get a single spot on her dress. Wherever she moved, his eyes followed, as one follows the light of a candle in a dark passage.

And towards the end of the day, Mr Callahan took off his filthy apron and his battered hat. He went to the little room in the back of the store, and returned wearing a clean, white apron.

Christmas came and passed, and New Year, and Noreen wore her gown and tiara every Saturday. And more and more customers came to see the girl in the angel gown. Mr Callahan put down fresh sawdust twice a day, and laid the fish out neatly in rows, and washed and cleaned the floors and window. He even cleaned the cat, and one night in January he painted the walls white as chalk. And his business began to prosper.

The children who had called Noreen *Fish Girl*, called her nothing at all for a while. But they finally found something which they seemed to think was even worse. *Fish Angel*, they called her. *Fish Angel*. But Noreen just smiled when she heard them, for she had chosen that very name for herself, a secret name, many weeks before.

And Saturday soon became Noreen's favourite day of the week, for that was the day she could work side by side with her father in what was, without a doubt, the neatest, cleanest fish store on the East Side of New York.

MYRON LEVY

THE BADDEST
WITCH IN THE WORLD

When the morning kindergarten cut jack-o'-lanterns from orange paper and pasted them on the windows so that the light shone through the eye and mouth holes, Ramona knew that at last Hallowe'en was not far away. Next to Christmas and her birthday, Ramona liked Hallowe'en best. She liked dressing up and going trick-or-treating after dark with Beezus. She liked those nights when the bare branches of trees waved against the streetlights, and the world was a ghostly place. Ramona liked scaring people, and she liked the shivery feeling of being scared herself.

Ramona had always enjoyed going to school with her mother to watch the boys and girls of Glenwood School parade on the playground in their Hallowe'en costumes. Afterwards she used to eat a doughnut and drink a paper cup of apple juice if there happened to be some left over. This year, after years of sitting on the benches with mothers and little brothers and sisters, Ramona was finally going to get to wear a costume and march around and around the playground. This year she had a doughnut and apple juice coming to her.

'Mama, did you buy my mask?' Ramona asked every day, when she came home from school.

'Not today, dear,' Mrs Quimby answered. 'Don't pester. I'll get it the next time I go down to the shopping centre.'

Ramona, who did not mean to pester her mother, could not see why grown-ups had to be so slow. 'Make it a bad mask, Mama,' she said. 'I want to be the baddest witch in the whole world.'

'You mean the worst witch,' Beezus said, whenever she happened to overhear this conversation.

'I do not,' contradicted Ramona. 'I mean the baddest witch.' 'Baddest witch' sounded much scarier than 'worst witch', and Ramona did enjoy stories about bad witches, the badder the better. She had no patience with books about good witches, because witches were supposed to be bad. Ramona had chosen to be a witch for that very reason.

Then one day when Ramona came home from school she found two paper bags on the foot of her bed. One contained black material and a pattern for a witch costume. The picture on the pattern showed the witch's hat pointed like the letter A. Ramona reached into the second bag and pulled out a rubber witch mask so scary that she quickly dropped it on the bed because she was not sure she even wanted to touch it. The flabby thing was the greyish-green colour of mould and had stringy hair, a hooked nose, snaggle teeth, and a wart on its nose. Its empty eyes seemed to stare at Ramona with a look of evil. The face was so ghastly that Ramona had to remind herself that it was only a rubber mask from the toy store before she could summon enough courage to pick it up and slip it over her head.

Ramona peeked cautiously in the mirror, backed away, and then gathered her courage for a longer look. That's really me in there, she told herself and felt better. She ran off to show her mother and discovered that she felt very brave when she was inside the mask and did not have to look at it. 'I'm the baddest witch in the world!' she shouted, her voice muffled by the mask, and was delighted when her mother was so frightened she dropped her sewing.

Ramona waited for Beezus and her father to come home, so she could put on her mask and jump out and scare them. But that night, before she went to bed, she rolled up the mask and hid it behind a cushion of the couch in the living-room.

'What are you doing that for?' asked Beezus, who had nothing to be afraid of. She was planning to be a princess and wear a narrow pink mask.

'Because I want to,' answered Ramona, who did not care to sleep in the same room with that ghastly, leering face.

Afterwards when Ramona wanted to frighten herself she would lift the cushion for a quick glimpse of her scary mask before she clapped the pillow over it again. Scaring herself was such fun.

When Ramona's costume was finished and the day of the Hallowe'en parade arrived, the morning kindergarten had trouble sitting still for seat work. They wiggled so much while resting on their mats that Miss Binney had to wait a long time before she found someone quiet enough to be the wake-up fairy. When kindergarten was finally dismissed, the whole class forgot the rules and went stampeding out the door. At home Ramona ate only the soft part of her tuna-fish sandwich, because her mother insisted she could not go out on an empty stomach. She wadded the crusts into her paper napkin and hid them beneath the edge of her plate before she ran to her room to put on her long black dress, her cape, her mask, and her pointed witch hat held on by an elastic under her chin – but today she was too happy and excited to bother to make a fuss.

'See, Mama!' she cried. 'I'm the baddest witch in the world!'

Mrs Quimby smiled at Ramona, patted her through the long black dress, and said affectionately, 'Sometimes I think you are.'

'Come on, Mama! Let's go to the Hallowe'en parade.' Ramona had waited so long that she did not see how she could wait another five minutes.

'I told Howie's mother we would wait for them,' said Mrs Quimby.

'Mama, did you have to?' protested Ramona, running to the front window to watch for Howie. Fortunately, Mrs Kemp and Willa Jean were already approaching with Howie dressed in a black cat costume, lagging along behind holding the end of his tail in one hand. Willa Jean in her stroller was wearing a buck-toothed rabbit mask.

Ramona could not wait. She burst out the front door yelling through her mask, 'Yah! Yah! I'm the baddest witch in the world! Hurry, Howie! I'm going to get you, Howie!'

Howie walked stolidly along, lugging his tail, so Ramona ran out to meet him. He was not wearing a mask, but instead had pipe-cleaners Scotch-taped to his face for whiskers.

'I'm the baddest witch in the world,' Ramona informed him, 'And you can be my cat.'

'I don't want to be your cat,' said Howie. 'I don't want to be a cat at all.'

'Why not, Howie?' asked Mrs Quimby, who had joined Ramona and the Kemps. 'I think you make a very nice cat.'

'My tail is busted,' complained Howie. 'I don't want to be a cat with a busted tail.'

Mrs Kemp sighed. 'Now, Howie, if you'll just hold up the end of your tail nobody will notice.' Then she said to Mrs Quimby, 'I promised him a pirate costume, but his older sister was sick and while I was taking her temperature Willa Jean crawled into a cupboard and managed to dump a whole quart of salad oil all over the kitchen floor. If you've ever had to clean oil off a floor, you know what I went through, and then Howie went into the bathroom and climbed up – yes dear, I understand you wanted to help – to get a sponge, and he accidentally knelt on a tube of toothpaste that someone had left the top off of – now Howie, I didn't say you left the top off – and toothpaste squirted all over the bathroom, and there was another mess to clean up. Well, I finally had to drag his sister's old cat costume out of a drawer, and when he put it on we discovered the wire in the tail was broken, but there wasn't time to rip it apart and put in a new wire.'

'You have a handsome set of whiskers,' said Mrs Quimby, trying to coax Howie to look on the bright side.

'Scotch tape itches me,' said Howie.

Ramona could see that Howie was not going to be any fun at all, even on Hallowe'en. Never mind. She would have fun all by herself. 'I'm the baddest witch in the world,' she sang in her muffled voice, skipping with both feet. 'I'm the baddest witch in the world.'

When they were in sight of the playground, Ramona saw that

70

it was already swarming with both the morning and the afternoon kindergarteners in their Hallowe'en costumes. Poor Miss Binney, dressed like Mother Goose, now had the responsibility of sixty-eight boys and girls. 'Run along, Ramona,' said Mrs Quimby, when they had crossed the street. 'Howie's mother and I will go around to the big playground and try to find a seat on a bench before they are all taken.'

Ramona ran screaming on to the playground. 'Yah! Yah! I'm the baddest witch in the world!' Nobody paid any attention, because everyone else was screaming, too. The noise was glorious. Ramona yelled and screamed and shrieked and chased anyone who would run. She chased tramps and ghosts and ballerinas. Sometimes other witches in masks exactly like hers chased her, and then she would turn around and chase the witches right back. She tried to chase Howie, but he would not run. He just stood beside the fence holding his broken tail and missing all the fun.

Ramona discovered dear little Davy in a skimpy pirate costume from the toy store. She could tell he was Davy by his thin legs. At last! She pounced and kissed him through her rubber mask. Davy looked startled, but he had the presence of mind to make a gagging noise while Ramona raced away, satisfied that she finally had managed to catch and kiss Davy.

Then Ramona saw Susan getting out of her mother's car. As she might have guessed, Susan was dressed as an old-fashioned girl with a long skirt, an apron, and pantalettes. 'I'm the baddest witch in the world!' yelled Ramona, and ran after Susan whose curls bobbed daintily about her shoulders in a way that could not be disguised. Ramona was unable to resist. After weeks of longing she tweaked one of Susan's curls, and yelled, '*Boing!*' through her rubber mask.

'You stop that,' said Susan, and smoothed her curls.

'Yah! Yah! I'm the baddest witch in the world!' Ramona was carried away. She tweaked another curl and yelled a muffled '*Boing!*'

A clown laughed and joined Ramona. He too tweaked a curl and yelled, '*Boing!*'

The old-fashioned girl stamped her foot. 'You stop that!' she said angrily.

'*Boing! Boing!*' Others joined the game. Susan tried to run away, but no matter which way she ran there was someone eager to stretch a curl and yell, '*Boing!*' Susan ran to Miss Binney. 'Miss Binney! Miss Binney!' she cried. 'They're teasing me! They're pulling my hair and boinging me!'

'Who's teasing you?' asked Miss Binney.

'Everybody,' said Susan tearfully. 'A witch started it.'

'Which witch?' asked Miss Binney.

Susan looked around. 'I don't know which witch,' she said, 'but it was a bad witch.'

'That's me, the baddest witch in the world,' thought Ramona. At the same time she was a little surprised. That others really would not know that she was behind her mask had never occurred to her.

'Never mind, Susan,' said Miss Binney. 'You stay near me, and no one will tease you.'

Which witch, thought Ramona, liking the sound of the words. Which witch, which witch. As the words ran through her thoughts Ramona began to wonder if Miss Binney could guess who she was. She ran up to her teacher and shouted in her muffled voice, 'Hello, Miss Binney! I'm going to get you, Miss Binney!'

'Ooh, what a scary witch!' said Miss Binney, rather absentmindedly, Ramona thought. Plainly Miss Binney was not really frightened, and with so many witches running around she had not recognized Ramona.

No, Miss Binney was not the one who was frightened. Ramona was. Miss Binney did not know who this witch was. Nobody knew who Ramona was, and if nobody knew who she was, she wasn't anybody.

'Get out of the way, old witch!' Eric R. yelled at Ramona. He did not say, 'Get out of the way, Ramona.'

Ramona could not remember a time when there was not someone near who knew who she was. Even last Hallowe'en, when she dressed up as a ghost and went trick-or-treating with Beezus and the older boys and girls, everyone seemed to know who she was. 'I can guess who this little ghost is,' the neighbours said, as they dropped a miniature candy bar or a handful of peanuts into her paper bag. And now, with so many witches running around and still more witches on the big playground, no one knew who she was.

'Davy, guess who I am!' yelled Ramona. Surely Davy would know.

'You're just another old witch,' answered Davy.

The feeling was the scariest one Ramona had ever experienced. She felt lost inside her costume. She wondered if her mother would know which witch was which, and the thought that her own mother might not know her frightened Ramona even more. What if her mother forgot her? What if everyone in the whole world forgot her? With that terrifying thought Ramona snatched off her mask, and although its ugliness was no longer the most frightening thing about it, she rolled it up so she would not have to look at it.

How cool the air felt outside that dreadful mask! Ramona no longer wanted to be the baddest witch in the world. She wanted to be Ramona Geraldine Quimby and be sure that Miss Binney and everyone on the playground knew her. Around her the ghosts and tramps and pirates raced and shouted, but Ramona stood near the door of the kindergarten quietly watching.

Davy raced up to her and yelled, 'Yah! You can't catch me!'

'I don't want to catch you,' Ramona informed him.

Davy looked surprised and a little disappointed, but he ran off on his thin little legs, shouting, 'Yo-ho-ho and a bottle of rum!'

Joey yelled after him, 'You're not really a pirate. You're just Mush Pot Davy!'

Miss Binney was trying to herd her sixty-eight charges into a double line. Two mothers who felt sorry for the teacher were helping round up the kindergarten to start the Hallowe'en parade, but as always there were some children who would rather run around than do what they were supposed to do. For once Ramona was not one of them. On the big playground someone started to play a marching record through a loudspeaker. The Hallowe'en parade that Ramona had looked forward to since she was in nursery school was about to begin.

'Come along, children,' said Miss Binney. Seeing Ramona standing alone, she said, 'Come on, Ramona.'

It was a great relief to Ramona to hear Miss Binney speak her name, to hear her teacher say 'Ramona' when she was looking at her. But as much as Ramona longed to prance along to the marching music with the rest of her class, she did not move to join them.

'Put on your mask, Ramona, and get in line,' said Miss Binney, guiding a ghost and a gypsy into place.

Ramona wanted to obey her teacher, but at the same time she was afraid of losing herself behind that scary mask. The line of kindergarteners, all of them wearing masks except Howie with his pipe-cleaner whiskers, was less straggly now, and everyone was eager to start the parade. If Ramona did not do something quickly she would be left behind, and she could not let such a thing happen, not when she had waited so many years to be in a Hallowe'en parade.

Ramona took only a moment to decide what to do. She ran to her cupboard inside the kindergarten building and snatched a crayon from her box. Then she grabbed a piece of paper from the supply cupboard. Outside she could hear the many feet of the morning and afternoon kindergartens marching off to the big playground. There was no time for Ramona's best printing, but that was all right. This job was not seat work to be supervised by Miss Binney. As fast as she could Ramona printed her name, and then she could not resist adding with a flourish her last initial complete with ears and whiskers.

Now the whole world would know who she was! She was Ramona Quimby, the only girl in the world with ears and whiskers on her last initial. Ramona pulled on her rubber mask, clapped

her pointed hat on top of it, snapped the elastic under her chin, and ran after her class as it marched on to the big playground. She did not care if she was last in line and had to march beside gloomy old Howie still lugging his broken tail.

Around the playground marched the kindergarten followed by the first grade and all the other grades while mothers and little brothers and sisters watched. Ramona felt very grown-up remembering how last year she had been a little sister sitting on a bench watching for her big sister Beezus to march by and hoping for a left-over doughnut.

'Yah! Yah! I'm the baddest witch in the world!' Ramona chanted, as she held up her sign for all to see. Around the playground she marched towards her mother, who was waiting on the bench. Her mother saw her, pointed her out to Mrs Kemp, and waved. Ramona beamed inside her stuffy mask. Her mother recognized her!

Poor little Willa Jean in her stroller could not read, so Ramona called out to her, 'It's me, Willa Jean. I'm Ramona, the baddest witch in the world!'

Willa Jean in her rabbit mask understood. She laughed and slapped her hands on the tray of her stroller.

Ramona saw Henry's dog Ribsy trotting along, supervising the parade. 'Yah! Ribsy! I'm going to get you, Ribsy!' she threatened, as she marched past.

Ribsy gave a short bark, and Ramona was sure that even Ribsy

knew who she was as she marched off to collect her doughnut and apple juice.

BEVERLY CLEARY

MOTHER MOUSE

The two children both slept in the nursery, the little girl in the bed by the wall and the little boy in the bed under the window. Between them were the toys, the boy's cars and building blocks and his crane and the girl's dolls' tables and chairs and her little kitchen. The children could start playing with them again straight away in the morning, because the toys spent the whole night exactly where they had been left the night before.

Or so they thought.

But under the floor of the nursery lived Mother Mouse, and Mother Mouse had seven children and fourteen grandchildren, all grown-up now. At night the children and grandchildren came up out of the hole. The boy-mice rode in the cars and built houses and castles with the building blocks and the girl-mice made tea in the kitchen and held parties on the chairs round the little tables. When it grew light they cleared everything away, put the things back where they had been and returned to Mother Mouse.

'Did you dance on the table?' asked Mother Mouse.

'No,' said the children and grandchildren, 'there was a new Mercedes that we drove around in and a new tea service with little blue flowers on it which we drank tea from.'

'I see,' said Mother Mouse. 'There were no such riches in my day. Your father and I were quite satisfied with the table. Your father wound up the musical box and we danced. All night.'

'Boring!' said the children.

'Hold your tongues, you spoiled brats,' said Mother Mouse. 'If your father were still alive you would have had a clip round the ear.'

76

Then they went to sleep, while above their heads the little boy and the little girl played with the cars and the building blocks and the crane and the dolls' tables and chairs and the kitchen.

Mother Mouse grew old.

'Oh, children,' she said, 'I have not much longer to live. Oh, children, how I should love to see the table just once more, and the musical box, and to dance round once again!'

'You do that, Ma,' said the children and grandchildren. 'We'll come and dance round with you.'

'Oh, children,' said Mother Mouse, 'I can't get on the table any more.'

But the mouse-boys whispered *smisple-smisple* in each other's ears. 'We can easily hoist you up,' they said.

When the little boy and the little girl were asleep that night, the mice-boys ran out at once and by the light of the moon they began to build a high tower. They gathered all the building-blocks together and stacked them on top of each other with the crane.

Red, blue, yellow, green, close up to the table. And they built a staircase around the tower and the staircase came out at the top, by the edge of the table.

Johnnie, the youngest mouse-grandchild, got into the new Mercedes and drove it down through the hole to Mother Mouse's house.

'Oh, child, what a luxury!' said Mother Mouse, stepping in through the car door, which really opened. 'Oh, if only your father could have seen this!'

You could not even hear the engine of the luxury car as it drove along and stopped at the entrance to the tower. Mother Mouse stepped shakily out.

'Oh, children, what times, what times,' she sighed. 'Nothing but innovations everywhere. Is that a kitchen? Oh, no! What a tea-service! Finer than the Queen's. And whose is this palace?'

'That is a tower, Ma,' said the children and grandchildren. 'Come on, we'll go up to the top.'

'Oh, oh, all those stairs!'

'Yes, Ma, then we can get on to the table.'

Mother Mouse climbed, step by step, with a sigh on every step. The little mouse-boys went in front, pulling, with the little mouse-girls behind, pushing. At every landing Mother Mouse had to take a rest. 'Oh, children, what an adventure!' Then came the last step, and there was the table, lying before her like a shining dance-floor.

'Oh, children, my old heart ...' sobbed Mother Mouse, walking slowly to the middle of the table. The children and grandchildren had hauled all the little tables and chairs up to the top and arranged them in a circle. They had found the old musical box, too, and hoisted it up. Johnnie wound it up and with a rusty *scrunch* it began to play 'The More We are Together'.

Mother Mouse stood up slowly. She stood on her hind legs and she stretched out her forepaws as if they were arms. 'The more we are together,' she sang croakily, and with stiff, swaying movements she began to dance.

She danced with her seven children and then with her fourteen grandchildren and after 'Together' came the French song '*Sur le pont d'Avignon*'. And after the dance they drank tea from the blue-flowered tea-service and Johnnie wound up the musical box again.

'Oh, children,' stammered Mother Mouse. 'Oh, children, that I should have lived to see the day.' And she stood up for the next dance.

'Oh, children,' she cried, twirling. 'Oh, your father ...'

Then she clutched at her heart and fell, still dancing.

Next morning, when the little boy and the little girl woke up, they saw a high tower of building blocks beside the table, with the new Mercedes standing in front of it. On the table stood all the

dolls' tables and chairs in a ring, and the flowered tea-cups were full of tea-leaves.

And there in the middle lay a dead mouse.

The children never did find out how it all happened, and when their mother dropped the dead mouse in the waste-paper basket she said 'Bah'.

She never knew that it was Mother Mouse.

PAUL BIEGEL
Translated by
PATRICIA CRAMPTON

A TREE FOR MISS JENNY MILLER

'I'm six today!' Jenny sang it like a song. 'Six today. Six today.'

She ran into the kitchen.

'Happy birthday!' said her mother.

'Happy birthday, six-year-old!' said her father.

Jenny sat down to have breakfast.

'I don't *feel* different today,' she said. She ate some bread and jelly.

'Do I *look* different?'

Her father took a good look.

'Mmm,' he said. 'There *is* something different.'

'What is it? What is it?' cried Jenny.

'Well,' said her father. 'There's a different kind of jelly on your face this morning!'

Jenny laughed at her nice silly father. Everything made her laugh today.

All morning she sang,

I'm six today!
Six today.
Six today.

The postman came by as Jenny sang her song.

'Six today! Is that so?' he said. 'Well, here's a letter for Miss Jenny Miller. She sounds six years old. So maybe it's for you.'

Jenny ran into the house with the letter.

'Am I Miss Jenny Miller?' she asked her mother.

'Yes, indeed!' said her mother. 'Sit down, Miss Jenny Miller, and I will read your letter to you.'

The letter said:

> The day I was six, someone gave me a wonderful present. I want you to have one just like it.
> I will bring it to you tomorrow.
> The present is a tree.

> Love,
> *Aunt Rachel.*

A tree!

A tree for a birthday present!

'But where can I put a *tree?*' asked Jenny.

'There is room in front of the house,' said her mother. 'And there is room in the backyard. Where do you want it?'

'I have to think about that,' said Jenny.

Jenny ran outside to the front of the house and looked around.

'It's so sunny out here,' she thought. 'Sometimes it's too sunny and too hot to play. But it's nice and cool under a tree. If I put the tree here, I can bring my doll outside and play house under the tree.'

Then Jenny ran into the backyard.

'But there's more room here,' she thought. 'If I put it here I can sit way up in the tree. I will see everyone, but no one else will see me. Yes, I want the tree here.'

Jenny fell asleep that night, thinking about the tree – how cool it was under her tree, how green it was up in the tree.

In the morning she said, 'How can Aunt Rachel bring a *tree* all the way from her house?'

'Mmm,' said her father. 'Maybe on her head?'

Jenny had to laugh when she thought about that.

Her mother said, 'In the car, of course.'

A tree in a car? Maybe this car was a truck!

So Jenny sat outside and looked for a truck with a tree.

But Aunt Rachel did not come in a truck. She came in her car, an old station wagon.

Jenny was puzzled.

Where was the tree?

'Happy birthday, Jenny dear!' said Aunt Rachel. Then she went out to the back of the station wagon and took something out. 'Here it is!' she cried. 'Jenny's tree!'

Jenny thought Aunt Rachel must be fooling, for she was holding

up something that looked like a tall plant. It was set in a ball of dirt, and it wasn't much taller than Aunt Rachel herself! How could that skinny old thing be a *tree*?

Jenny said, 'Thank you,' but she wanted to cry.

They had lunch, and there was still some pink birthday cake. But Jenny did not want any.

'What's the matter?' her mother asked.

'Nothing,' said Jenny.

They waited until Father came home to plant the tree.

'Where do you want to put it?' he asked Jenny.

Jenny said, 'In the backyard,' but she wanted to say, 'I don't care! I don't care!'

Father made a deep hole. First he put some tree food in, and next the little tree. Then he packed the dirt around the tree and watered it.

'You will have to water it every day this week,' he told Jenny.

Jenny wanted to cry out, 'I won't! I don't care if it grows! Skinny old thing!'

Aunt Rachel took a good look at Jenny, then she said, 'If your mother says yes, will you come home with me, Jenny? I have something to show you.'

Jenny loved to visit Aunt Rachel, and her mother said yes. It was fun to drive home with her aunt. It was fun to sleep in her aunt's big bed. It was fun to have Aunt Rachel's pancakes for breakfast next morning.

Jenny almost forgot about the tree.

'Let's have our cocoa outside,' said Aunt Rachel, 'in the back-yard.'

Jenny took the cups out on a tray.

'Where shall we sit?' she asked.

'Look around,' said her aunt, 'and find the very best place!'

The place Jenny liked best in her aunt's backyard was the big green tree with the little green bench right under it.

So they sat down on the bench and had cocoa.

'What did you want to show me, Aunt Rachel?' Jenny asked.

'This tree,' said her aunt.

How tall it was! How green!

'This is *my* birthday tree,' said Aunt Rachel.

'Your birthday tree!' cried Jenny. 'But it's so *big*!'

'This tree was my birthday present when I was six,' said her aunt. 'When I got it, it was just as small as yours. Some birthday presents are to play with and some are to grow with. We grew up together, my tree and I.'

Jenny looked up again at the tree.

'Will *my* tree ever be this big?' she asked.

'Yes, I think so,' said her aunt.

Jenny thought about her little tree, growing and growing.

All at once she jumped up.

'Can we go home now, Aunt Rachel?' she said. 'I have to get back to water my tree.'

LILIAN MOORE

NAUGHTY LITTLE THURSDAY

The farmer's wife came out of the kitchen door and walked across the farmyard. Mrs Hen, sitting on her three eggs in the open barn, watched her. She put down her clothes basket and pegged shirts and sheets, towels and trousers, pillowcases and pullovers along the line until there wasn't an inch of space left. It was Monday. Mrs Hen knew it and shifted about on her eggs. It was time for them to hatch and she had enough of sitting there keeping them warm. If only she could follow the farmer's wife back indoors, there would be crumbs for her. But she couldn't. She had to stay there until her chickens came out of their shells.

With her leathery long thin claws, she gently moved an egg. She listened. Could she hear a faint, very faint tap? She thought she could. She listened again. Yes, there it was. Tap, tap, tap, tap. It went on and on and, before long, a fine line, as delicate as a pencil line, ran across the shell. She prodded it gently with her beak. It opened a little. Mrs Hen helped it to widen. Soon a tiny yellow beak appeared and, after it, a small bald-looking head. Her

chicken pushed with his shoulders and stood there among the ruins of the egg, thin, flat-feathered and scrawny. But his mother was pleased with him. She thought he was beautiful.

'You're Monday, my little one,' she told him, drawing him under her glossy russet-coloured feathers. 'You're Monday, because you hatched out on washing day.'

The new chick peered out from under his mother's wing. 'I'm Monday, Monday, Monday!' he chirped cheekily. He didn't want to be smothered by feathers, he pushed himself out with his stick-like legs and got back up on his tiny splay-feet. He staggered about unsteadily and cheeped as he poked his beak about in the straw and corn.

'I want a playmate. Make my brothers hurry up and come out of their shells.'

'I only wish I could,' sighed Mrs Hen moving fussily to try to get comfortable. 'I've had more than enough of sitting here. When I think of the corn I could be pecking and the crumbs that the farmer's wife would throw out for me, it makes me quite cross.' She chucked, chucked, chucked away to herself and gave each of the eggs a tap – quite a firm, cross tap with her beak.

Tuesday came and there was no tapping to be heard from either of the two unhatched eggs. Wriggling about, Mrs Hen tried to get comfortable. On Tuesdays, Mrs Parkinson, the farmer's wife's mother, always visited. In her basket there was always a cake that she had baked herself. And what cakes she baked! Mrs Hen had tasted crumbs from them all. Today, when she saw Mrs Parkinson arrive at the door, her mouth watered. Her beak began to open and shut.

'If only I could have some cake crumbs,' she moaned sadly. And, when the door closed and Mrs Parkinson and her cake had gone inside the farmhouse, Mrs Hen could not stop herself from giving each of the eggs another sharp peck.

'Get on with it,' she clucked. 'Do you expect me to sit here all the week?'

As if in reply, a first faint tap came from one of the eggs. Mrs Hen sat very still and listened. The tapping went on. She moved the egg so that she could tap too. There was no doubt about it, the second egg was hatching. Firmer and firmer became the tapping until the first faint crack appeared. The chicken tapped and poked, tapped and poked, and, at last, got its beak through. Mrs Hen helped, and his damp, ugly, large head came right out of the shell.

'My little lovely one,' clucked his mother. She caressed him.

'You're Tuesday,' she told him. 'You're my own little Tuesday, because you came on the same day as Mrs Parkinson and her cake.'

Beady-eyed Tuesday was even perkier than his brother. He wouldn't let his mother take him under her feathers. He didn't want to be petted. He struggled up on his spindly legs, he tried to move his fragile wings.

'I'm hungry,' he cheeped. 'Find me something to eat. I'm hungry.'

'Now I've two fine chicks,' thought Mrs Hen, looking at the unsteady matchstick-legged pair. 'Soon we'll all go looking for crumbs,' she told them. 'There's only one more egg to hatch.'

'Hurry up, Mother, hurry up,' they both cried.

'I'm doing my best,' she told them and she fluffed and she fluffed and she fluffed up her feathers until she looked like a soft ball.

She sat and watched the red sun go down behind the chimney pots on the farmhouse roof. Soon it was dark everywhere. The two new chicks slept and Mrs Hen listened and waited.

When morning came and it was light again, Mrs Hen shifted her egg with her sharp pointed claws. She looked for a crack. There wasn't one. She listened with her head down for a tap. There wasn't one. Now she was really cross. 'You've been in there long enough,' she clucked angrily. 'Come out. Do you hear me? Come out!'

The two chicks, whose feathers were dry now and who looked less ugly, strutted on their stick-like legs and chirped, 'We want crumbs. We want crumbs,' although they didn't know yet what crumbs were.

'Be quiet, you two,' their mother ordered. 'How do you expect me to hear if your brother is tapping? I want . . . Goodness me!' she interrupted herself, for she had just seen their neighbour Mrs Richardson come into the farmyard. 'Of course, it's Wednesday, the day she comes for her cream. Well, perhaps your brother will be Wednesday.'

But he wasn't. Mrs Richardson came out with her jug of cream and went through the farmyard back to her house. The two chickens went on pecking among the corn and straw and Mrs Hen went on sitting on her last egg. Mrs Hen watched the farmer's wife wash one of the dogs in a big tin bath. He barked because he hated the water. She watched the farmer lead the cows back to the shed for milking. She watched the farmhand fetch bundles of fresh straw with his fork. She sat and watched everything that went on, because she couldn't leave her egg. She was spitting-cross because she had to sit and sit and sit.

All night long she went on sitting. The morning came and with a sigh Mrs Hen knew it was Thursday when she saw the farmer's wife loading her car with vegetables to go to market to sell them.

'I just can't believe it,' she fussed, 'Thursday, and I'm still sitting here.'

She rolled her egg out from under her feathers, not very gently, and she looked it all over. She tapped it on one side. She tapped it on the other. Then, holding up her beak with exasperation she brought it down so hard that she forced a crack.

'There,' she clucked triumphantly, 'if you won't make the effort,

I will. You're coming out, my lad, for I'm not sitting here any longer.'

'No!'

Mrs Hen couldn't believe her ears. Her feathers stood on end. Quite distinctly, she heard a 'no' from inside the shell.

'What do you mean, "no"?' she asked.

'I mean no, no, no! I'm not coming out,' squeaked her chick from inside the shell.

'Oh, yes you are and quick, so get tapping!'

'No, I'm not. I'm staying here in the warm.'

Mrs Hen looked like a porcupine with her feathers stiff with anger. She thrust her beak into the crack and opened it.

'Your brothers are waiting for you,' she tried to tempt him. 'They are both getting stronger each day.'

'I don't want to see them. They'll bully me. They're big. I'm only little.'

'And you'll stay little and grow with your feet in your ears if you don't come out of that shell,' Mother Hen hissed into the crack.

'I don't care!'

There was only one thing Mrs Hen could do and she did it. She pointed her beak and forced it down sharply into the crack. The shell opened enough for her to see two large beady eyes and a yellow beak. The chicken looked at his mother and said, 'Go away.'

That was enough for Mrs Hen. After all these days of waiting her chick had said 'Go away.' So she went. She turned and walked away, clucking furiously and saying, 'All right then, I'll go. I'll go to the farmhouse with your brothers for lovely soft cake crumbs. Come on, Monday. Come on, Tuesday.'

They went, all three of them, and suddenly it was quite quiet. The chicken knew he was all alone.

'Crumbs?' he chirped. 'I wonder what crumbs are?'

He began to peck at his shell. 'I think I'd like crumbs,' he thought. And he pecked and tapped and pecked and tapped. Before his mother and his brothers had got very far, he was out of his shell. Thin, damp-feathered, all head and just a scrawny body on matchstick legs, he staggered uncertainly after them calling out, 'Wait for me! I want some crumbs! Wait for me!'

Mrs Hen looked back. She forgot all those hours and days of waiting. She forgot how cross she had been. She forgot how cheeky he had been. To her he looked beautiful.

'So you're little Thursday after all!' she clucked. 'Come on, my precious one. Come with us to the farmhouse for some crumbs.'

And off they went in a tottering line, Mrs Hen, then Monday, then Tuesday, and last of all, little Thursday, naughty little Thursday.

BARBARA IRESON

THE ONE THAT GOT AWAY

'And what have we to remember to bring tomorrow?' Mrs Cooper asked, at half past three. Malcolm, sitting near the back, wondered why she said 'we'. *She* wasn't going to bring anything.

'Something interesting, Mrs Cooper,' said everyone else, all together.

'And what are we going to do then?'

'Stand up and talk about it, Mrs Cooper.'

'So don't forget. All right. Chairs on tables. Good-bye, Class Four.'

'Good-bye, Mrs Cooper. Good-bye, everybody.'

It all came out ever so slow, like saying prayers in assembly. 'Amen,' said Malcolm, very quietly. Class Four put its chairs on the tables, collected its coats and went home, talking about all the interesting things it would bring into school tomorrow.

Malcolm walked by himself. Mrs Cooper had first told them to find something interesting on Monday. Now it was Thursday and still he had not come up with any bright ideas. There were plenty of things that he found interesting, but the trouble was, they never seemed to interest anyone else. Last time this had happened he had brought along his favourite stone and shown it to the class.

'Very nice, Malcolm,' Mrs Cooper had said. 'Now tell us what's interesting about it.' He hadn't known what to say. Surely anyone looking at the stone could see how interesting it was.

Mary was going to bring her gerbil. James, Sarah and William had loudly discussed rare shells and fossils, and the only spider in the world with five legs.

'It can't be a spider then,' said David, who was eavesdropping.

'It had an accident,' William said.

Isobel intended to bring her pocket calculator and show them how it could write her name by punching in 738051 and turning it upside down. She did this every time, but it still looked interesting.

Malcolm could think of nothing.

When he reached home he went up to his bedroom and looked at the shelf where he kept important things; his twig that looked like a stick insect, his marble that looked like a glass eye, the penny with a hole in it and the Siamese-twin jelly-babies, one red, one green and stuck together, back to back. He noticed that they were now stuck to the shelf, too. His stone had once been there as well, but after Class Four had said it was boring he had put it back in the garden. He still went to see it sometimes.

What he really needed was something that could move about, like Mary's gerbil or William's five-legged spider. He sat down on his bed and began to think.

On Friday, after assembly, Class Four began to be interesting. Mary kicked off with the gerbil that whirred round its cage like a

89

hairy balloon with the air escaping. They they saw William's lame spider, James's fossil, Jason's collection of snail shells stuck one on top of the other like the leaning tower of Pisa, and David's bottled conkers that he had kept in an air-tight jar for three years. They were still as glossy as new shoes.

Then it was Malcolm's turn. He went up to the front and held out a matchbox. He had chosen it very carefully. It was the kind with the same label top and bottom so that when you opened it

you could never be sure that it was the right way up and all the matches fell out. Malcolm opened it upside down and jumped. Mrs Cooper jumped too. Malcolm threw himself down on hands and knees and looked under her desk.

'What's the matter?' Mrs Cooper said.

'It's fallen out!' Malcolm cried.

'What is it?' Mrs Cooper said, edging away.

'I don't know – it's got six legs and sharp knees ... and sort of frilly ginger eyebrows on stalks – He pounced. 'There it goes.'

'Where?'

'Missed it,' said Malcolm. 'It's running under your chair, Mary.'

Mary squeaked and climbed onto the table because she thought that was the right way to behave when creepy-crawlies were about.

'I see it!' Jason yelled, and jumped up and down. David threw a

book in the direction that Jason was pointing and James began beating the floor with a rolled-up comic.

'I got it – I killed it,' he shouted.

'It's crawling up the curtains,' Sarah said and Mrs Cooper, who was standing by the curtains, moved rapidly away from them.

'It's over by the door,' Mary shrieked, and several people ran to head it off. Chairs were overturned.

Malcolm stood by Mrs Cooper's desk with his matchbox. His contribution was definitely the most interesting thing that anyone had seen that morning. He was only sorry that he hadn't seen it himself.

JAN MARK

THE BOOK OF BEASTS

He happened to be building a palace when the news came, and he left all the bricks kicking about the floor for Nurse to clear up – but then the news was rather remarkable news. You see, there was a knock at the front door and voices talking downstairs, and Lionel thought it was the man come to see about the gas, which had not been allowed to be lighted since the day when Lionel made a swing by tying his skipping-rope to the gas-bracket.

And then, quite suddenly, Nurse came in, and said, 'Master Lionel, dear, they've come to fetch you to go and be King.'

Then she made haste to change his smock and to wash his face and hands and brush his hair, and all the time she was doing it Lionel kept wriggling and fidgeting and saying, 'Oh, don't, Nurse,' and, 'I'm sure my ears are quite clean,' or, 'Never mind my hair, it's all right,' and, 'That'll do.'

'You're going on as if you were going to be an eel instead of a King,' said Nurse.

The minute Nurse let go for a moment Lionel bolted off without waiting for his clean handkerchief, and in the drawing-room there were two very grave-looking gentlemen in red robes with fur, and gold coronets with velvet sticking up out of the middle like the cream in the very expensive jam tarts.

They bowed to Lionel, and the gravest one said:

'Sire, your great-great-great-great-great-grandfather, the King of this country, is dead, and now you have got to come and be King.'

'Yes, please, sir,' said Lionel. 'When does it begin?'

'You will be crowned this afternoon,' said the grave gentleman who was not quite so grave-looking as the other.

'Would you like me to bring Nurse, or what time would you like me to be fetched, and hadn't I better put on my velvet suit with the lace collar?' said Lionel, who had often been out to tea.

'Your Nurse will be removed to the Palace later. No, never mind about changing your suit; the Royal robes will cover all that up.'

The grave gentlemen led the way to a coach with eight white horses, which was drawn up in front of the house where Lionel lived. It was No. 7, on the left-hand side of the street as you go up.

Lionel ran upstairs at the last minute, and he kissed Nurse and said:

'Thank you for washing me. I wish I'd let you do the other ear.

93

No – there's no time now. Give me the hanky. Good-bye, Nurse.'

'Good-bye, ducky,' said Nurse; 'be a good little King now, and say "please" and "thank you", and remember to pass the cake to the little girls, and don't have more than two helps of anything.'

So off went Lionel to be made a King. He had never expected to be a King any more than you have, so it was all quite new to him – so new that he had never even thought of it. And as the coach went through the town he had to bite his tongue to be quite sure it was real, because if his tongue was real it showed he wasn't dreaming. Half an hour before he had been building with bricks in the nursery; and now – the streets were all fluttering with flags; every window was crowded with people waving handkerchiefs and scattering flowers; there were scarlet soldiers everywhere along the pavements, and all the bells of all the churches were ringing like mad, and like a great song to the music of their ringing he heard thousands of people shouting, 'Long live Lionel! Long live our little King!'

He was a little sorry at first that he had not put on his best clothes, but he soon forgot to think about that. If he had been a girl he would very likely have bothered about it the whole time.

As they went along, the grave gentlemen, who were the Chancellor and the Prime Minister, explained the things which Lionel did not understand.

'I thought we were a Republic,' said Lionel. 'I'm sure there hasn't been a King for some time.'

'Sire, your great-great-great-great-great-grandfather's death happened when my grandfather was a little boy,' said the Prime Minister, 'and since then your loyal people have been saving up to buy you a crown – so much a week, you know, according to people's means – sixpence a week from those who have first-rate pocket-money, down to a halfpenny a week from those who haven't so much. You know it's the rule that the crown must be paid for by the people.'

'But hadn't my great-great-however-much-it-is-grandfather a crown?'

'Yes, but he sent it to be tinned over, for fear of vanity, and he had had all the jewels taken out, and sold them to buy books. He was a strange man; a very good King he was, but he had his faults – he was fond of books. Almost with his latest breath he sent the crown to be tinned – and he never lived to pay the tinsmith's bill.'

Here the Prime Minister wiped away a tear, and just then the carriage stopped and Lionel was taken out of the carriage to be crowned. Being crowned is much more tiring work than you would suppose, and by the time it was over, and Lionel had worn the Royal robes for an hour or two and had had his hand kissed by everybody whose business it was to do it, he was quite worn out, and was very glad to get into the Palace nursery.

Nurse was there, and tea was ready: seedy cake and plummy cake, and jam and hot buttered toast, and the prettiest china with red and gold flowers on it, and real tea, and as many cups of it as you liked. After tea Lionel said:

'I think I should like a book. Will you get me one, Nurse?'

'Bless the child,' said Nurse, 'you don't suppose you've lost the use of your legs with just being a King? Run along, do, and get your books yourself.'

So Lionel went down into the library. The Prime Minister and the Chancellor were there, and when Lionel came in they bowed very low, and were beginning to ask Lionel most politely what on earth he was coming bothering for now – when Lionel cried out:

'Oh, what a worldful of books! Are they yours?'

'They are yours, your Majesty,' answered the Chancellor. 'They were the property of the King, your great-great – '

'Yes, I know,' Lionel interrupted. 'Well, I shall read them all. I love to read. I am so glad I learned to read.'

'If I might venture to advise your Majesty,' said the Prime Minister, 'I should *not* read these books. Your great – '

'Yes?' said Lionel, quickly.

'He was a very good King – oh, yes, really a very superior King in his way, but he was a little – well, strange,'

'Mad?' asked Lionel, cheerfully.

'No, no' – both the gentlemen were sincerely shocked. 'Not mad; but if I may express it so, he was – er – too clever by half. And I should not like a little King of mine to have anything to do with his books.'

Lionel looked puzzled.

'The fact is,' the Chancellor went on, twisting his red beard in an agitated way, 'your great – '

'Go on,' said Lionel.

'Was *called* a wizard.'

'But he wasn't?'

'Of course not – a most worthy King was your great – '

'I see.'

'But I wouldn't touch his books.'

'Just this one,' cried Lionel, laying his hands on the cover of a great brown book that lay on the study table. It had gold patterns on the brown leather, and gold clasps with turquoises and rubies in the twists of them, and gold corners, so that the leather should not wear out too quickly.

'I *must* look at this one,' Lionel said, for on the back in big letters he read 'The Book of Beasts'.

The Chancellor said, 'Don't be a silly little King.'

But Lionel had got the gold clasps undone, and he opened the first page, and there was a beautiful Butterfly, all red, and brown, and yellow, and blue, so beautifully painted that it looked as if it were alive.

'There,' said Lionel 'isn't that lovely? Why – '

But as he spoke the beautiful Butterfly fluttered its many-coloured wings on the yellow old page of the book, and flew up and out of the window.

'Well!' said the Prime Minister, as soon as he could speak for the lump of wonder that had got into his throat and tried to choke him, 'that's magic, that is.'

But before he had spoken the King had turned the next page, and there was a shining bird complete and beautiful in every blue feather of him. Under him was written, 'Blue Bird of Paradise', and while the King gazed enchanted at the charming picture the Blue Bird fluttered his wings on the yellow page and spread them and flew out of the book.

Then the Prime Minister snatched the book away from the King and shut it up on the blank page where the bird had been, and put it on a very high shelf. And the Chancellor gave the King a good shaking, and said:

'You're a naughty, disobedient little King,' and was very angry indeed.

'I don't see that I've done any harm,' said Lionel. He hated being shaken, as all boys do; he would much rather have been slapped.

'No harm?' said the Chancellor. 'Ah – but what do you know about it? That's the question. How do you know what might have been on the next page – a snake or a worm, or a centipede or a revolutionist, or something like that.'

'Well, I'm sorry if I've vexed you,' said Lionel. 'Come, let's kiss and be friends.' So he kissed the Prime Minister, and they settled down for a nice quiet game of noughts and crosses, while the Chancellor went to add up his accounts.

But when Lionel was in bed he could not sleep for thinking of the book, and when the full moon was shining with all her might and light he got up and crept down to the library and climbed up and got 'The Book of Beasts'.

He took it outside on to the terrace, where the moonlight was as bright as day, and he opened the book, and saw the empty pages with 'Butterfly' and 'Blue Bird of Paradise' underneath, and then he turned the next page. There was some sort of red thing sitting under a palm tree, and under it was written 'Dragon'. The Dragon did not move, and the King shut up the book rather quickly and went back to bed.

But the next day he wanted another look, so he got the book out into the garden, and when he undid the clasps with the rubies and turquoises, the book opened all by itself at the picture with 'Dragon' underneath, and the sun shone full on the page. And then, quite suddenly, a great Red Dragon came out of the book, and spread vast scarlet wings and flew away across the garden to the far hills, and Lionel was left with the empty page before him, for the page was quite empty except for the green palm tree and the yellow desert, and the little streaks of red where the paint brush had gone outside the pencil outline of the Red Dragon.

And then Lionel felt that he had indeed done it. He had not been King for twenty-four hours, and already he had let loose a Red Dragon to worry his faithful subjects' lives out. And they had been saving up so long to buy him a crown, and everything!

Lionel began to cry.

Then the Chancellor and the Prime Minister and the Nurse all came running to see what was the matter. And when they saw the book they understood, and the Chancellor said:

'You naughty little King! Put him to bed, Nurse, and let him think over what he's done.'

'Perhaps, my Lord,' said the Prime Minister, 'we'd better first find out just exactly what he *has* done.'

Then Lionel, in floods of tears, said:

'It's a Red Dragon, and it's gone flying away to the hills, and I *am* sorry, and oh, do forgive me!'

But the Prime Minister and the Chancellor had other things to think of than forgiving Lionel. They hurried off to consult the police and see what could be done. Everyone did what they could.

They sat on committees and stood on guard, and lay in wait for the Dragon, but he stayed up in the hills, and there was nothing more to *be* done. The faithful Nurse, meanwhile, did not neglect her duty. Perhaps she did more than anyone else, for she slapped the King and put him to bed without his tea, and when it got dark she would not give him a candle to read by.

'You are a naughty little King,' she said, 'and nobody will love you.'

Next day the Dragon was still quiet, though the more poetic of Lionel's subjects could see the redness of the Dragon shining through the trees quite plainly. So Lionel put on his crown and sat on his throne and said he wanted to make some laws.

And I need hardly say that though the Prime Minister and the Chancellor and the Nurse might have the very poorest opinion of Lionel's private judgement, and might even slap him and send him to bed, the minute he got on his throne and set his crown on his head, he became infallible – which means that everything he said was right, and that he couldn't possibly make a mistake. So when he said:

'There is to be a law forbidding people to open books in schools or elsewhere' – he had the support of at least half his subjects, and the other half – the grown-up half – pretended to think he was quite right.

Then he made a law that everyone should always have enough to eat. And this pleased everyone except the ones who had always had too much.

And when several other nice new laws were made and written down he went home and made mud-houses and was very happy. And he said to his Nurse:

'People will love me now I've made such a lot of pretty new laws for them.'

But Nurse said: 'Don't count your chickens, my dear. You haven't seen the last of that Dragon yet.'

Now the next day was Saturday. And in the afternoon the Dragon suddenly swooped down upon the common in all his hideous redness, and carried off the Football Players, umpires, goal-posts, football, and all.

Then the people were very angry indeed, and they said:

'We might as well be a Republic. After saving up all these years to get his crown, and everything!'

And wise people shook their heads and foretold a decline in the National Love of Sport. And, indeed, football was not at all popular for some time afterwards.

Lionel did his best to be a good King during the week, and the people were beginning to forgive him for letting the Dragon out of the book. 'After all,' they said, 'football is a dangerous game, and perhaps it is wise to discourage it.'

Popular opinion held that the Football Players, being tough and hard, had disagreed with the Dragon so much that he had gone away to some place where they only play cats' cradle and games that do not make you hard and tough.

All the same, Parliament met on the Saturday afternoon, a convenient time, when most of the Members would be free to attend, to consider the Dragon. But unfortunately the Dragon, who had only been asleep, woke up because it was Saturday, and he considered the Parliament, and afterwards there were not any Members left, so they tried to make a new Parliament, but being an M.P. had somehow grown as unpopular as football playing, and no one would consent to be elected, so they had to do without a Parliament. When the next Saturday came round everyone was a little nervous, but the Red Dragon was pretty quiet that day and only ate an Orphanage.

Lionel was very, very unhappy. He felt that it was his disobedience that had brought this trouble on the Parliament and the Orphanage and the Football Players, and he felt that it was his duty to try and do something. The question was, what?

The Blue Bird that had come out of the book used to sing very nicely in the Palace rose-garden, and the Butterfly was very tame, and would perch on his shoulder when he walked among the tall lilies. So Lionel saw that *all* the creatures in the Book of Beasts could not be wicked, like the Dragon, and he thought:

'Suppose I could get another beast out who would fight the Dragon?'

So he took the Book of Beasts out into the rose-garden and opened the page next to the one where the Dragon had been, just a tiny bit, to see what the name was. He could only see 'cora', but he felt the middle of the page swelling up thick with the creature that was trying to come out, and it was only by putting the book down and sitting on it suddenly, very hard, that he managed to get it shut. Then he fastened the clasps with the rubies and turquoises in them and sent for the Chancellor, who had been ill on Saturday week, and so had not been eaten with the rest of the Parliament, and he said:

'What animal ends in "cora?"'

The Chancellor answered:

'The Manticora, of course.'

'What is he like?' asked the King.

'He is the sworn foe of Dragons,' said the Chancellor. 'He drinks their blood. He is yellow, with the body of a lion and the face of a man. I wish we had a few Manticoras here now. But the last died hundreds of years ago – worse luck!'

Then the King ran and opened the book at the page that had 'cora' on it, and there was the picture-Manticora, all yellow, with a lion's body and a man's face, just as the Chancellor had said. And under the picture was written, 'Manticora'.

And in a few minutes the Manticora came sleepily out of the book, rubbing its eyes with its hands and mewing piteously. It seemed very stupid, and when Lionel gave it a push and said, 'Go along and fight the Dragon, do,' it put its tail between its legs and fairly ran away. It went and hid behind the Town Hall, and at night when the people were asleep it went round and ate all the pussy-cats in the town. And then it mewed more than ever. And on the Saturday morning, when people were a little timid about going out, because the Dragon had no regular hour for calling, the Manticora went up and down the streets and drank all the milk that was left in the cans at the doors for people's teas, and it ate the cans as well.

And just when it had finished the very last little ha'porth, which was short measure, because the milkman's nerves were quite upset, the Red Dragon came down the street looking for the Manticora. It edged off when it saw him coming, for it was not at all the Dragon-fighting kind; and, seeing no other door open, the poor, hunted creature took refuge in the General Post Office, and there the Dragon found it, trying to conceal itself among the ten o'clock mail. The Dragon fell on the Manticora at once, and the mail was no defence. The mewings were heard all over the town. All the pussies and the milk the Manticora had had seemed to have strengthened its mew wonderfully. Then there was a sad silence, and presently the people whose windows looked that way saw the Dragon come walking down the steps of the General Post Office spitting fire and smoke, together with tufts of Manticora fur, and the fragments of the registered letters. Things were growing very serious. However popular the King might become during the week, the Dragon was sure to do something on Saturday to upset the people's loyalty.

The Dragon was a perfect nuisance for the whole of Saturday, except during the hour of noon, and then he had to rest under a tree or he would have caught fire from the heat of the sun. You see, he was very hot to begin with.

At last came a Saturday when the Dragon actually walked into the Royal nursery and carried off the King's own pet Rocking-Horse. Then the King cried for six days, and on the seventh he was so tired that he had to stop. Then he heard the Blue Bird singing among the roses and saw the Butterfly fluttering among the lilies and he said:

'Nurse, wipe my face, please. I am not going to cry any more.'

Nurse washed his face, and told him not to be a silly little King. 'Crying,' said she, 'never did anyone any good yet.'

'I don't know,' said the little King, 'I seem to see better, and to hear better now that I've cried for a week. Now, Nurse dear, I know I'm right, so kiss me in case I never come back. I *must* try if I can, to save the people.'

'Well, if you must, you must,' said Nurse; 'but don't tear your clothes or get your feet wet.'

So off he went.

The Blue Bird sang more sweetly than ever, and the Butterfly shone more brightly, as Lionel once more carried the Book of Beasts out into the rose-garden, and opened it – very quickly, so that he might not be afraid and change his mind. The book fell open wide, almost in the middle, and there was written at the bottom of the page, 'The Hippogriff', and before Lionel had time to see what the picture was, there was a fluttering of great wings and a stamping of hoofs, and a sweet, soft, friendly neighing; and there came out of the book a beautiful white horse with a long, long, white mane and a long, long, white tail, and he had great wings like swan's wings, and the softest, kindest eyes in the world, and he stood there among the roses.

The Hippogriff rubbed its silky-soft, milky-white nose against the little King's shoulder, and the little King thought: 'But for the wings you are very like my poor, dear, lost Rocking-Horse.' And the Blue Bird's song was very loud and sweet.

Then suddenly the King saw coming through the sky the great straggling, sprawling, wicked shape of the Red Dragon. And he knew at once what he must do. He caught up the Book of Beasts and jumped on the back of the gentle, beautiful Hippogriff, and leaning down he whispered in the sharp white ear:

'Fly, dear Hippogriff, fly your very fastest to the Pebbly Waste.'

And when the Dragon saw them start, he turned and flew after them, with his great wings flapping like clouds at sunset, and the Hippogriff's wide wings were snowy as clouds at the moon-rising.

When the people in the town saw the Dragon fly off after the Hippogriff and the King they all came out of their houses to look, and when they saw the two disappear they made up their minds to the worst, and began to think what would be worn for Court mourning.

But the Dragon could not catch the Hippogriff. The red wings were bigger than the white ones, but they were not so strong, and so the white-winged horse flew away and away and away, with the Dragon pursuing, till he reached the very middle of the Pebbly Waste.

Now, the Pebbly Waste is just like the parts of the seaside where there is no sand – all round, loose, shifting stones, and there is no grass there and no tree within a hundred miles of it.

Lionel jumped off the white horse's back in the very middle of the Pebbly Waste, and he hurriedly unclasped the Book of Beasts and laid it open on the pebbles. Then he clattered among the pebbles in his haste to get back on to his white horse, and had just jumped on when up came the Dragon. He was flying very feebly, and looking round everywhere for a tree, for it was just on the stroke of twelve, the sun was shining like a gold guinea in the blue sky, and there was not a tree for a hundred miles.

The white-winged horse flew round and round the Dragon as he writhed on the dry pebbles. He was getting very hot: indeed, parts of him even had begun to smoke. He knew that he must certainly catch fire in another minute unless he could get under a tree. He made a snatch with his red claws at the King and Hippogriff, but he was too feeble to reach them, and besides, he did not dare to over-exert himself for fear he should get any hotter.

It was then that he saw the Book of Beasts lying on the pebbles, open at the page with 'Dragon' written at the bottom. He looked and he hesitated, and he looked again, and then, with one last squirm of rage, the Dragon wriggled himself back into the picture, and sat down under the palm tree, and the page was a little singed as he went in.

As soon as Lionel saw that the Dragon had really been obliged to go and sit under his own palm tree because it was the only tree there, he jumped off his horse and shut the book with a bang.

'Oh, hurrah!' he cried. 'Now we really *have* done it.'

And he clasped the book very tight with the turquoise and ruby clasps.

'Oh, my precious Hippogriff,' he cried, 'you are the bravest, dearest, most beautiful – '

'Hush,' whispered the Hippogriff modestly. 'Don't you see that we are not alone?'

And indeed there was quite a crowd round them on the Pebbly Waste: the Prime Minister and the Parliament and the Football Players and the Orphanage and the Manticora and the Rocking-Horse, and indeed everyone who had been eaten by the Dragon. You see, it was impossible for the Dragon to take them into the book with him – it was a tight fit for even one Dragon – so, of course, he had to leave them outside.

They all got home somehow, and all lived happy ever after.

When the King asked the Manticora where he would like to live he begged to be allowed to go back into the book. 'I do not care for public life,' he said.

Of course he knew his way on to his own page, so there was no

danger of opening the book at the wrong page and letting out a
Dragon or anything. So he got back into his picture, and has never
come out since: that is why you will never see a Manticora as long
as you live, except in a picture-book. And of course he left the
pussies outside, because there was no room for them in the book –
and the milk-cans too.

Then the Rocking-Horse begged to be allowed to go and live on
the Hippogriff's page of the book. 'I should like,' he said, 'to live
somewhere where Dragons can't get at me.'

So the beautiful, white-winged Hippogriff showed him the way
in, and there he stayed till the King had him taken out for his
great-great-great-great-grandchildren to play with.

As for the Hippogriff, he accepted the position of the King's Own
Rocking-Horse – a situation left vacant by the retirement of the
wooden one. And the Blue Bird and the Butterfly sing and flutter
among the lilies and roses of the Palace garden to this very day.

E. NESBIT

THE AWFUL BABY

Once, even before breakfast, even before Richard was dressed,
things were passed over the fence from next door. First came a big
basket. It was full of baby napkins, baby bottles, jars of baby food
and baby clothes. Next came a car seat. Then came the fat baby,
Liza, who usually lived next door.

'She's our baby for today,' said Mummy. 'Her mother has to go
to town.'

Richard didn't want the fat baby, not for a whole day. She
couldn't talk. She couldn't walk. She pulled things about and she
crawled. And the first thing she did was to crawl across the kitchen
floor to the cupboards. *Clatter! Crash!* Liza pulled out saucepans.

'Oh, you busy one,' laughed Mummy, not at all cross. She gave
Liza a wooden spoon to bang.

105

Liza threw the spoon away. Richard gave it back to her. She threw the spoon right across the kitchen. Richard ran to fetch it and Liza crawled off, plop-plop, out of the kitchen. She crawled into the bedroom. Into the bathroom. Into the sitting-room. She grabbed at the coffee table trying to pull herself upright. It wobbled. It fell. Liza yelled.

Mummy came rushing in and gathered her into her arms, kissing her cheek, crooning to her. Then and there, Richard decided that Liza was awful, but he watched while Mummy bathed her. When she tried to wash Liza's toes she kicked out her feet. *Splash!* Richard was wet on his face and his arm and his shirt. And when he tried to dry Liza's toes she curled them away, then squirmed and wriggled so he couldn't catch them. Later, she grabbed and pulled at him when he sat in his own car seat and she sat in hers on the way to the supermarket. She wanted his teddy. Richard held Ted tightly. Liza yelled until the car stopped.

Oh, botheration! Mummy had forgotten to bring Liza's stroller. So she put Liza on one hip, flung her bag over one shoulder and they went into the supermarket. 'Fetch me a trolley, please, Richard,' Mummy said.

Richard wheeled the trolley and Mummy took what she needed from the shelves and dropped them into it. Liza took things which Mummy didn't need. She dropped them in the trolley, or on the floor. It was Richard who picked them up and put them on the shelves. She really was an awful baby!

Near the soap powder shelves, Mummy sat Liza on the trolley's baby seat. She liked riding there. She swung her legs. She waved her fat arms and smiled at everyone. People looked and smiled back at Liza, even when she made grabs at them. No one looked at Richard.

They stopped at the deep-freeze cabinet. Richard held the door open so that Mummy could stretch in and take out a chicken and some margarine. Liza stretched the other way. She tugged at a pink carton on top of a display stand. Pull, pull, pull! It slid towards her then toppled down. Its flap dropped open. *Plop! Smash! Splosh!* Broken eggs splattered the trolley and Liza and the floor. She yelled.

Mummy snatched Liza up out of the trolley into her arms. Now Mummy was sploshed with sticky egg, its yellow yolk and white bits of shell. Liza screamed. She buried her head in Mummy's shoulder. People rushed to help. Someone mopped up Mummy. Someone mopped up Liza. Someone mopped up the trolley. Someone mopped up the floor. No one noticed Richard.

He wheeled the trolley to the cashier's desk. 'We'll pay for the broken eggs,' said Mummy.

'That's all right,' said the cashier. 'It was an accident. Your baby has had a nasty fright.'

Liza hiccupped.

'She's *not* our baby,' said Richard.

The cashier hadn't heard him. She said, 'Just pay for what you need.'

Mummy fumbled for her shoulder bag. She couldn't find it. She didn't have it. Everything was in it – money, wallet, car keys. Where could it be? She remembered locking the car door, putting Liza on a hip and the bag over one shoulder. Yes! She remembered that. Where was the bag now?

'Should anyone find a shoulder bag, please bring it to the desk,' said the cashier into her microphone. Everyone in the supermarket heard the announcement. Richard certainly did. He was running back to the soap powder shelves. Mummy had put Liza into the trolley there, but she hadn't left her bag. And it wasn't by the cereals, or the bread, or honey. He looked in the stand where the egg cartons were stacked. No bag there either.

Richard turned to the refrigerator cabinet. He stood on his toes and opened the door to look in. Mummy's bag was on top of the margarine. Stretching, stretching he could grasp its strap. He pulled gently. Down came an icy-cold bag and some margarine as well. Back went the margarine into the freezer and off went Richard with the shoulder bag, icy cold and flapping against his legs all the way to the cashier's desk.

'You're a clever boy to find Mummy's bag,' she said.

'I don't know what I'd do without Richard, specially today,' said Mummy. 'He's my best help, isn't he, Liza?'

Liza smiled and babbled baby-talk to Richard and stretched out her fat little arms to him, putting egg on his shirt.

'Your baby thinks so, too,' said the cashier.

'She's not our baby,' Richard said but the girl didn't listen because she said, 'Your baby's put egg on you, too.'

So they took Liza home and gave her another bath. And Richard had a bath. And Mummy had a shower while Richard minded Liza. She crawled very close to him and tried to pull herself upright on his leg. He gave her a hug and they both fell over in a heap. They laughed and laughed. She really was a nice, fat, cuddly, crawly baby – Richard's baby for that day.

JEAN CHAPMAN

THE DISCONTENTED KING

There was once a King who ruled over a pleasant country full of green hills, blue rivers and little busy towns. He lived in a square stone castle of medium size with tall stone towers, on which the sun shone from morning till night.

All round the castle was a park full of stately trees, and under the trees ran the King's deer that he sometimes hunted. The room where the King sat and signed papers and fixed his great red seal to them was a high sunny room, very warm and comfortable, overlooking a rose-garden, and beyond the rose-garden he could see the green park. Just outside the window was a tall spreading elm tree in which the white pigeons sat all day and made sweet cooing music. The King had a red robe with silver flowers on it and a great black horse for riding on when he travelled about his country. But still he was not happy. He was a discontented King, and it did not make things any better that he could not tell exactly why he was discontented.

The Queen was beautiful and graceful. She was nearly always cheerful and had a good temper. She was gay, amusing, and very fond of the King. She did not sit all day long on a silk sofa eating sweets and fanning herself, but was active and liked making things. She made cushion-covers and pillowcases and long trailing gowns and tall elegant head-dresses. She liked riding about in the park

too; but best of all she liked putting on her oldest dress and going into the kitchen when the chief cook was away and baking pastries and pies and sweetmeats and little sugar-rolls with cherries on top; she did not of course always wear her oldest dress. She had a blue robe with gold flowers on it, and a white horse for travelling round the country with the King. With such a Queen as his wife, the King ought to have been happy, but he was not. He was a discontented King, and it did not make it any better that he could not tell exactly why he was discontented.

The King and Queen had one daughter, who was gay and happy like her mother, but was not so fond of sewing and cooking. Instead she liked sitting in her little room high up in one of the castle towers and gazing out over the green fields to where, on clear days, she could just see the sea. She did not do this all day. Sometimes she would read, and sometimes she would help her mother or father. Sometimes she would even help her mother when she went into the kitchen to cook; especially when she was baking the little sugar-rolls with cherries on top. Sometimes she was so happy that she sang like a blackbird. She had a green robe and a dappled grey pony for riding about the country on, beside her father and mother. With such a daughter for a Princess, the King ought to have been happy, but he was not. He was a discontented King, and it did not make it any better that he did not know exactly why he was discontented.

One day the King was sitting alone in his special room. He had done his signing and sealing for the day and was looking out of the window across the green lawns. The white pigeons were cooing peacefully in the great elm tree. It was a beautiful day, but still he was not happy. The Queen was in the kitchen, making little square tarts with slices of orange in them; the Princess could be heard chirruping away like a blackbird as she combed her long yellow hair in her little room at the top of the tower. She looked out of the window from time to time, to where her father's black horse and her mother's white one and her own dappled grey pony were grazing in the big meadow.

In the kitchen the Queen had a feeling that the King was not very happy, so when she had put her little orange tarts in the oven, she went up to the Princess's room and asked her to come

down and talk to the King. The Princess had by now finished combing her hair and had done it up in a gold net with small gold leaves round the edge of it. She stopped singing when her mother told her the King was not happy.

'Oh dear,' she sighed, 'is Father not happy again?'

'I'm afraid not, my dear,' said the Queen. 'Let us go down and see if we can suggest something to cheer him up.'

They went down to the King's room and sat down one on each side of him.

'It is a beautiful day,' said the Queen. 'Would you like to go hunting?'

'You go,' said the King, not exactly rudely, for he was never rude to the Queen; but still he did not want to go hunting.

'Well, what about a game of draughts with the new set made of red and white ivory?' said the Princess. 'I love playing draughts.'

111

'Well, have a game with your mother,' said the King, not exactly rudely, for he was never rude to the Princess; but still he did not want to play draughts.

'What about a swim in the lake?' said the Queen.

'Let the fishes swim,' said the King. 'It is what they are for.'

'What about some music, Father?' suggested the Princess. 'You know you love music, and you have not yet heard the three new trumpeters who have come from Bohemia to join the royal band.'

'I have heard them practising all the morning,' said the King. 'Three trumpeters cannot practise in a castle like this without *everybody* hearing them. Not that they are not very good trumpeters, but when you feel as I do, the last thing you want to hear is a trumpet. I am tired of music. As a matter of fact,' went on the King unhappily, 'I am tired of everything. I am tired of hunting, I am tired of signing papers, I am tired of playing games, and I am tired of music and dancing and all the things I used to like best.'

The Queen and the Princess both looked very sad and the Princess began to cry a little.

'Oh, my dears,' said the King, sorry to see the Princess's tears, 'I am not tired of you. Oh, not at all. But I am tired of everything else. Listen to those silly pigeons cooing in that tree. I am tired of them. Above all I am tired of this castle.'

'But it is a lovely castle,' said the Queen, who was thinking of her orange tarts baking in the kitchen, and all the shining pots and pans on the shelves.

'It is a beautiful castle,' said the Princess, who was thinking of her little room in the tower, where she kept all her books and her games and her clothes and the shining mirror and hairbrush and comb on her dressing-table.

The King got up and put one hand on the Queen's shoulder and the other hand on the Princess's.

'My dears,' he said, 'if you do not mind, we will leave this castle and find another one. The truth is, I am tired of it, and I shall not be happy as long as we are here. I am sorry if this distresses you, but it is the only thing to do. We shall go tomorrow, all three of us.'

The Queen and the Princess did not like this idea, but they said nothing. They knew it was of no use to argue when the King was feeling like this.

'You, my dear,' he said to the Queen, 'may take your sewing-basket and your favourite lady-in-waiting and a little serving-maid to help you if you want to cook. And you,' he said, turning to the Princess, 'may pack up some of your favourite belongings, and you shall have a room to yourself just like your own room here.'

So it was arranged. The Queen agreed because she was a cheerful and contented person who usually did as the King wished. Besides she wanted to get back to the kitchen to see to her little square tarts – which, indeed, were only just saved from burning. They were all to set off next morning. The Lord Chamberlain was to go on in front in order to take possession of any castle that the King might fancy and to turn out any people that might happen to be living there. He was to have a small army with him, just a few knights and men, in case of difficulty. It may not seem polite or kind to turn people out of their homes, but really most people are glad of a change, and it is considered an honour to have the King living in your house. That is why the army was a very small one. It was not thought likely that there would be any difficulty. The three trumpeters from Bohemia were also to go on ahead to announce the King's arrival.

The Queen took her waiting-lady and her serving-maid and some of her favourite things; and the Princess packed up her most treasured belongings, as the King had said. Next morning the King put on his red robe with the silver flowers on, and the Queen put on her robe of blue with the gold flowers, and the Princess put on her green robe. The King got up on his black horse, and the Queen got up on her white one, and the Princess got up on her dappled grey pony. The three trumpeters blew a cheerful blast on their three trumpets, and the Lord Chamberlain rode on ahead with the knights and men. The servants rode behind. It was a beautiful morning, and everyone chattered happily. As they went out of the gates into the park, the white pigeons were cooing gently and peacefully in the elm tree.

'Really,' said the Queen, 'this is not such a bad idea. Perhaps we all needed a change.'

'I'm so excited,' said the Princess. 'This is quite an adventure.'

And the King laughed and began to sing a little. This was so unusual that even the black horse wondered what had happened to his master. He neighed gladly, and so did the Queen's white horse and the Princess's dappled pony.

They rode on for two days, and on the third day the weather changed. It became cold and cloudy. They had reached the edge of the King's country and were now by the seashore. There was a big stone castle standing on the cliff just above the sea.

'This will do,' said the King. 'We will live here.'

The Chamberlain went to the owner of the castle, who was an old man living there with his wife and only a very few servants. The old man and his wife were very glad to move to a smaller house at the edge of their grounds. The three trumpeters blew a loud blast, and the King and Queen and all the others rode into the courtyard.

They soon made themselves comfortable. The King took as his stateroom a large hall overlooking the sea. The Queen had a pleasant room beside it, and was soon unpacking her sewing materials and other things with the help of her lady-in-waiting. The Princess had a big room in the tower. It was not unlike her own room at home, but it was much larger and instead of overlooking the green fields it overlooked the stone courtyard.

The Lord Chamberlain and the knights also found themselves rooms, and the three trumpeters were told to practise their trumpeting near the stables, as far away from the King as they could get.

For a month they all lived together in the castle by the sea. Everyone was contented, even the King. He had found new forests to hunt in. He even went out in a boat and fished. The Queen had soon found her way to the kitchen. It was not such a good kitchen as her own and nothing like so clean. However, she and the servants set to work and turned it out, and before long she was cooking there as well as she had ever done at home. The Princess at first missed her view over the green park, but from her window over the courtyard she could see people coming and going, and this amused her. She carolled away in her big room, or read her books, or went down the steep little path to the sea and played on the sands.

Then one day the Queen noticed that the King was looking miserable. She and the Princess went and talked to him.

'What is wrong, my dear?' asked the Queen.

'I don't know,' said the King. 'One thing is certain. We must move from this castle. I don't like it and it doesn't suit me.'

'Is it the noise of the sea outside your window?' asked the Princess.

'Well, it's certainly very noisy,' said the King.

'We could change your room,' said the Queen, 'and give you one on the other side.'

'I don't think it's the noise of the sea altogether,' said the King. 'I just don't like the place. It's too large. Much too large. I ought to have known that to begin with. What on earth did you let me come to a great barracks of a place like this for?'

He was never exactly rude to the Queen, but this question was almost rude. He looked out of the window.

'There's something wrong with this place. I miss something, but I don't know what it is. At any rate I can't stay here a day longer.'

The Queen and the Princess would cheerfully have stayed there for another six months, but they knew it was no use arguing.

By next morning everything was packed up once more and off they all went. The Lord Chamberlain and the trumpeters went first, with the knights and men-at-arms. Then came the King in his red robe with the silver flowers on it, riding his black horse; and the Queen in her blue robe with the gold flowers, riding her white horse; and the Princess in her green robe on her dappled grey pony. Everyone felt cheerful. As for the waiting-women and servants, they were always glad of a change.

They rode on for two days and on the third day they came to a castle standing by the shore of a great blue lake.

'This will do,' said the King, riding up to the Lord Chamberlain. 'This is just what we want. Take it.'

The castle was not difficult to take, for the owner was away, and the only people in it were three or four old servants, who did not at all mind having the royal family to live there.

Once more they settled down. The King had a room overlooking the lake, and the Queen found herself another beside it. The Princess had a little room at the top. It overlooked the lake and she could see the swans floating gracefully on its surface. True, her room was dark and rather bare, but she made it as comfortable as she could and was soon singing away as she combed her yellow hair.

The King liked the new castle.

'It's a nice size,' he said to the Queen. 'That other place was much too big. Can't think how we ever lived there a day, much less a month.'

The Queen agreed that the new castle was much smaller. The kitchen, indeed, was very small – too small if anything. There was scarcely room for all the pots and pans and jars and bowls and dishes and plates that a good kitchen must have. Still, she managed to make it more or less as she wanted, and was soon busy making some of the little sugar-rolls with cherries on top that the Princess loved so much.

'This place isn't going to be bad at all,' said the Princess.

'Of course it isn't,' said the King. 'I told you it was just what we were looking for. Such a nice size – not too big and not too small.'

Then he went down to a kind of pavilion by the lake, took off his red robe, and put on a bathing costume. Soon he was swimming peacefully in the lake, while the swans glided around.

The weather was fine, and for a month everything went on well. Then the Queen again noticed that the King did not look altogether happy. She went and spoke to the Princess.

'I'm afraid this may mean another move,' she said.

The King had indeed grown tired of swimming. He found the swans greedy and ill-tempered, beautiful as they were. He did not like playing draughts here any more than he had done at home. There was no creature in the neighbourhood worth hunting, and the noise of the three Bohemian trumpeters practising once more annoyed him.

He found the Queen in the kitchen.

'Why are you wearing that old dress?' he asked. 'You look dreadful in it.'

'Why, my love,' said the Queen, much surprised, 'you always say you like me best in this old dress, for then you know I am happy among my jars and dishes.'

'Nonsense,' said the King, not exactly rudely, for he never spoke to the Queen really rudely, but still he did not like her in her old cooking dress.

'Go and put on your blue robe with the gold flowers on it, for we must be moving,'

'What, again?' asked the Queen, pretending to be surprised.

'You really want us to move again?' asked the Princess, who had just come in.

Yes, the King insisted on setting out once more and next morning, for the third time, off they went. The Lord Chamberlain went in front with the knights and trumpeters, then came the Queen in her blue robe with the gold flowers, riding her white horse; and the King in his red robe with the silver flowers, riding his black horse; and the Princess in her green robe, riding her grey pony. Then came the waiting-women and the servants, who were laughing and chatting merrily, for they never minded a move.

For two days they travelled like this, and on the third day the weather became terribly hot. The Princess sang no more, the Queen lost her cheerful looks, and even the horses began to pant and grumble. There was no more laughing and joking among the servants. They came to a great bare desert covered with stones, and at the edge of it there was a castle.

'This will do,' said the King to the Lord Chamberlain. 'Take it.'

The Chamberlain said nothing, for he was much too hot to speak, and the trumpeters blew a feeble blast on their trumpets. In the castle lived a wicked knight with four fierce dogs, but the men-at-arms drove them out, and soon the King and his party were settled in the castle. The weather grew cooler. Everybody was soon happy again. The King and the knights rode their horses over the desert. The Queen embroidered a beautiful veil in her cool sewing room overlooking the garden. The Princess made herself comfortable in a little round room in a round tower at the top of the castle. The King had a handsome chamber over the main gateway, and there he would sit signing and sealing the important papers that came every day by a special messenger.

'Now this is not so bad,' he said. 'That other place was really too small, and the one before was much too big, but this one is just right.'

The Queen did not like to tell him that the kitchen was in such a state that she had not the heart to do any cooking. Instead, she went back to her embroidery.

But the cool weather did not last long. In another month it was just as hot as ever. Once more the King became unhappy. He looked out of the window of his great stateroom. There was something missing, but he did not know what it was. He was much too unhappy to do anything.

'What a miserable place this is!' he said to the Queen and the Princess one day. 'I really can't think how we ever came to settle here.'

'Why, it's very comfortable,' said the Princess, who had grown to be quite content with the castle at the edge of the desert. 'I have a lovely little room, and I can watch the queer creatures that come and play round the walls. My room is quite round, and I have never had a round room before.'

The King took no notice, but said to the Queen:

'Why are you always wearing your best robe nowadays? Why do I never see you in that homely old dress you use for cooking?'

The Queen did not like to tell him that she could do no cooking because the kitchen was so inconvenient, so she said nothing.

'All the same,' said the King, 'you'd better keep it on, for we must go travelling again. I couldn't stay another minute.'

He was not exactly rude to the Queen, for he was never quite rude to her, but he spoke sharply all the same.

Well, off they set once more in the hot, hot weather. The Lord Chamberlain went first, very hot in all his Chamberlain's robes, and the knights and the men-at-arms went with him. Then came the King in his red robe with the silver flowers, and the Queen in her blue robe with the gold flowers, and the Princess in her green robe, which she used for travelling about the kingdom. The King rode his black horse, and the Queen her white one, and the Princess her dappled pony. Then came the waiting-people and the servants, who were always glad of a change; they were not laughing and joking much, for the weather was terribly hot.

For two days they rode like this, and all the time the road ran uphill. The weather gradually became cooler, and this pleased the horses, which had grown very tired. Presently they came to mountainous country, and just beyond a thick fir-wood they saw a handsome castle looking across a valley to a great range of snow-mountains.

The King called the Lord Chamberlain to him.

'Will it do, Your Majesty?' asked the Lord Chamberlain.

'It will,' answered the King. 'Take it.'

The castle in the mountains belonged to a knight who was away at the wars, and his lady was glad to leave it and go and live with her parents for a time, as she had become very lonely. So the three Bohemian trumpeters, who had grown skilful after all their months of practice, blew a splendid blast on their trumpets, and everyone rode into the courtyard.

'Now this is something like it,' said the King. He chose himself a noble room on the first floor, and the Queen had a fine sitting-room beside it. The Princess once more climbed to the top of the castle, where she found herself a little room with a view towards the snow-mountains. They all settled down and life began once more. The Queen did not find things easy, for she had no more material for sewing. She had used it all up. The kitchen was small and there was no room for her as well as the cook who prepared the ordinary meals. The Princess had read all her books. The trumpeters practised no more, for they had become so skilful that they needed no more practice for the time being. The Queen and the Princess took to playing draughts with each other to pass the time away. They became used to the new life, and soon the Princess was chirping away as merrily as ever. The King went hunting wolves in the great black forest at the castle gates.

'A much better place than that dreadful old wicked knight's castle at the edge of the desert,' he said. 'And a lot better than those other two castles we tried.'

And they all agreed with him and hoped they would stay there some time.

Then it began to snow. Soon no more messengers could reach them because of the snow, so that the King had no more papers to sign and seal. He had nothing at all to do, for there was no more hunting, and he was forced to join the knights and the men-at-arms in games of snowballing in the castle grounds. They snowballed each other in order to keep warm, for the weather continued very cold.

At the end of a month the Queen once more noticed that the King was looking unhappy. He was sitting in his stateroom muffled up in his red robe with the silver flowers on it, and several robes, one of them of fur, on top of it. He was looking discontentedly out of the window at the great black pine trees with their snow-laden branches. He felt that he ought to be happy. Yet there was something missing, though he could not tell what it was. He had often said he had too much work to do, and now he had none. All the same, he was unhappy.

'Of all the castles we have lived in,' said the King, 'this is the worst. What is the good, I ask you, of being stuck away in a place like this, where nobody visits us unless it is a lost wolf in search of a dead rat or a starving bird? The castle by the sea was bad enough, but it was better than this. So was the one by the lake, and so was the one by the desert. That one was at least warm, but this is cold, cold, cold!'

The Queen said nothing. She and the waiting-woman had already packed up their belongings and were ready to go.

'And *draughty*!' the King went on. 'In all my life I have never lived in so draughty a place. Listen to the wind howling up and down these miserable cold passages. I can't stay here another minute – not another minute!'

'This time,' said the Queen, 'I really think we ought to go home. We've tried four castles already, and you haven't liked any of them.'

'Just as you like,' said the King. 'I don't care where we go so long as we get out of this draughty old ruin!'

'Hadn't we better wait till the snow melts and the weather's a bit warmer?' said the Queen.

'Certainly not. It will probably never melt. We must go at once, do you hear – at once!'

It was no use arguing. Once more everything was packed up, and they all set out. The King's red robe with the silver flowers was covered with a black fur cloak, and the Queen's blue robe with the gold flowers was covered with a brown fur cloak, and the Princess's green robe was covered with a white fur cloak. But how cold they all were! When they had gone a mile or two, the poor Princess was nearly weeping with the cold. The Queen was very

120

sorry the King had made them all set off while the weather was cold, but she said nothing. Only she was determined that once they got home, nothing would make her leave it again in a hurry. Everyone was cold, and nobody chattered and laughed. The Chamberlain whistled to keep his spirits up, until the King told him to stop. The King was in a very bad temper. He was angry with the Queen for having allowed him to set out in such weather, and he was angry with himself for being so headstrong and discontented.

After some hours the wind blew stronger, and more snow began to fall. A terrible storm broke over them. They could no longer see which way they were going. They stumbled on as best they could. It was by now night-time, and the moon, which ought to have been shining, was lost in the black storm. It was as much as they could do to keep together. The Princess was now crying piteously. There was nothing to do but to struggle on. How the snow fell! How the wolves howled among the trees! How the wind blew in their faces and stung their cheeks!

'What a fool I have been!' said the King to himself. 'Why did I ever allow myself to leave home with my dear Queen and the poor little Princess? We shall never reach home alive, and it will all be my fault.'

But in the end, when they were tired out, and the horses could hardly go another step, the storm calmed down. The road had been going downhill steadily, and the weather became warmer. Although they did not know where they were, they knew they must be out of the mountains. When daylight came, they were in the middle of a thick mist. There was nothing to do but to go on until the mist cleared.

At last, in the middle of some open country dotted with trees, they saw a huge shape towering out of the mist. It was a castle. They could just make out its square shape and pointed towers. Everyone stopped.

'It will do,' said the King in a tired voice to the Chamberlain. 'Take it.'

Three blasts were sounded on the three trumpets, and the Chamberlain and the knights and men-at-arms rode forward through the mist.

Presently the Chamberlain came back to where the King sat on his horse waiting. He told the King that the castle had been left by its owners and was now in the hands of robbers.

'What a careless fellow the owner must be to leave his castle like that!' said the King. 'Send in the men-at-arms and turn the robbers out.'

The knights and the men-at-arms made short work of the robbers. After half an hour's fighting the leader of the men-at-arms came out and told the King that the robbers had been driven off and were now lost in the mist. Once more the three trumpeters sounded their trumpets, and the royal party rode through the castle gateway. Then the mist began to clear. But already the Queen had recognized her home.

Yes, it was really their old home. They had come upon it in the mist without at first knowing it. Here they were at last, half dead with hunger and tired out, at the very gates of their own castle.

But what a mess the robbers had left! Everything was dirty and neglected. The furniture had not been polished, windows had been broken and not mended, nothing had been cleaned or washed for months.

After everybody had had a meal and a rest, the servants set to work and made the place as tidy and comfortable as possible, and it was not long before the King and the Queen and the Princess settled down to enjoy being at home again.

The Queen began to make cakes in her own kitchen, and to embroider and sew as she used to; the Princess was overjoyed to have her own little room in the tower overlooking the green park, and soon she was singing away and combing her hair as if she had never been away for a day, let alone several months.

As for the King, a whole pile of important papers arrived that very evening, and all these needed signing and sealing, so that he had work for a week. After all, he thought, as he sat down to his table and began work, home was not so bad, and all he had wanted was a little change. Then he looked up and listened to something he could hear outside the high window. The sun was shining. Far away in the meadow his own black horse and the Queen's white one and the Princess's dappled grey pony were feeding contentedly. Near at hand, the great elm tree spread its shady branches over the garden. The sound that had caught the King's ear was the cooing of the white pigeons in its leaves. What a peaceful, contented sound it was! That was what had been missing in all the other castles he had been to. There had been no cooing pigeons in the castle by the sea, or the castle by the lake, or the castle beside the desert, or the castle in the mountains. No, only in his own castle could he hear the peaceful noise of these contented birds. How wrong he had been to think the noise silly! It was the pleasantest noise in all the world, except for two others – one was the talking of the Queen, who was nearly always good-humoured and cheerful, and the other was the singing of his little Princess as she combed her hair in the room upstairs in the tower.

When he had finished his work for the day, he sent for the Princess and asked her to play a game of draughts with him, and the Queen brought in some fresh orange tarts and some sugar-rolls with cherries on top. It was the happiest time they had spent since the King made them all set out on their long journey.

JAMES REEVES

TAILOR GREEN AND THE GRAND COLLECTION

It was a fine day in early spring when the tailor came to Humblehurst. He was tall and thin and wore round spectacles on his friendly face. He drove an old cart piled high with his belongings, and he sang this song to his pony as they clip-clopped along:

Sprocket me bobbins
and riddle me rhee,
the Good Lord made me
a tailor to be.

The tailor looked round him at the gloomy little town and smiled at everyone he saw.

But the people of Humblehurst just stared back. They were not used to strangers.

The tailor's belongings rattled in the cart. There were tables and chairs, a bed with shiny knobs, a sewing-box and rolls and rolls of material.

The pony stopped outside a small shop with a notice which read FOR SALE. The tailor jumped down from the cart and opened the door.

Inside, the shop was empty, musty and dusty.

The tailor took a deep breath and set to work. He found his broom and began to sweep. Clouds of dust filled the air and made him cough. He scrubbed and polished, rubbed and dusted until lunchtime.

124

Then the tailor sat down with a sigh and unpacked his sandwiches.

As he was munching, a sudden movement caught his eye. A little girl was standing shyly in the doorway. She had been watching him at work.

'Hello,' said the tailor, but she did not wait to hear him. She ran away as fast as she could go. The tailor was sorry. He liked talking to people. But no one seemed at all friendly in Humblehurst.

All afternoon he carried in his things and arranged them in the shop. And as he worked, he sang:

> *Sprocket me bobbins*
> *and riddle me rhee,*
> *the Good Lord made me*
> *a tailor to be.*

As the sun went down over the hill the tailor lit his fire to warm a bowl of soup for his supper. On the mantelshelf stood a jar with twelve gold coins – all the money he had in the world.

'That will have to last until I get my first customers,' he thought to himself.

The next day the tailor was up bright and early. He fetched the last parcel out of his cart and carefully unwrapped a long wooden board, which read:

E. W. GREEN

TAILOR

All clothes made to measure

The tailor fixed the board above his shop window.

Then he looked up and down the High Street. People were hurrying here and there but no one seemed very interested in the new shop.

Sadly the tailor went back inside.

Later that afternoon the tailor was sorting through his coloured ribbons. Behind him the door creaked, just a little, and there stood the child again. She wore an old grey dress, one size too big, and her feet were bare. She was watching him with round, blue eyes.

'Hello,' said the tailor, carrying on with his work.

The little girl was very shy. But she was also curious.

'What are you doing?' she asked, taking a step into the room and looking round.

'I'm sorting out my ribbons,' he replied. 'Getting ready to make fine clothes for the people here.'

'What lovely cloth,' said the child, gently touching a roll of golden velvet.

'I once dressed a countess in that,' said the tailor.

The kettle on the fire began to steam.

'Would you like a cup of tea?' he asked.

'Thank you,' said the child and sat down by the fire to warm her feet.

While they drank, the tailor asked questions about the town and the child asked questions about how to make fine clothes. The time slipped by.

126

'I must go now,' said the child, as the sun went down behind the hill.

'Do come again,' said the tailor.

And she did come again, the very next day. There were still no customers in the shop, so the tailor said, 'Let's get to work on the garden.'

He found his spade, fork and trowel, strong leather boots and a bundle of seed packets.

All day long they worked in the garden, digging and clearing and planting.

In the afternoon the postman came by.

'Lovely day,' said the tailor. But the postman didn't stop. The child sighed.

'They're all too busy to notice,' she said.

All through the summer the child came to see the tailor as often as she could. She helped him in the garden. She learnt about sewing and cottons and threads.

But still no one came to order any clothes. The tailor looked anxiously at his jar of gold coins. Now there were only ten.

One day the tailor was walking in his garden. Some bright blue harebells caught his eye.

'That's exactly the colour of her eyes,' he said to himself. Then he had an idea.

He hurried into his shop and began to work. All morning he cut and pinned and tacked. All afternoon he sewed and measured. As he worked he sang this song:

> Sprocket me bobbins
> and riddle me rhee,
> the Good Lord made me
> a tailor to be.

By tea time, when the child came running up the path, the tailor had finished his work.

'Hello,' he said, 'I've a surprise for you – it's in the shop.'

There on the counter lay a beautiful blue dress.

'Oh,' gasped the little girl, 'a dress ... and shoes to match.' She slipped them on and ran back to the tailor.

'It's beautiful,' she said. 'How did you think of anything so pretty?'

'Well,' replied the tailor, 'sit down, and I'll tell you my secret.'

He held up a bunch of blue flowers. 'Do you know what these are?' he asked.

The child shook her head.

'Harebells,' he told her, 'wild harebells. The Good Lord made all the flowers in the world. He chose their colours and shapes. That's where my ideas come from.'

The child's eyes were round with surprise. She had never thought of anyone making the flowers or choosing their colours and shapes. She fingered the dress and looked at the harebells.

'The Good Lord must be very clever,' she said.

The next day, the tailor was in the garden when the child came.

'I tried to tell them about the flowers at home,' she said, 'but they wouldn't listen.'

'Never mind,' said the tailor.

Just then the Mayor hurried by. He was looking worried.

'The Mayor!' whispered the tailor. 'Now let's think. What clothes would we make for him, if we could?' He looked round his garden.

'Those!' said the child, pointing to the tall gold and purple irises.

'Yes,' said the tailor, getting excited. 'Purple suit, golden cloak with fur trim, purple hat with long gold feather ... exactly right!'

After that, it became a game they often played.

They made up clothes for all the people in the town. And all from the flowers in the tailor's garden: babies in snowdrop white, edged with green; lovely dresses for the ladies, with layers of frills like the hollyhocks, or smooth and stately as the lilies.

'If only they could actually wear them,' sighed the child one day, when they had just chosen a new red uniform for the fire brigade. 'The whole town would be as beautiful as your garden.'

Then the tailor had an idea.

'That's it,' he said, clapping his hands together. 'We'll have a Collection!'

'What's a Collection?' asked the child.

But the tailor was so excited, he did not answer. He reached for his notebook, took a pen from his top pocket and began to draw.

'First,' he said, 'we draw all the clothes we have thought of. Remember the Mayor?'

'Yes,' she replied. 'Purple and gold, like the irises.'

The tailor began to draw the suit, the hat and the long gold feather.

'Then,' said the tailor, 'we make them, and announce A COLLECTION.'

'What happens then?' asked the child.

'We throw a party and show everyone the clothes we have made,' explained the tailor. 'If they like them they will buy them. Perhaps they will ask me to make more for their friends and relations.'

'A party,' breathed the child. 'A Collection!' And she danced round the room.

So for weeks and weeks the tailor sewed and cut and pinned and tacked. The child watched him and learnt all she could. Soon she was helping, and as they worked, they sang:

> *Sprocket me bobbins*
> *and riddle me rhee,*
> *the Good Lord made me*
> *a tailor to be.*

The child was so excited, she began to tell people about the Collection.

'Clothes,' they scoffed, 'fine clothes. We haven't time for such things.' But secretly they were very curious. What would the clothes be like? Who had they been made for?

'When is this Collection?' they asked, trying not to look interested.

'Next Saturday,' announced the child, 'at the tailor's shop. There will be tea and cakes and music, too.'

'A lot of nonsense. Never heard of such a thing!' said the

townspeople. But they all wrote COLLECTION in the space for Saturday in their diaries.

At last all the clothes were finished. 'Now it's time for the invitations,' said the tailor.

Everyone was to be invited. Together they wrote the invitations out and the child ran off to deliver them.

'Now let me see,' said the tailor to himself. 'We shall need food; that's a job for Aunt Bertha. My brother's band will provide the music. And there must be people to wear the clothes ...' So he started to write letters to his friends and relations.

Saturday came at last. The tailor got up early and went downstairs. The very last gold coin lay in the jar on the shelf.

'What if no one comes?' he thought anxiously. 'I have no more money and all my materials are made into clothes.'

He began to whistle to cheer himself up. And as he dressed, he sang his song:

> *Sprocket me bobbins*
> *and riddle me rhee,*
> *the Good Lord made me*
> *a tailor to be.*

130

After that he felt much better.

At eleven o'clock Aunt Bertha arrived with baskets full of cakes and buns. Next came the tailor's friends and relations. Soon the shop was full of people trying on clothes, putting out chairs, arranging flowers and setting out the food.

The tailor got out his pony and went to the railway station to collect his brother and the band.

'Where is everybody?' asked the tailor's brother as they drove back through the empty town.

'They must all be at my shop,' replied the tailor, getting quite excited.

But when they arrived at the shop, they had a terrible shock. There was no one there. The chairs were gone, there was no food on the tables and worst of all – the pile of new clothes was nowhere to be seen!

'Thieves!' cried the tailor. 'They've taken everything.'

Just then the child came running down the street. 'Follow me,' she shouted, and began to lead the pony back up the High Street.

131

'Wh-wh-what's happening?' stammered the tailor. 'Where are my beautiful clothes?'

'It's all right, I've arranged everything,' said the child, stopping outside the Town Hall. 'This way.' And she hurried the tailor and all the musicians up the grand staircase.

The great doors opened and the tailor gasped. There, in the vast hall, sat the Mayor, the Lady Mayoress, all the important people – and everyone else in the whole town. And they were all looking at him!

The child stepped forward.

'Ladies and Gentlemen,' she said clearly, 'we are proud to present . . . the Collection.'

In walked the tailor's nephew, George, wearing the green and yellow postman's uniform. The tailor cleared his throat and explained that the idea came from the tall yellow daffodils in the spring.

Next came the fireman's uniform, red and gold like the tulips.

The school uniforms; pretty as Michaelmas daisies for the girls, bright as bluebells for the boys.

There were suits and dresses, coats and hats, shoes and boots to suit everyone.

The tailor explained each one as it was shown.

'And finally,' he said, holding up his hands for silence, 'the best of my collection . . . the Mayor.'

In walked the tailor's Uncle Charles, wearing the purple and gold suit that was like the great summer irises in full bloom. He looked magnificent.

'Hurrah,' shouted everyone at once. 'What a grand Collection!'

When the cheering had died down, the Mayor rose to his feet.

'My friends,' he said, 'I should like to thank the new tailor, Mr Ernest Green, for a most enjoyable day. Never in my life have I seen such fine clothes. Why, not even King Solomon was dressed so splendidly.'

'Hear, hear!' shouted everyone.

'And furthermore,' declared the Mayor in his best-occasion voice. 'I wish to make it known that I shall be purchasing the Mayoral suit this very evening.'

'What does he mean?' whispered the child.

'He's going to buy the clothes we designed for him,' replied the tailor. 'Hurray!'

Next day the child came round to the tailor's at tea-time. They sat in front of the fire and talked about the grand Collection.

A big pile of orders for new clothes lay on the table and three gold coins winked in the jar on the shelf.

'We have so much work to do now, I shall need some help,' said the tailor. 'How would you like to be my assistant?' The child's eyes shone.

'Oh, yes please,' she said.

So the child and the tailor began to make clothes for the people of Humblehurst, and as they worked they sang:

> *Sprocket me bobbins*
> *and riddle me rhee,*
> *the Good Lord made me*
> *a tailor to be.*

And very soon it was hard to say which were more beautiful – the people in their new clothes, or the gardens of flowers they planted around their houses!

MERYL DONEY

A TERRIBLE TALE OF A HOUSE ON A HILL

Once upon a time, there were two handsome fowls who lived together in a pretty little house on the top of a hill. They were – or so they said – of French descent, so everyone called them Monsieur Poulet and Madame Poulet, which sounded very grand, and pleased them very much. Now, they had only one trouble: they had no chicks of their own; so what do you think they did? Why, they adopted a little lonely mouse, who had no father or mother, and they all three lived together in the house on the hill, and were very happy.

At the foot of the hill, on the other side of a river, there was another house, but it was, oh! so very different from the one on the hill.

The door was half off, the chimney smoked, and all the windows were broken. If you had peeped inside you would have found lots of cobwebs, and a very dirty floor, and an untidy fireplace. This was the home of Mr Reynard the fox and his four little foxes.

But this was not a happy home by any means. And this was because Mr Reynard was a very lazy man, who never would work if he could possibly help it, and it never worried him very much if the little foxes had no food. All he did was to sit by the table smoking his pipe and drinking cider – he was such a thirsty fellow – whilst the young foxes got hungrier and hungrier.

At last, one day the larder was quite empty, and the little hungry foxes, all four of them, began to howl for food. They made such a noise that at last Reynard was aroused. He put down his pipe and began to scold the baby foxes in a way which was quite disgraceful. He used shocking language, and the little things were very much ashamed of their father.

But after a little while he began to think that something must be done, so, going to the door, he pointed up the hill to the house where Mr and Mrs Poulet lived, and said, 'See, my children, a nice fat cock and hen live up at that house. The cock will be away at the farmyard, but I think I can catch the hen and bring her back for dinner.'

'Hurrah!' cried all the little foxes. 'I'll make up the fire to roast her,' cried the first little fox. 'And I'll make the stuffing,' cried the second. 'And I'll lay the table,' said the third. 'And I'll look on till the eating begins,' said the youngest, who was a lazy fox, like his father.

Mr Reynard threw a sack over his shoulder and started off up the hill.

But he was wrong in thinking that Mr Poulet had gone out, for there had been trouble at the pretty house on the hill that morning. Mr Poulet and the mouse had both got out of bed on the wrong side. They were both very late when they came down to breakfast, and before long it was clear that things were not as they ought to be.

When at last they sat down to the nice breakfast Mrs Poulet had prepared, they were as cross and rude as they could be. Mr Poulet said the porridge was burnt; the mouse said the bread was too thick and the butter too thin; and when Mrs Poulet told him to be quiet, he said, 'Shan't.' At this Mr Poulet lifted a wing, intending to box his ears, and in doing so upset the milk jug.

Mrs Poulet got up from the table in despair, and started to clear away. Now, as a rule, the little mouse helped to wash up and make the beds, and Mr Poulet fetched the water from the well before he went to business.

But this morning the mouse pretended not to hear when Mrs Poulet called him; and Mr Poulet said that for his part he had a cold, and should stay indoors today; so he took the newspaper and settled down in front of the fire. Poor little Mrs Poulet did the washing up and made the beds all by herself, and then, feeling very sad at heart over the scene which she had just witnessed in the home which, up to now, had been such a happy one, Mrs Poulet took her little bucket and went off to the well for the water.

She little thought that more trouble was already on the way to that little house on the hill. She had only just left the back door when the fox knocked at the front door. The mouse opened it, and when he saw who was there, he scuttled away as fast as he could.

It was very fortunate that he did, but, perhaps, after all, Mr Reynard would not have bothered very much about him. You see he was a very little chap, and Mr Reynard wanted a much bigger dinner for his family of four.

Mr Poulet was so busy reading the daily paper that he did not know who the visitor was until the fox had caught him by the neck, saying, 'Well, this is luck! I didn't expect to find you at home.'

And before poor Mr Poulet could either kick or scream he found himself in a dark sack, jogging along on the fox's back. The terrified little mouse ran to meet Mrs Poulet, and told her what had happened to her poor husband. 'Ah! what a day of trouble,' said the poor little hen. 'Now, what can I do to save him?'

She thought for a moment, then she said, 'Go into the store cupboard and bring out four bottles of my very best cider.' Then she took two of the bottles and flew down the hill as fast as she could. She knew the way the fox would go, and that he would not go very quickly, and she got to the foot of the hill before the fox was in sight. Then she put the two bottles just where the fox would be sure to see them, and hurried off home for two more bottles. These she put further on along the road, close to a tree; then she hurried back to the tree where she had left the first bottles, and hid herself to see what would happen. Presently the fox came in sight.

He was walking slowly, for the sack was heavy, and he was fat and lazy, and the sun was hot, and he was very thirsty; his tongue was hanging out of his mouth. When he saw the bottles of cider, he cried out for joy, and, putting the sack down, he opened and drank both bottles. Then he took up his sack and walked on, still more slowly now, and the little hen followed him in a state of great excitement. When he reached the other two bottles he said he felt thirstier than ever. He put the sack down, emptied both bottles, and then leaning back against the tree, went fast asleep.

As soon as she heard him snoring, the hen flew home for her work-box, and the mouse came scampering after her to see whatever she was going to do. Taking her scissors, the hen cut a long slit in the sack, and Mr Poulet's head came through it in no time. He was very hot and frightened, and his feathers were all ruffled, but his wise little wife would not let him rest. 'Be off at once,' she said, 'and find a stone as large as yourself, and bring it here. Hurry up! there is no time to lose.' Mr Poulet ran off without a word, and soon he came back pulling a large stone, the little mouse pushing up behind.

'Now roll it into the sack,' said the hen. This, too, they did. Then

137

the hen began to sew up the slit in the sack as fast as she could go, for she was afraid the fox would wake up. However, he was still snoring loudly when she had finished; and though the sun was hotter than ever, and the road was uphill, it did not take them long to reach the pretty little house on the hill.

In they scampered, quite breathless, and having fastened all the windows and bolted the doors, they sat down to rest. 'Now let this be a lesson to you both,' said Mrs Poulet severely, as she sat and fanned herself. 'If only you had not been so cross this morning there need have been none of this trouble.'

But so far as the fox was concerned they were all quite safe. For when the fox awoke he had a very bad headache through sleeping in the sun, and he never noticed the trick the hen had played on him. He put the sack over his shoulder and staggered off towards his home; but when he tried to cross the river the heavy sack weighed him down, and before he could scramble back to the bank, he was carried away and drowned.

But the little foxes did not get their nice dinner, and there they stayed in the tumble-down house, getting hungrier and hungrier, until one day their aunt, Reynard's sister, heard of their plight, and took them all to live with her, and trained them to get their own dinner; but she always warned them to let Mr and Mrs Poulet alone, and never go near the house on the hill. So Mr and Mrs Poulet lived in peace, and so grateful to her were her husband and the little mouse, that ever after they did all the housework between them.

ANON.

THE FIG-TREE BEGGAR
AND THE
WILFUL PRINCESS

There was once a boy named Khotan, who was very lazy. He was so lazy he refused to feed himself. He would open his mouth wide and wait until his mother cut his food into small pieces. Then he would chew the pieces slowly and smile happily. He did this until he was seventeen years old!

When Khotan was seventeen, his mother died. The villagers thought that now Khotan would surely find work and begin to feed himself. But no. Khotan just walked into the forest, lay down under a fig tree, opened his mouth wide, and waited until the ripe figs fell off the tree and into his mouth.

One morning a man from another village was passing through the forest and heard cries for help. 'H-e-l-p! I'm starving. I'm dying. H-e-l-p!' He ran quickly towards the cries and saw a young man stetched out on his back under a sweet fig tree, calling, 'H-e-l-p!'

As the man knelt down to see if the boy were ill, Khotan smiled up at him and said, 'Be so kind as to shake the branches of the fig tree. The wind has stopped blowing and I haven't had one fig all day.'

'You lazy good-for-nothing!' the man said, and shook the tree in anger, scattering figs in all directions. Then he turned and stomped off.

Khotan jumped up. He grabbed a handful of figs and threw them at the man. They missed him and fell into the river. The man did not return, so Khotan lay down again under his tree.

The figs floated slowly downstream until, in the late afternoon, they came to the place where Chaidiao, the Princess of the province, was bathing. She saw them and reached out and tasted one. It was delicious. She tried another. It too was delicious. There was one more, and she ate that.

Then she told her father, the Chow, about the figs and asked for more of the same. But none quite like them could be found. Yet Chaidiao could not forget their taste. She looked for them during the day and dreamed of them at night. Finally she told her father she would marry the man who would bring her those figs. She would marry him and none other.

'What nonsense!' her father said. 'What wilfulness!' But the Princess talked so incessantly about the figs, that at last the Chow declared that all the men of the province should appear at the meeting hall.

When they gathered in the meeting hall, the Chow announced:

'The Princess has promised to marry the man who will bring her a certain fruit. Are all the men of the province present?'

'No. Khotan would not come,' someone called out. 'He said he cannot leave his tree.'

'Then carry him!' the Chow ordered. 'Every man must be present.'

The Chow's servants went to speak with Khotan. They offered to carry him, but he refused to abandon his tree. Only when they promised to pick him a good supply of figs to take with him did he agree to being carried to the palace.

'Khotan, the fig-tree beggar!' the servants announced when they arrived at the meeting hall.

The Chow looked in horror at Khotan. Not because Khotan was dressed in rags, his face streaked with dirt, his hair caked with mud, but because of what he carried in his arms: FIGS. And the very ones the Princess had described.

'Daughter,' the Chow asked, 'are the figs in this man's lap the figs you have been looking for?'

'Yes, father,' she answered happily. 'Yes, these are my figs!'

'Then prepare for your wedding, my wilful daughter, for your husband has arrived!'

Khotan and Chaidiao were married the next day by a Buddhist monk.

The Chow was so angry that his daughter had chosen such a husband that he banished them both from the province. They were placed in a barge without oars and left to drift down the river towards the open sea.

Khotan remained in the position in which he had been placed, staring with a wide happy grin at his beautiful bride. Chaidiao stared fearfully back at him, wondering what would happen.

But nothing happened. Khotan just sat there.

The day passed and then the night. Khotan did not move. The next morning Chaidiao was hungry and restless. Now she hoped Khotan *would* do something. But no. He just sat there.

On the second evening the barge got stuck in the mud along the shore. Chaidiao sat up expectantly, waiting for Khotan to speak, to move, to look for food. No. Khotan just sat where he was.

The next morning when Khotan woke up, Chaidiao was gone. Suddenly Khotan was hungry, very hungry. And where was his wife? Where was Chaidiao?

Khotan went into the forest to find her, and came to a Buddhist monastery. The monks gave him rice and rice seedlings, and he brought them back to the barge. But the Princess had not returned.

Khotan set the seedlings in the shade and sat down to eat the rice. Without thinking he finished all the rice, then he realized: when Chaidiao returns, *if* Chaidiao returns, what will she eat?

It was almost dark when Chaidiao came out of the forest, her arms filled with fruits and wild berries. She went to the barge but

Khotan was not there. She began to look for him along the river's edge and saw him bending over a row of rice seedlings he had just planted.

So they began to live together. Khotan worked in the rice fields and Chaidiao gathered fruit and tended their garden. In the evening they slept near the barge.

After many months the gods above noticed Khotan, the once lazy beggar, working hour after hour in the hot rice fields. They decided to reward him, and in the midst of a dreadful thunderstorm, they forged a bronze gong and gave it to the lightning to carry down to the earth.

The next morning Khotan found the beautiful gong lying in the middle of the rice fields. 'I shall give it to Chaidiao as a present,' he thought, and he struck it once to hear its sound.

Immediately the rags he was wearing fell from him and he was dressed in silk clothes. He struck it a second time: he became tall and straight. A third time: his face shone with beauty. A fourth time: servants surrounded him, kneeling before him. A fifth time: musicians joined them. And the sixth time: wisdom entered his heart.

Khotan then returned to the boat surrounded by the servants and musicians. Chaidiao, thinking he was some great foreign prince, bowed her head to the ground.

'Great one! Honoured one!' she said. 'How may I serve you?'

'Food!' he answered.

Chaidiao prepared rice and fruit and served the prince. But when he insisted that she cut up his food into tiny pieces, she looked at him more closely. She looked right into his eyes.

'Khotan?' she whispered.

And the great foreign prince smiled, and, looking into her eyes, whispered back, 'Chaidiao?'

Then Khotan designed a magnificent wooden ship, and while his servants built it, his musicians played for him and Chaidiao.

Soon news of the foreign prince reached the province of the Chow, and the Chow sent an invitation to the prince, asking him and all his royal retinue to the palace.

The Chow went down to the river to greet the royal party. And when he saw his own daughter walking off the ship at the side of the foreign prince, he could not stop himself from crying out in astonishment: 'CHAIDIAO!'

'Yes, Father,' she answered. 'You invited us, and we have returned.'

So it was that Khotan and Chaidiao came to live again in the province of the Chow. And when the Chow died, Khotan, the fig-tree beggar, became Chow. He was considered a wise and generous ruler by all. And he was. Except ... he had one peculiarity that no one understood: he refused all invitations to dinner and never ate in public.

Why? Well, he much preferred to stretch out on the floor of his bedroom while his wife cut his food into tiny pieces and dropped them into his open mouth ... one by one.

Retold by DIANA WOLKSTEIN

GOOSE FEATHERS

Of course, Debby was only eight years old. It was not surprising that she thought a skunk was a black and white kitten. But Tim was nine and three-quarters and there were things happening to him too. It was that way with the feathers. It was that way with the hundreds of goose feathers that Mrs Wiggin had stored in the feather house.

'Now that the new teacher is coming here to live we must have some new pillows,' said Mrs Wiggin. 'We must make some new pillows for the four-poster bed.'

'Oh, she doesn't need pillows,' said Tim.

But they all went into the feather house and closed the door. Piles of fluffy white feathers lay on the table.

'Here are the pillow tickings,' said Mrs Wiggin. 'We'll stuff them full of feathers.'

'For the teacher,' said Debby.

'Aw,' said Tim. 'I hope they're hard.'

Mrs Wiggin scooped up handfuls of feathers. She put them into the tick that Tim held for her. Debby was clapping her hands to make the feathers skip about. When she giggled, a cloud of them would flutter up. It took only a breath of air to move them. They sailed lightly up and then floated down again on the table.

'The baby's crying,' said Tim.

'Oh, dear,' said his mother. 'I was hoping she would sleep until we finished these. I'll have to go and feed her. You hold this, Debby, and Tim can put the feathers in. I'll be back in a few minutes. If you go out, be sure to close the door behind you.'

'Yes,' said Tim.

He stuffed the feathers in. He pushed them in fast to make the pillow as hard as he could. It couldn't be too hard for that teacher, he thought.

'Hold it straight, Debby,' he said.

'My arms ache,' said Debby. 'They ache up into my neck.'

'Rest your arms on the table. Hold the bag wide open,' Tim said.

'Oh, ouch, ouch!' squealed Debby. 'There's a feather tickling my nose. Take it off.'

'Hold still, Debby. Blow it off yourself.'

'Oh, ouch!' she squealed. 'It won't go.'

'Hold still!' cried Tim. 'You're stirring all the feathers up.'

'Oh, ouch!' cried Debby.

She wriggled and kicked. She waved the pillow tick around her head. She made a big wind with the pillow tick. The feathers swirled about.

'They're all over me! Take them off, Tim. Take them off. They tickle!'

The feather house was full of floating feathers. They were like a snowstorm.

'Stop it. Stop it!' cried Tim, and he tried to catch Debby.

'Let me go!' she screamed. 'Let me go!'

She jerked away from Tim. She opened the door and ran out.

'Come back with that sack,' called Tim, and he ran out of the feather house after her.

They ran past the woodshed and into the potato field. The feathers flew off Debby as she ran. Half-way across the field Tim caught her.

'Give me that sack,' he cried.

But the pillow tick flew up in the air and out of it floated a cloud of feathers. There was a strong breeze blowing and off went the feathers towards the woods.

Debby watched them as long as she could see them.

'There go some of the teacher's feathers,' she said.

'You're a bad girl,' said Tim. 'Now there won't be enough to make the pillows too hard.'

'Tim! Timothy Wiggin!'

It was his mother calling. Tim and Debby looked towards the house.

'Why, it's snowing,' said Debby. 'Look! It's snowing hard.'

But Tim's heart jumped so high that it almost went out through the top of his head. He began to run across the potato field as fast as he could. Mrs Wiggin was running towards the feather house. Great flakes of snow were floating from the open door.

Tim had left the door open! The feathers were drifting like snow across the yard and into the apple orchard. They were drifting like a blizzard into the apple orchard.

Mrs Wiggin stood with the baby under her arm. She was looking into the empty feather house. Tim stood looking in too. And Debby. There were about six feathers left in it.

Then they all turned and watched the feathers. They sifted past the house and past the little apple trees. Some of them hung in the apple trees. They hung in the apple trees like apple blossoms. But most of them floated away on the breeze.

'There go two good pillows,' Mrs Wiggin said at last. 'Two good big pillows. Something always happens, seems so to me, seems so.'

Tim said nothing.

And Debby said nothing too.

The feathers flew around all the evening. They fluttered up and they fluttered down. Mr Wiggin came back from the woods with feathers in his hair. Sarah, the cow, wore a crown of them between her horns. Trot, the dog, chased them. He thought they were

butterflies. The pigs snuffed and grunted. The feathers stuck to their noses. The geese looked surprised. Were they losing their feathers again?

Only the birds were happy. They scurried and hurried about. They were gathering feathers – the robins, the bobolinks, the bluebirds, and the meadowlarks. They cheeped and sang as they gathered the feathers to line their nests.

All the birds had warm feather beds that summer, but there were no new pillows for the four-poster bed.

'Accidents will happen, seems so to me, seems so,' said Mr Wiggin.

'Yes, they do in this topsy-turvy family,' Mrs Wiggin said. 'But we can put the children's pillows in the front room.'

'Oh, yes!' cried Debby. 'Then the teacher won't have to be without any.'

'Aw!' said Tim. 'Why do we have to have a teacher?'

EMMA L. BROCK

SILLY BILLY

Little White Goat lived on a farm with lots of other goats. He was always getting into mischief, leaving the herd of goats and wandering off on his own. Then he would get into trouble. The farmer's wife was always having to search for him among the farm buildings where Little Goat would hide.

She told her husband, 'That silly little goat is always in trouble. He won't stay with the other goats and I never know where to find him. Yesterday, I found him chasing the chickens – then he followed me into the kitchen and started eating the tablecloth – he nearly pulled it off, then all my dishes would have been broken. You'll have to keep him fastened up. He's nothing but a nuisance.'

The farmer laughed. 'Don't get so upset, my dear. He's young yet, but he'll settle down soon, so stop worrying.'

The next day the farmer milked the cows and put the milk churns in the dairy. Then he drove the cows into the meadow.

While he was away that naughty little goat got loose and wandered across the farmyard to the dairy. He pushed open the door and went inside.

There he saw a big bowl of cream on the table. He sniffed it – 'atchoo!' it went up his nose. Then he tasted it – it tasted so good that he drank it all up.

He looked on a shelf and found a big cheese. He reached up and began to eat it. 'Yum, yum!' He liked that better than the cream.

Then he looked around and saw the milk churns. He tried to take off the lid to look inside, but the churn tipped over, the lid came off and out splashed the milk, all over the goat and all over the floor.

Little White Goat rushed outside as the milk churn rolled and clattered after him. He slipped and slid over the river of milk as it flowed out of the dairy into the farmyard.

Little Goat dashed across the farmyard scattering the hens and chickens. They set up such a squawking and cackling that the farmer's wife came out to see what all the noise was about.

When she saw Little White Goat she was very angry. 'What have you done, you silly-billy? Be off with you!'

She picked up a broom and chased him away. Then she went into the dairy to clear up the mess.

When the farmer came home she had such a tale to tell.

'That silly goat has been in trouble again. He got into the dairy, drank the cream, ate the cheese and upset a churn of milk all over the floor. I've been clearing up all day. I'm tired of that troublesome goat, he'll have to go. Can't *you* do something about him?'

'There now! Don't take on so! He's only young yet but he'll soon settle down. I'll put him in the orchard tomorrow. He'll be out of your way there,' her husband replied, trying hard to soothe her.

The next day the farmer drove Little Goat into the orchard. Then he shut the gate and spoke to him.

'Now stay there today and don't get in any more trouble. See if you can be good for a change.'

Little Goat bleated as he kicked up his heels and cantered away. The farmer went back to the farm and soon was driving his tractor into a field to start ploughing.

Silly Billy wandered around the orchard looking for mischief. There was nothing to do except eat grass and stare at the trees above him. Then he did see what he could do, for the trees were loaded with apples and some of the branches were low enough for him to reach. He stood on his hind legs and reached up. He shook the branches until the apples fell down. 'Bump, bump, bumpety bump' they tumbled down, some bumping on his head, but he didn't mind. He crunched the apples happily, although he wasn't to know that they were green and unripe and quite sour. When he was full he lay down to rest.

He did not rest long for soon he began to feel ill. He rolled over and over in agony with terrible pains in his stomach. He staggered to his feet and bleated loudly for help.

The farmer's wife was in the farmyard feeding the hens and chickens and she heard his bleating. She hurried to the orchard to find out what was the matter. When she saw Little Goat staggering about in such pain she was very sorry.

She helped him to the stable and put him to rest on some straw.

'There, there! You poor little goat, what is the matter? You look so ill and in such pain. I'll fetch my husband, he'll know what to do. I won't be long, so you rest there until I come back.'

She hurried to the field and called and called but her husband could not hear her for the noise from the tractor. Then he saw her waving frantically so he stopped the tractor and ran to her.

'What's the matter?' he asked.

'Little Goat is very ill, he was staggering around the orchard in such pain, so I put him in the stable. Do come and see him, he might die!'

They hurried to the stable and the farmer looked at Little Goat, then prodded him gently while Little Goat bleated plaintively.

'He's certainly in pain and I know why. I ought to have known better. I should never have put him in the orchard. He's been eating sour unripe apples, that's why he is ill. He has colic.'

'But he couldn't reach them,' said his wife.

'You don't know goats, my dear. If they want something to eat they'll find a way of getting it. Perhaps this will teach him a lesson. I'll give him a dose of medicine to stop the pain. He'll be all right tomorrow, you'll see.'

Sure enough Little Goat was better the next day and was allowed out in the farmyard. He was very quiet and didn't even chase the chickens. The farmer's wife was very pleased and told her husband.

'Little Goat has been very good today. He's followed me around quietly all day long. Perhaps he won't get into any more trouble.'

She was wrong!

The next day was wash day and she hung all her washing on the line. Soon it was blowing in the breeze.

The farmer came towards her leading Little Goat and carrying a rope in his hand.

'What are you going to do?' she asked.

'I'm going to make sure that Little Goat is safe today. I'll fasten him to the tree on the lawn. Then he can't wander away and get into trouble.'

'Good! I can get on with my work now,' said his wife and she went indoors while the farmer went off to the field in his tractor.

Little Goat walked round and round the tree until he felt quite dizzy. Then he ate some of the juicy, green grass. Then he looked around – and guess what he saw! A lovely line of washing, blowing in the breeze! He wished he was free to go and look at it. Suddenly he had a clever idea. He nibbled and gnawed at the rope which tied him to the tree, and soon he was free. He certainly was a clever, inquisitive, mischievous goat, for he walked very quietly across the grass to the washing line. Then he knocked down the wooden prop which held the line high, so now he could reach the washing easily.

He fancied a pair of red socks and began to eat them. 'Yum, yum!' They tasted very good. Then he nibbled delicately at a towel – mmm, quite tasty! But what was on the rest of the menu? A bright blue striped shirt! He began to chew that. Ah! this tasted best of

all, so he ate big holes in it. He was so busy eating he did not hear the farmer's wife come out to fetch her washing.

When she saw the goat she went *mad*! She grabbed a broom and chased him.

'Get away from my washing, you scoundrel! Look what you've done! This is the last straw – you'll have to go!' She chased him round the farmyard while the hens and chickens squawked in terror as they tried to get out of the way. At last she chased him into the stable and shut the door.

'Stay there! *You*'ll be in trouble when I tell my husband what you've done,' she panted breathlessly.

When the farmer came back from the fields, she met him at the gate.

'Wait till I tell you what that silly goat has been up to today.'

'But I tied him up this morning, so how could he be in trouble again?' he asked.

'I'll tell you how. He got loose from the rope, then he went to my washing line and ate your socks, made holes in my best towel and ruined your blue striped shirt. He ate so much of it that it's only fit for a duster now. He bit through the rope – that's how he got loose.'

'Where is he now?' asked the farmer.

'In the stable. You'll have to get rid of him. Take him to market and sell him, for I'm fed up with him.'

'Now, now! Don't take on so. It isn't the end of the world, you know. He's only young and full of mischief. He'll settle down soon – you'll see! Tomorrow he can go with the big goats. He won't be able to get out of that field, I'll make sure of that.' The farmer sighed as he put away the tractor and went indoors.

Next day Little Goat was taken to the field away from the farm and stayed there with the big goats. He liked it there for he could roam around and eat the juicy green grass.

After a while he became restless and wandered away from the big goats and came to the far end of the field. There he managed to squeeze through a gap in the hedge – and he was out on the open road.

'Oh this is great fun,' he thought as he clip-clopped along the road. Suddenly he heard a loud noise – he turned and saw a big milk lorry rushing towards him. He leapt to the roadside just in time. That scared him so he kept to the side of the road where he was safe.

Soon he came to a busy main road. He looked around him, bewildered by all the noise; cars, lorries and buses were whizzing by, making him terrified. He tried to get away, dodging in and out of the traffic. Drivers slammed on their brakes and stopped as Little Goat stood bleating with fright, in the middle of the traffic jam.

A police car drove up and stopped while a policeman jumped out to see what was the matter. 'What's going on here? Who's blocking the road?' he asked.

One of the motorists laughed and answered,

'You might ask that silly goat standing in the middle of the road – he's the culprit!'

The policeman hurried towards the goat and grabbed hold of him. Silly Little Goat was only too glad to be taken away from the traffic.

The drivers laughed and one asked, 'Are you arresting the goat, Constable?'

The policeman saw the funny side of the problem. 'Yes!' he answered. 'I'm taking him into custody for obstructing the traffic.'

By this time the second policeman had joined them. He directed the traffic and soon the road was clear.

'What are we going to do with him?' he asked as they walked back to the car.

'Get the tow rope from the boot of the car and we'll fasten the goat to the back bumper.'

Soon they were driving slowly along the road with Silly Billy trailing behind them.

People stared and laughed when they saw the goat, and the children became very excited to see such a funny sight. They followed on the pavement, keeping up with the car, for they wanted to see where the police were taking him.

At last they reached the police station. The goat was untied and taken inside while one policeman stayed outside and explained what had happened, as the children clamoured to know all about it.

As for the goat, he was put in a cell and locked up until the police could find his owner.

Back at the farm at the end of the day the farmer went to drive the goats back to the farm. He looked for Little Goat; he searched all over the field and came to the gap in the hedge. Then he knew where Little Goat had gone – he had run away!

He hurried back to the farm, driving the goats in front of him. Then he called to his wife as he went indoors.

'Little Goat has run away. I'll have to go and look for him before it's dark.'

'Wait a minute!' his wife answered. 'Don't go yet. Why don't you ring up the police first? They may know something – someone may have found him and reported it to the police.'

'All right! I'll fasten the goats up for the night and then ring up,' he answered.

Soon he was back and picked up the phone and asked for the police.

'Has anyone reported finding a little white goat, because I've lost one? What's that? You've got one locked up in a cell ... He's what? He's trying to knock the door down! ... All right – I'll come right over ... Yes! I'll bring my truck. Thank you very much.'

'What did they say?' asked his wife.

'It's all right, my dear, don't worry. Little Goat is safe. They've locked him up in a police cell. I'll fetch him at once before he kicks the door down – I won't be long.'

Off went the farmer with his truck and soon arrived at the police station. As soon as Little Goat saw him he quietened down. He was led out of the cell and put in the truck.

'Make sure you keep him off the roads in future. He could have caused a nasty accident, or got killed,' said the policeman as they fastened the goat securely in the truck.

'I'll make sure of that – don't worry,' answered the farmer. 'Thank you very much for looking after him.'

As they drove away Little Goat was very quiet. This time he had really learned his lesson. He did not want to get run over. He did not want to be locked up in a police cell ever again. All he wanted was to get safely back home to the farm.

So, at last Little Goat had grown up and he never, never got into trouble again.

GLADYS LEES

THE PAGE BOY AND THE SILVER GOBLET

There was once a little page boy who was in service in a stately castle on the Scottish west coast. He was a pleasant, good-natured little fellow and carried out his duties so willingly that he was popular with everyone, including the great earl whom he served every day and the fat old butler for whom he ran errands. The castle stood on the edge of a cliff overlooking the sea and although the walls on that side were very thick, there was a small postern door which allowed only one person to pass through to a narrow flight of steps cut out of the cliff side and leading down to the seashore. The shore was a pleasant place on summer mornings when one could bathe in the shimmering sea.

On the other side of the castle were gardens and pleasure grounds opening on to a long stretch of heather-covered moorland and beyond was a chain of lofty mountains. The little page boy was very fond of going out on the moor when his work was done. He could then run about as much as he liked, chasing bumblebees, catching butterflies, looking for birds' nests when it was nesting time and watching the young birds learning to fly.

The old butler was very pleased that he should go out on the moor for he knew that it was good for a healthy little lad to have plenty of fun in the open air. But before the boy went out the old man always gave him one warning. 'Now, mind my words, laddie, and keep away from the fairy knowe on the moor, for the little folk are not to be trusted.'

This knowe of which he spoke was a little green hillock which stood on the moor about fifty yards from the garden gate and the local people said that it was the abode of the fairies who would punish any rash mortal who went too near them. It was also known as Boot Hill and according to the great earl the hillock had been made hundreds of years before when visiting noblemen cleaned the earth and mud from their boots on the hill before entering the castle. Because of the various stories the country folk would walk a good half mile out of their way, even in broad daylight, rather than run the risk of going near the hillock and bringing the little folk's displeasure down upon themselves. At night, they said, the fairies walked abroad, leaving the door of their dwelling open so that any foolish mortal who did not take care might find himself inside.

Now, the little page boy was an adventurous lad, and instead of being frightened of the fairies he was very anxious to see them and visit their abode, just to find out what it was like. One night, when everyone else was asleep, he crept out of the castle by the little postern door and stole down the steps, then along the seashore to a path leading up on to the moor.

He went straight to the fairy knowe and to his delight he found that what the local people had said was true. The top of the knowe was tipped up and from the opening came rays of light streaming into the darkness. His heart was beating fast with excitement, but gathering his courage he stooped down and slipped inside. He found himself in a large room lit by numberless tiny candles and there, seated round a polished marble table, were scores of tiny folk: fairies, elves and gnomes, dressed in green, yellow, pink, blue, lilac and scarlet; in fact, all the colours of the rainbow.

The little page boy stood in a dark corner watching the busy scene in wonder, thinking how strange it was that there should be such a number of those tiny beings living their own lives all unknown to men and yet not far away from human dwellings. Suddenly an order was given, by whom he could not tell.

'Fetch the cup,' cried the unknown voice and instantly two little fairy pages dressed in scarlet darted from the table to a cupboard in the wall of the compartment. They returned staggering under the weight of a most beautiful silver goblet, richly embossed and lined inside with gold.

The silver cup was placed on the middle of the table and, amid clapping of hands and shouts of joy, all the fairies began to drink out of it in turn. The page boy could see from where he stood that no one poured wine into the cup and yet it appeared to be always full. The wine that was in it was not always of the same kind, but sometimes red and sometimes white. Each fairy, when he grasped the stem, wished for the wine he desired, and lo, in a moment the cup was full of it. 'It would be a fine thing if I could take that cup home with me,' thought the page boy. 'No one will believe that I have been here unless I have something to show for it.' So he bided his time and waited.

Presently the fairies noticed him and, instead of being angry at his boldness in entering their abode, as he expected, they seemed very pleased to see him and invited him to take a seat at the table. But not long after he sat down they became rude and insolent, whispering together and peering at him and asking why he should be content to serve mere mortals. They also told him that they were aware of everything that went on in the castle and made fun of the old butler whom the page boy loved. They laughed at the food served in the castle and said it was only fit for animals. When any fresh, dainty food was set on the table by the scarlet-clad fairy pages they would push the dish across to him saying: 'Taste it, for you will not have the chance to taste such good things at the castle.'

At last, he could stand their teasing remarks no longer; besides, he knew that if he wanted to secure the silver cup he must not lose any more time in doing so as they all appeared to be turning against him. Suddenly he stood up and grabbed the cup from the table, holding the stem of it lightly in his hand.

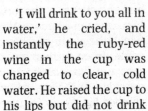

'I will drink to you all in water,' he cried, and instantly the ruby-red wine in the cup was changed to clear, cold water. He raised the cup to his lips but did not drink from it. With a sudden jerk he threw the water over the burning candles and instantly the room was in darkness. Then, clasping the precious cup tightly in his arms, he sprang to the opening of the knowe through which he could see the stars gleaming clearly in the sky. He was just in time, for the opening like a trap door fell with a crash behind him. Soon he was speeding along the moor with the whole troop of fairies at his heels. They were wild with rage and from the shrill shouts of fury the page boy knew that if they overtook him he could expect no mercy at their hands.

The page boy's heart began to sink, for fleet of foot though he was, he was no match for the fairy folk who were steadily gaining on him. All seemed lost, when a mysterious voice sounded out of the darkness:

> *If you would gain the castle door,*
> *Keep to the black stones on the shore.*

It was the voice of some poor mortal, who, for some reason or other, had been taken prisoner by the fairies and who did not want such a fate to befall the adventurous page boy; but the little fellow did not know this. He had once heard that if one walked on the wet sands which the waves had washed over the fairies could not touch him. The mysterious voice brought the saying into his mind. He dashed panting down the path to the shore, his feet sank into the dry sand and his breath came in little gasps. He felt as if he must drop the silver cup and give up the struggle, but he persevered and at last, just as the foremost fairies were about to lay hands on him, he jumped across the water mark on to firm, wet sand from which the waves had just receded. He was now safe. The little folk could go no further but stood on the dry sand uttering cries of rage and disappointment while the page boy ran triumphantly by the edge of the sea carrying the precious cup in his arms. He climbed lightly up the steps in the rock and disappeared through the postern door into the castle.

For many years afterwards, long after the little page boy had grown up and had become a stately butler who trained other little page boys to follow in his footsteps, the beautiful goblet remained in the castle as a witness to his adventure.

GRANT CAMPBELL

THE TERRIBLY PLAIN
PRINCESS

Once upon a time there was this terribly plain Princess. I won't beat about the bush – she was terribly plain. All the visitors at the Royal Christening remarked upon it.

'How extraordinarily plain she is,' said her aunt as she handed over a solid silver spoon as a christening present.

'Quite exceptionally so,' said her cousin-once-removed as she put a solid gold napkin ring into the Princess's tiny hands.

I say tiny hands, but her hands were a great deal larger than those of most Royal Princesses. Her mouth was wider, too, and her nose was hopelessly snubbed. She also had twenty-three freckles over her nose and cheeks.

The King and Queen watched anxiously as the pile of presents grew higher and the comments on the Princess's plainness grew franker. Finally, the Lord High Chamberlain presented the child with a portrait of himself wearing his full robes of office.

'We shall be hard put to find her a husband,' he said gloomily, shaking his head with the worry of it all. The poor Queen could bear it no longer. She burst into tears and sobbed all over the King's best ermine cloak, which did it no good.

The Princess, whose name was Sophia, lived on an island with her mother, Good Queen Matilda, and her father, Good King Ferdinand. The island was the Island of Toow and was one of a group of islands with original names like the Island of Wun and the Island of Thri. Further over to the right was the Island of Faw but nobody talked about that one. It was uninhabited and a bit of an eyesore with trees and wild flowers all over the place and no street lighting. All the islands were surrounded by seas of an incredible blue and a golden sun shone all the time.

The terribly plain Princess thrived in this beautiful kingdom,

but any hopes that she might grow out of her plainness faded with the passing of the years. She didn't look like a Princess and she didn't behave like one. Sometimes her Royal cousins from Thri and Wun would come over to visit.

They would play very genteel games like 'The farmer's in his Royal den,' and 'Here we go gathering Royal nuts in May,' but the Princess Sophia was bored by it all. She would slip away to find Bert, the gardener's boy. He was her one and only true best friend in all the world – or so she told him.

Bert was also terribly plain. He had a snub nose, large hands, a wide mouth and twenty-eight freckles. He worked very hard because the gardener was bone idle and spent most of his time sleeping in a wheelbarrow in the shade of a Royal pear tree.

Bert trimmed the hedges, and weeded the paths and raked the leaves off the grass. When Bert wasn't working in the gardens he was busy with his secret plan to grow a giant blue marigold. He confided this secret to no one but the Princess Sophia – and the cook and most of his relations (and he came from a very large family).

The Princess loved to help him, and together they mixed powders to sprinkle and solutions to spray. They grew a giant orange marigold and some small blue marigolds but never a giant blue one. It was very disappointing for Bert but he was a sunny sort of boy and he refused to give up hope.

When the terribly plain Princess was fifteen, Good King Ferdinand sent for the Lord High Chamberlain.

'Look here,' he said, 'what are you doing about finding a husband for the Princess Sophia?'

The Lord High Chamberlain bowed low.

'Everything is in hand, Your Majesty,' he said proudly. 'I think I may say in all modesty, and without fear of contradiction, though I say it myself as shouldn't –'

'Get on with it, man,' said the King. It was rather unkingly of him but his nerves were frayed by sleepless nights spent worrying about his daughter's future.

The Lord High Chamberlain tried again. 'Bearing in mind the Princess Sophia's terrible plainness of face and largeness of hands, I have now discovered the ideal husband for your daughter.'

The King sighed.

'I suppose he, too, is terribly plain,' he said.

'On the contrary, Your Majesty, Prince Archibald is of Royal and noble countenance.'

162

The King began to feel much happier.

'And where does this Prince live?' he asked.

'On the Island of Ayte,' said the Lord High Chamberlain.

The King lowered his voice to a whisper.

'And what is it that makes the Prince an ideal husband for the Princess Sophia?' he asked.

The Lord High Chamberlain lowered his voice also.

'Your Majesty,' he said, 'the Prince Archibald is terribly short-sighted – in a Royal sort of way. I doubt if he will notice that his bride is terribly plain.'

Good King Ferdinand was delighted. He told Good Queen Matilda who was delighted and together they told the Princess Sophia who was horrified.

'But I don't want to marry him,' she protested and she stamped her foot and looked plainer than ever. 'I want to marry Bert, the gardener's boy, and help him grow a giant blue marigold.'

'But dearest child,' said her mother. 'The gardener's boy is terribly plain and Prince Archibald is of Royal and noble countenance.'

'Royal and noble poppycock!' said the Princess. 'I want to marry Bert.'

But her protestations went unheeded and the date was set for the wedding. You may well be wondering what Bert had to say about all this. The fact is that he didn't say anything because he had designed a square parasol to shelter the marigolds from the sun's rays at midday and was trying to decide the best position for it.

On the Island of Ayte, Prince Archibald was not looking forward to his coming betrothal either, because he was a confirmed bookworm. His rooms in

163

the palace had books where books should be and books where books shouldn't be. Scattered among the books were various pairs of spectacles to help him with his reading. (There were times when his parents worried about him.)

The day of the Royal wedding dawned bright and clear. The Royal party set sail from the Island of Ayte in the Good Ship Aytee, bound for the Island of Toow.

The Princess Sophia waited on the quayside with Good King Ferdinand and Good Queen Matilda and the Lord High Chamberlain and hundreds of lesser mortals. The terribly plain Princess wore a beautiful gown of white and gold lace and a rather thick veil. As the Prince's ship drew alongside the quay a great cheer went up from the Princess's supporters and the Prince put down his book and went up on deck. It was a proud moment for the people of Toow when the Prince Archibald, of Royal and noble countenance, prepared to meet the terribly plain Princess Sophia.

But it was not to be. It so happened that the Prince Archibald had forgotten to take off his reading spectacles and put on his walking-about spectacles. Instead of stepping on to the ship's gangplank he missed it by a good few inches and stepped straight into the incredibly blue sea!

Now, although the people of Toow were nice, well-mannered people, it isn't every day you can see a Royal Prince plopping into the water like that. I have to admit that they all fell about laughing. Some of them laughed so much that *they* fell into the water as well.

Poor Prince Archibald was very upset. As soon as he was fished out of the water he gave orders to sail back to Ayte and turned to the next chapter in his book. The terribly plain Princess Sophia was also upset. She ran away to find Bert and weep on his shoulder, but when she did find him he was at the top of a step-ladder, adjusting the square parasol over his precious marigold plants. The princess fell to her knees on the grass below him, and wept terribly plain tears all over the marigold.

When Bert came down five minutes later to see what was going on he could hardly believe his eyes. The marigolds were beginning to grow! The plants grew taller and taller and produced giant buds which burst into bloom. Yes! You've guessed it. Bright blue marigolds!

That's almost the end of the story. Bert was awarded a medal – the Gardener's Silver Cross – and he was allowed to marry the Princess. They went to live on the Island of Faw where they raised many new and wonderful plants with the help of Princess Sophia's terribly plain tears. (She could cry to order by thinking how nearly she had married Prince Archibald!) Oh yes! They also raised a large family of happy, but terribly plain, children!

PAMELA OLDFIELD

THE RUNAWAY SHOES

In a faraway part of the world, there is a little town called Pokey-doke. And on the edge of this town is a little red house. Mr and Mrs Nickelodeon Kumquat live there.

One day Mr and Mrs Nickelodeon Kumquat cleaned and polished their good shoes. Mrs Kumquat set them all out on the back stoop to dry. As soon as she went back inside the house, all four shoes began talking at once.

'Goody,' said the first shoe.

'Now's our chance,' said the second shoe.

'To run away,' said the third shoe.

'Let's go!' said the fourth shoe.

So they hopped down the steps and they tiptoed down the path and they walked across the lawn and they RAN across the road and into a field.

But Mr Nickelodeon Kumquat saw them go. He was looking out of a window.

'Mrs Kumquat,' he cried. 'Come quickly. Our shoes are running away. We must catch them and bring them home.'

Mr and Mrs Nickelodeon Kumquat rushed out of the house in their bedroom slippers. They jumped down the steps and they leaped down the path and they bounced across the lawn and they RAN across the road and into the field.

When the shoes saw Mr and Mrs Nickelodeon Kumquat running after them, they all began to talk at once.

'Perhaps we'd better hide,' said the first shoe.

'And wait for a while,' said the second shoe.

'Until they get past us,' said the third shoe.

'Let's run!' said the fourth shoe.

Licketysplit across the field ran the shoes. Out in the middle of the field they saw a cow.

'Oh, Cow,' said the first shoe.

'Will you do us a favour?' said the second shoe.

'Just put one shoe on each foot,' said the third shoe.

'And make believe you always wear shoes,' said the fourth shoe.

'Gladly,' said the cow. 'Moo-oo-oost gladly.'

So the cow put on the shoes and stood still, looking up at the sky and pretending to watch for the stars to come out.

As Mr and Mrs Nickelodeon Kumquat ran past the cow, Mr
Kumquat shouted over his shoulder,

'Did you see any shoes run past you?'

'Not I,' said the cow. 'I didn't see any shoes run past me.' And
she told the truth, too.

But just then Mrs Kumquat stopped running.

'Mr Kumquat,' she said. 'Did you ever see a cow with shoes on
before?'

'Why, no,' said Mr Kumquat. 'Come to think of it, I never did.
Those must be our shoes on that cow!' So they turned around and
started to run back.

'Oh my!' said the first shoe.

'They're coming back!' said the second shoe.

'We didn't fool them!' said the third shoe.

'Let's run!' cried the fourth shoe.

So they said thank you politely to the cow and the four shoes
ran licketysplit down to the edge of the brook. There they saw a
crocodile. Don't ask me how he happened to be there. He just was.

'Oh, Crocodile,' said the first shoe.

'Will you do us a favour?' said the second shoe.

'Just put one shoe on each foot,' said the third shoe.

'And make believe you always wear shoes,' said the fourth
shoe.

'Well,' said the crocodile, 'it's hardly the sort of thing I'd want
to do every day in the week, but all right.'

So he put on the shoes and he stood still at the edge of the brook.

He hummed a little song his mother had taught him when he was small and he pretended he was singing himself to sleep.

As Mr and Mrs Nickelodeon Kumquat ran past the crocodile, Mr Kumquat shouted over his shoulder, 'Did you see any shoes run past you, Crocodile?'

'Not I,' said the crocodile. 'I didn't see any shoes run past me.' And he told the truth, too.

But just then, Mr Kumquat stopped running.

'Mrs Kumquat,' he said. 'Did you ever see a crocodile with shoes on before?'

'Why, no,' said Mrs Kumquat. 'Come to think of it, I never did. Those must be our shoes on that crocodile!' So they turned around and started to run back towards the crocodile.

'Oh my!' said the first shoe.

'They're coming back!' said the second shoe.

'We didn't fool them!' said the third shoe.

'Let's run!' cried the fourth shoe.

So they said thank you politely to the crocodile and the four shoes ran licketysplit right into the middle of the woods and Mr and Mrs Nickelodeon Kumquat never saw where they went. So Mr and Mrs Kumquat had to go home in their bedroom slippers.

All day long the four shoes had a wonderful time. They walked up the sides of trees and walked along the branches. They hopped into mud puddles. They floated on the brook like little boats.

In the afternoon they started off towards town. When they came to a barn, they walked up one side and over the roof and down the other side. When they came to a fence they walked on top of it. Sometimes they even walked on the telephone wires!

'It's getting late,' said the first shoe.

'We'd better go home,' said the second shoe.

'But, gosh –' said the third shoe.

'We're awfully dirty,' said the fourth shoe.

And they certainly were. They didn't look at all like the same shoes Mr and Mrs Nickelodeon Kumquat had cleaned and polished that morning.

So the four shoes walked down the main street and walked into the shoemaker's shop and hopped up on the shelf.

In a few minutes the shoemaker turned around and saw them.

'Well my goodness,' he said. 'Those shoes belong to Mr and Mrs Nickelodeon Kumquat. I mended them last month. I wonder how they got here.'

He thought for a while and then he said, 'Mr and Mrs Nickelodeon Kumquat must have left them here when I was out for lunch.'

So the shoemaker cleaned and polished the shoes until they looked brand new. Then he put them back on the shelf.

Later, when the shoemaker wasn't looking, the four shoes hopped down from the shelf and skipped up the street. They went straight back to the little red house where Mr and Mrs Kumquat live.

There they stood, lined up in a row on the steps when Mr Nickelodeon Kumquat opened the door just before suppertime.

'Mrs Kumquat,' he cried. 'Come quickly!'

Mrs Nickelodeon Kumquat came.

'Why, there are our shoes!' she said. 'Now how do you suppose they got there?'

'Well,' said Mr Nickelodeon Kumquat with a wink, 'that's just where you put them this morning, isn't it?'

And he told the truth, too.

EDNA PRESTON

THE KIDNAPPING OF LORD COCKEREL

Not very long ago, a man and his wife lived in a small flat in the centre of a noisy city. Every morning, they were woken by the sound of the milk train clattering through a nearby tunnel; every evening, there was a great blowing of horns, stamping of feet and calling of 'Paper! Paper!' by news-boys as tired people made their way home from work. For many years, they didn't bother very much about the clamour; after all, it was company. They had no children and would have been dreadfully quiet all by themselves. But one midsummer day, when they had to close their windows because of the roar of the buses and stop up their ears because of the screech of brakes, the man put down his knife and fork and pushed back his chair.

'Alice,' he said. 'I've got an idea. We'll go and live in the country.'

'In the *country*, George?' questioned his wife in surprise. A dreamy look came into her eyes. 'You mean, the *real* country? With haystacks? And pigs?'

'*Certainly* with pigs. We'll have a farm. We'll sell the flat. We'll buy a cottage. We'll have animals, and vegetables, and take things as they come, see? We'll GO.'

Then he finished up his steak-and-kidney pudding, and together they studied the railway timetable to find out when the next train might be travelling to the country. The *real* country. With pigs.

There was one that very afternoon.

So you see *that* was how George and Alice began. The cottage they found was dark and rickety. There were tiny windows and crooked floors, a gate that was half off its hinges, and a cellar full of cobwebs and mice. But there were outhouses, a vegetable patch, a pigsty . . . and best of all, a bit of meadow land.

They worked hard, and soon had everything to rights. Little by little, they began to stock the farm.

The first animal to be bought was a cow, for they needed milk for themselves and could sell what was left over. Then a pig, and half a dozen chickens. A cat, to keep the mice away. A dog, to guard the house. And a donkey.

They hesitated a bit about the donkey, but the man said it would cost nothing to feed – it could live in the meadow and sleep in one of the outhouses. And it would be useful for carrying things to the market, when they had enough to sell.

'Cabbages . . . and eggs . . . and cooking apples . . .' he explained. 'We shall soon build up a business. We must take things as they come.

'What's the matter?'

Alice was looking worried.

'There's one thing that bothers me,' she said. 'We'll have to get up very early to look after all these animals. There isn't a milk train here, or motor horns and the alarm clock got broken when we moved house.

'What shall we do?'

They thought. It really was a problem. They were so accustomed to noise . . . with so much silence, one could almost sleep for ever. And then what would happen? What would happen if they *never* woke up?

'I have it!' George thumped the table. 'A cockerel. That's what we need. A cockerel always crows, just as dawn is breaking. That'll wake us, come what may.'

So they bought a cockerel.

What a voice he had, that cockerel! His was the loudest in the yard by far. How proud he was of it, too.

'Cock-a-doodle-doo! Wake up, you people, do!' he screamed, as the first pale glimmer of sun lighted the horizon. The other animals groaned and grunted and muttered crossly that they were busy dreaming and did not want to be disturbed. But George and Alice rolled out of bed and started mixing the chicken feed and milking the cow. There was a lot to do on a farm, and they had to begin early or they would not finish by bedtime.

To begin with, it was a happy arrangement, and all went well. But soon the animals began to be irritated by the cockerel. It was one thing being told that dawn was breaking; it was quite another to hear that loud, raucous cry so often – during one's noontime nap, when one was searching for truffles, or pulling up worms. And he was so beautiful.

'I'm smarter than you!' he would crow. 'What stupid things you do!' The cockerel strutted about among the brown hens, pushing them out of the way and helping himself to the tastiest morsels.

'I am the Lord of you all,' he announced. 'It is well known that the man and his wife cannot get out of bed without my instructions. The success of the farm depends entirely on my own efforts. You are indeed fortunate to have me among you. Why, even the sun does not rise until he has heard me! That is my cousin, up there on the church steeple. You can see that he is covered in gold; every Sunday, human beings come into the building and sing songs to him.

'They are not very good songs,' mused the cockerel critically, 'but then human beings do not have very good voices. They cannot crow.'

After that, he insisted on being called 'Lord Cockerel' by the other animals.

'Respect, where respect is due!' he called severely. 'What? What? What? Respect me!'

At last, the rest of the farmyard creatures said that they could stand it no longer.

'He needs to be taught a lesson,' they decided. 'We'll kidnap him, and shut him up in the corn shed for a week or two. There's plenty to eat there, so he won't be hungry, and it will show him that ordinary folk can manage quite well without such an outcry.'

'Yes! That's a glor-i-ous idea,' mewed the cat.

Kidnapping Lord Cockerel wasn't so easy as they had thought it was going to be. He was so alert and watchful, stepping proudly

among them and darting his fierce yellow eyes in all directions. Once, Pig lumbered up behind him with a sack, and was just about to drop it over his head when Lord Cockerel turned and saw him.

'What? What? What? What are you going to do?' he cackled.

'Just gathering acorns,' answered Pig hastily. 'Tra-la ... tra-la ... tum tiddly um tum...' He wandered off.

On another occasion, Cow almost succeeded in pushing him into her milking pail. But she stumbled and kicked it over in her efforts, and Lord Cockerel made a great fuss about the spilled milk. 'A stupid thing to doooo!' he crowed crossly.

They had almost given up hope when Cat thought of a plan.

'It's a very de-vi-ous plan,' she mewed. 'I will pretend I have hurt my tail. I will hide under the sacks in the corn shed and cry for help. When Lord Cockerel comes in to see what has happened, I will run out quickly and shut the door on him, and push the bolt across on the outside with my paw. I can do that,' she explained, 'because I am a member of the CAT family. Cats are clever. Everybody knows that.'

The plan worked splendidly. Cat made a pitiful outcry, mewing that her tail was caught in a trap. Lord Cockerel stalked into the corn shed to advise her, and in half a second she had whisked past him, slammed the door and pushed home the bolt.

He was caught.

It was no use crowing, either. The corn shed was a long way from the farmhouse. No one would hear him.

The aimals were delighted with the success of their trick. The yard was peaceful and friendly; it seemed a different place. The donkey dozed in the meadow ... the swallows nested in the eaves ... the hens made dustbaths for themselves and fluttered and gossiped together.

At last, dusk fell.

'There's just one thing,' Cat reminded them, as she dropped in for a last taste of milk. 'Someone will have to rouse the Farmer in the morning, otherwise he won't get up. Human beings never do. They are not like us. They would sleep all day as well as all night if there were no interruption.'

The aimals nodded their heads and nudged each other.

'Cat is sensible,' they said. 'Let Pig rouse the Farmer in the morning. He has a good, loud grunt. But who will wake Pig?'

'The swallows in the eaves will wake me,' answered Pig. 'They always start the day early. They twitter and flutter like ever so.'

So they all went to bed and slept.

Sure enough, as soon as it was light the swallows began tweeting and fidgeting. Pig opened one eye ... then the other. He yawned. Then, feeling important, he lumbered over to the farmhouse, took up a position beneath the bedroom windows, and grunted:

'SNORK
    SNORK
        SNUMP!'

'George,' whispered Alice. 'That pig's making a dreadful noise. He

174

must have got a stomach-ache. Best take him to the Vet, before it gets any worse!'

George raised himself on his elbow, and listened.

'SNORK
  SNORK
    SNUMP!'

'You're right, Alice. I'll just have a bite of breakfast, and we'll be off. Luckily, the Vet'll be in the village at nine. It's his day. He'll soon put him right. You may be sure of that.'

He lurched out of bed, pulled on his trousers and sweater, and swallowed some hot tea. Then, without more ado, he chivied Pig into the wheelbarrow and wheeled him off...

The other animals watched them go. They felt a little uneasy.

Hours later, the wheelbarrow returned, with a crestfallen Pig.

'What happened, old chap?' asked Donkey sympathetically.

'The Vet said I had over-eaten,' answered Pig crossly. 'I'm to have nothing but warm water and bicarbonate for a week. Such an idea! I shall starve to death. *You* can wake the Farmer next time. I shan't.'

He stumped heavily back to his sty and slammed the door.

'Poor fellow!' mooed Cow. 'Tomorrow morning, I'll go. Leave it to me. The farmer understands my language. I often call to him when it is milking time, to remind him to bring a pail. I'll wake him.'

'You are sure to be more successful, my dear,' agreed Cat. She did not want to go herself, for she was fond of her sleep and had no intention of rising early. 'I *think* what to do, *they* do it,' she purred.

As soon as she heard the swallows moving in the rafters, Cow raised her head, threw back her shoulders and ambled purposefully towards the farmhouse.

Under the window grew a fine hawthorn hedge. Cow took a mouthful or two, for she was partial to hawthorn and found the prickly bits especially delicious. Then:

'MOO!'

Alice was at the bedroom window in a second, peering under the curtain. 'George,' she cried desperately. 'That cow's on the

175

flower bed! She's trampling on the roses! She's eating the hedge! Stop her! Stop her! Get her off!'

'Well! Did you ever hear such a thing?' marvelled George, staring blearily over his wife's shoulder. 'Drat her! We'll empty a load of water over her – that'll make her change her ways!' And without another word, he filled the slop pail and tipped it over the sill.

Sssssssssplashshshshshshshs!

Cow stepped back hastily. She disliked water, except for drinking purposes, and some of it had gone in her eye. Hurriedly, she made her way back to the barn, stamping her feet and rubbing up against the straw to warm herself.

'Raining?' questioned Donkey pleasantly. He was half awake.

'It's *not* raining!' snapped Cow. 'I expect I've caught pneuuuuuuuumonia. Moo! I shan't wake him tomorrow morning. That's certain. It's *your* turn.'

Donkey sniffed.

But nobody else volunteered. The animals were beginning to feel uncomfortable. Perhaps they had been rather silly to kidnap Lord Cockerel after all. He *was* good at waking people up. No one could deny that.

'What about Dog?' muttered Donkey hopefully. 'Let Dog do it. A dog is Man's Best Friend.'

But Dog wouldn't.

'Let them sleep,' he growled. 'They like sleeping. Why shouldn't they? They'll get up some time, I dare say ... next week ... or the week after. In time for Christmas. They won't want to miss the puddin', you see. *She*'ll cook it. *He*'ll eat it. They look forward to that. It's what they like, puddin'. Mind you, I prefer a good bone myself, nicely matured, and with a maggot or two. But there's no accounting for tastes.'

'What about Cat?'

'Me?' squeaked Cat. 'The idea! I don't *do* things of that kind. I tell other people how to do them. It's what we call delegation. I know howwww, you see, so I tell them. But my voice is far, far too delicate to emulate an alarm clock.'

She rolled the word emulate round her tongue. It was a long word. Nobody knew what it meant.

'*All* right,' snuffed Donkey. 'I will, then. I'll wake him. But only once.'

Night fell. It was damp and misty. Owls hooted from the elm trees and there wasn't a moon at all – only a pale sort of wish-wash where she might have been.

'It's a pity to disturb a person's rest,' thought Donkey to himself, in his muddled way. 'I'll go and wake the Farmer *now*, before he goes to sleep. Then the job'll be done. That's a brilliant idea, that is. Brains ... that's what's needed. Brains.'

He pushed open the door of the outhouse with his nose and made his way towards the farm. But it wasn't where he thought it should have been. He had forgotten how difficult it is to find anyone, anything, anywhere, at night. He blundered and stumbled ... he scraped his shins against the water trough ... he tripped over Dog's feeding bowl ...

'George,' whispered Alice.

'Ah?'

'I hear burglars.'

'Burglars?'

'In the yard. Listen.'

Bump, bump, bump.

Then, 'EEE OOR!' sounded through the darkness.

'EE OOR! EEEEEE OR! I might as well make as much row as I can,' muttered Donkey, 'in case I'm in the wrong place.'

He took an enormous breath.

'EEEE OORR!'

'It's that donkey, my dear,' grunted George. 'We'll throw something in his direction – to send him away. Stupid creature. He thinks it's morning.'

A piece of soap hurtled out of the bedroom window.

'Carrots?' questioned Donkey, as he caught it neatly. 'Ugh! Soap!'

Blowing bubbles, spluttering, hiccuping, he galloped across the farmyard and disappeared into the meadow. They could hear his footsteps growing fainter ... fainter ... Then silence.

'He'd better sleep outside in future,' the Farmer decided. 'Maybe he doesn't like being in a shed.'

George and Alice finished undressing, pulled the eiderdown up to their chins, and slept.

177

Well, all stories have an ending. Before many hours had passed, it was heard that *somebody* had pulled back the bolt on the door of the corn shed. *Who* did it, nobody knew.

'It was the wind, I dare say,' mewed Cat drowsily. 'Or weasels. Ask no questions, you'll be told no lies. Anyway, Lord Cockerel is at large again. We ALL know that. Listen!'

'Cock-a-doodle-doo!' shrilled from corner of the rickyard.

But it did not sound quite so jaunty as before.

'Get up, good people, do!' called a familiar voice. Lord Cockerel fluttered towards them, clearing his throat.

'Been away for a brief holiday,' he explained. 'And – listen will you? I don't want to be called Lord Cockerel any more. Just Cockerel. Or Cocky, for short. See? Cocky!'

He has been known as Cocky for some time, now. And he is *much* more thoughtful than he used to be. When the animals are dozing, he only crows in a whisper. Like this:

'*Cock-a-doodle-doo.*'

The rest of them have really grown quite fond of him.

'We all have our peculiarities,' explained Cat, washing carefully behind her left ear. 'What one can't do another can.'

The animals nodded. They knew *that* was right. Why, who would expect Donkey to lay eggs, or Dog to fill the milk churns?

'Furthermore,' went on Cat, yawning and arching her back, 'nobody tells the truth, the whole truth, and nothing but the truth – *all* day long.

'Who *could* have let Cocky out? I know, mind you. But I shan't say.

'Mew!'

JEAN KENWARD

'FRAIDY MOUSE

Once upon a time there were three grey mice, and they lived in a corner of a barn.

Two of the mice weren't afraid of anything, except the brown tabby cat who lived in the farmhouse. Two of the mice said, 'Hi! Look at us. We're tricky and we're quicky and we're fighty and we're bitey. We're not afraid of anything, except the tabby cat.'

But the third little mouse said, 'Don't look at me. I'm afraid of everything. I'm a 'Fraidy Mouse.'

'Fraidy Mouse's brothers said, 'Don't be ridiculous. There's nothing to be frightened of, except the tabby cat.'

'Fraidy Mouse shivered, 'I've never seen a tabby cat. Does Tabby Cat stamp with his feet? Does he growl?'

'Fraidy Mouse's brothers said, 'Don't be absurd. Tabby Cat sits by the door of the barn.

> He sits on the ground,
> He's big and he's round.
> He doesn't move a muscle
> Till he hears a little rustle.
> Then he'll jump. Thump!
> And he'll eat you till you're dead.'

Then 'Fraidy Mouse's brothers said, 'But Tabby Cat's indoors now. So off we go together to be bold, brave mice.'

'Fraidy Mouse was left alone, sitting in the barn. In case he should see something fearsome and frightening, he closed his eyes tightly and fell fast asleep.

While 'Fraidy Mouse was sleeping, the farmer passed the barn. He was carrying a sack full of big brown potatoes. One of the potatoes fell out and rolled about. It rolled to the door of the barn. And there it stayed.

'Fraidy Mouse woke up. He saw that big potato. 'Mercy me! It's Tabby Cat, sitting by the door!

He's sitting on the ground,
And he's big and he's round.
He won't move a muscle
Till he hears a little rustle.
Then he'll jump. Thump!
And he'll eat me till I'm dead.'

'Fraidy Mouse kept so still that all his bones were aching. Then his brothers came back, and they said, 'Hi, 'Fraidy Mouse!'

'Fraidy Mouse whispered, 'Hush! Oh hush! Don't you see the tabby cat sitting by the door?'

'Fraidy Mouse's brothers said, 'Don't be idiotic. That's not a tabby cat. That's a big potato.' And they laughed. 'Fraidy Mouse's brothers rolled around laughing, until they were exhausted and had to go to sleep.

But poor little 'Fraidy Mouse cried himself to sleep.

While the mice were sleeping, the farmer passed the barn. He picked the potato up and carried it away. 'Fraidy Mouse twitched in his sleep – dreaming. He dreamed he was a tricky, quicky little mouse.

As the sun went down, the big brown tabby cat came padding to the barn. And he sat by the door. 'Fraidy Mouse twitched in his sleep again – dreaming. He dreamed he was a fighty, bitey little mouse.

After a while, the mice woke up. The first thing they saw in the twilight was the cat, a big round brown thing sitting by the door. 'Fraidy Mouse's brothers hid away in holes. They stared out with frightened eyes, too terrified to speak.

'Fraidy Mouse thought they were teasing him again, pretending to be frightened of a big brown potato. He wouldn't get caught like *that* again!

He called out, 'Hi there! You silly old potato!' The tabby cat was so surprised he didn't move a muscle. 'Fraidy Mouse called again, 'I'm only small and 'Fraidy. But I'm not afraid of *you*, you silly old potato. And neither are my tricky, quicky, fighty, bitey brothers.'

Tabby Cat said to himself, 'What a mouse! If that's a little 'Fraidy Mouse, the smallest, most afraid mouse, his brothers must be terrible. I shan't come here again.'

Then Tabby Cat stalked away, pretending not to hurry. And 'Fraidy Mouse said, 'Funny! That potato's got a tail!'

'Fraidy Mouse's tricky, quicky, fighty, bitey brothers came creeping from their holes, and they said, 'Oh, 'Fraidy Mouse! How brave you were to talk to the tabby cat like that!'

'Fraidy Mouse thought, 'Tabby Cat! That wasn't a potato. I was talking to a real live tabby cat. Oh my!'

Then his legs gave way, and he fell on his back. And his brothers said, 'He's resting. It's tiring being so brave!'

ANNE WELLINGTON

J. ROODIE

J. Roodie was wild and bad, although he was only nine. Nobody owned him, so he lived in a creek bed with his animals, who had nasty names. His dog was called Grip, which was what it did to passers-by. He had a bad-tempered brumby called Kick, and a raggedy crow called Pincher. Pincher swooped down and stole kids' twenty cents worth of chips when they came out of the fish and chip shop. J. Roodie had trained him to do that.

Nobody ever went for a stroll along the creek, because they knew better. J. Roodie kept a supply of dried cow manure and used it as ammunition, because he didn't have pleasant manners at all. He never had a bath and his fingernails were a disgrace and a shame.

There was a cottage near the creek with a FOR SALE notice, but no one wanted to live near J. Roodie. Everyone muttered, 'Someone should do something about that awful J. Roodie!' but nobody knew what to do and they were too scared to get close enough to do it, anyhow.

J. Roodie painted creek-mud scars across his face, and blacked out his front teeth. He drew biro tattoos over his back and he stuck a metal ring with a piece missing through his nose so that it looked pierced. He swaggered around town and pulled faces at babies in prams and made them bawl, and he filled the kindergarten sandpit with quicksand. Luckily the teacher discovered it before she lost any pupils.

He let Grip scare everyone they met, and he let Kick eat people's prize roses, and he was just as much a nuisance going out of town as he was going in. But nobody came and told him off, because they were all nervous of tough J. Roodie and his wild animals.

One day he was annoyed to see that the FOR SALE notice had been removed from the cottage and someone had moved in. He sent Grip over to scare them away.

Grip bared his fangs and slobbered like a hungry wolf at the little old lady who had just moved in.

'Oh, what a sweet puppy!' said the little old lady whose name was Miss Daisy Thrimble. Grip had never been called 'sweet' before, so he stopped slobbering and wagged his tail. Miss Daisy Thrimble gave him a bath and fluffed up his coat with a hair dryer. 'I'll call you Curly,' she said. 'Here's a nice mat for you, Curly.'

Grip felt self-conscious about going back to J. Roodie with his coat all in little ringlets, and besides, the mat was cosier than a creek bed, so he went to sleep.

J. Roodie waited two days for him and then he sent Pincher to the cottage. Miss Daisy was hanging out washing. 'Caaaaawwrk!' Pincher croaked horribly, flapping his big, raggedy, untidy wings and snapping his beak.

'What a poor little lost bird,' said Miss Daisy. She plucked Pincher out of the sky and carried him inside. She filled a saucer with canary seed and fetched a mirror and a bell. 'I'll call you Pretty Boy,' she said. 'And I'll teach you how to talk.'

Pincher already knew some not very nice words that J. Roodie taught him, but Miss Daisy Thrimble looked so sweet-faced and well behaved that Pincher didn't say them. He tapped the bell with his beak, and looked in the little mirror, and decided that it was very nice to have playthings.

J. Roodie grew tired of waiting for Pincher, and he sent Kick to scare Miss Daisy away. Kick pawed the lawn and carried on like a rodeo and rolled his eyes till the whites showed.

'Oh, what a darling little Shetland pony!' said Miss Daisy. She caught Kick and brushed away the creek mud and plaited his mane into rosettes tied up with red ribbons. 'There's a cart in the shed,' she said. 'You can help me do the shopping. I'll call you Twinkle.'

Kick snorted indignantly, but then he saw his reflection in a kitchen window and was amazed that he could look so dignified. He stopped worrying about his new name when Miss Daisy brought him a handful of oats.

J. Roodie marched over to the cottage and yelled, 'YAAAAH!' at the top of his voice. He jumped up and down and brandished a spear and rattled some coconuts with faces painted on them, which were tied to his belt. They looked just like shrunken heads. 'WHEEEEEE!' yelled J. Roodie. 'GRRRRRRR!'

'What a dear little high-spirited boy!' said Miss Daisy. 'But you certainly need a bath.' She dumped J. Roodie into a tub and when she had finished scrubbing, he was as clean and sweet-smelling as an orange. Miss Daisy dressed him in a blue checked shirt and nice clean pants and brushed his hair. 'There,' she said. 'I shall call you Joe. I'll be proud to take you into town with me in my little cart.'

She sat Joe Roodie next to her, and Kick, called Twinkle now,

184

trotted smartly into town, and Grip, called Curly now, ran beside and didn't nip anyone they met.

People said, 'Good morning, Miss Daisy. Is that your little nephew?'

'His name is Joe,' Miss Daisy said proudly. 'I think he lived in the creek bed before he came to stay with me.'

'He can't have,' they said. 'J. Roodie lives in the creek bed and he'd never let anyone else live there.'

'J. who?' asked Miss Daisy, because she was rather hard of hearing. 'Do you know anyone called J. something or other, Joe?'

Joe Roodie didn't answer right away. He'd just felt in the pockets of his new pants and found a pocket knife with six blades, and a ball of red twine, and some interesting rusty keys, and eleven marbles.

'We'll buy some apples and make a pie for our supper,' said Miss Daisy. 'Maybe we could invite that J. boy they said lives in the creek. What do you think, Joe?'

Joe Roodie hadn't tasted apple pie for as many years as he hadn't had a bath, and his mouth watered.

'There used to be a kid called J. Roodie in the creek bed,' he said. 'But he doesn't live there any more.'

ROBIN KLEIN

185

THE CHRISTMAS
ROAST

Once a man found a goose on the beach. The November storms had been raging several days before. She had probably swum too far out, been caught, and then tossed back to land again by the waves. No one in the area had geese. She was a real white domestic goose.

The man stuck her under his jacket and took her home to his wife. 'Here's our Christmas roast.'

They had never kept an animal and had no coop. The man built a little shed out of posts, boards and roofing board right next to the house wall. The woman put sacks in it and put an old sweater on top of them. In the corner they put a pot with water in it.

'Do you know what geese eat?' she asked.

'No idea,' said the man.

They tried potatoes and bread, but the goose wouldn't touch anything. She didn't want any rice either, and she didn't want the rest of their Sunday cake.

'She's homesick for the other geese,' said the woman.

The goose didn't resist when they carried her into the kitchen. She sat quietly under the table. The man and the woman squatted before her, trying to cheer her up.

'But we aren't geese,' said the man. He sat on a chair and tried to find some band music on the radio. The woman sat beside him, her knitting needles going clickety-clack. It was very cosy. Suddenly the goose ate some rolled oats and a little cake.

'She's settling down, our lovely Christmas roast,' said the man. By next morning the goose was waddling all over the place. She stuck her neck through the open doors, nibbled on the curtains, and made a little spot on the doormat.

The house in which the man and woman lived was a simple one. There was no indoor plumbing, only a pump. When the man pumped a bucket full of water, as he did every morning before going to work, the goose came along, climbed into the

bucket and bathed. The water spilled over, and the man had to pump again.

In the garden there was a little wooden house, which was the toilet. When the woman went to it, the goose ran behind her and pressed inside with her. Later she went with the woman to the baker and then to the dairy store.

When the man came home from work on his bicycle that afternoon, the woman and the goose were standing at the garden gate.

'Now she likes potatoes, too,' reported the woman.

'Wonderful,' said the man and stroked the goose on the head. 'Then by Christmas she will be round and fat.'

The shed was never used, for the goose stayed in the warm kitchen every night. She ate and ate. Sometimes the woman set her on the scales, and each time she was heavier.

When the man and the woman sat with the goose in the evening, they both imagined the most marvellous Christmas food.

'Roast goose and red cabbage. They go well together,' said the woman and stroked the goose on her lap.

The man would rather have had sauerkraut than red cabbage,

but for him the most important thing was the dumplings. 'They must be as big as my head and all the same size,' he said.

'And made with raw potatoes,' added his wife.

'No, with cooked ones,' asserted the man. Then they agreed that half the dumplings should be made with raw potatoes and half with cooked ones. When they went to bed, the goose lay at the foot and warmed them.

All at once it was Christmas.

The wife decorated a small tree. The husband biked to the shop and bought everything they would need for the great feast. He also bought a kilo of extra-fine rolled oats.

'Even if it's her last,' he said with a sigh, 'she should at least know that it's Christmas.'

'I've been wondering,' began the woman, 'how, do you think, should we ... I mean ... we still have to ...' But she couldn't get any further.

The man didn't say anything for a while. 'I can't do it,' he said finally.

'I can't either,' said the woman. 'I could, if it were just any old goose. But not this one. No, I can't do it, no matter what.'

The man grabbed the goose and fastened her on to his baggage carrier. Then he rode his bicycle to a neighbour's. In the meantime, the woman cooked red cabbage and made the dumplings, one just as big as the next.

The neighbour lived far away, to be sure, but still not so far that it was a day's journey. Nevertheless, the man did not come home until evening. The goose sat contentedly behind him.

'I never saw our neighbour. We just rode around,' he said ashamedly.

'It doesn't matter,' said the woman cheerfully. 'While you were gone, I thought it over and decided that adding something else to the dinner would just spoil the good taste of the red cabbage and the dumplings.'

The woman was right, and they had a good meal. At their feet the goose feasted on the extra-fine rolled oats. Later all three sat together on the sofa in the living room and enjoyed the candlelight.

The next year, for a change, the woman cooked sauerkraut to go with the dumplings. The year afterwards there were broad

noodles to go with the sauerkraut. They were such good things
that nothing else was needed to go with them.

And so time passed. Goose grew very old.

MARGRET RETTICH
Translated by ELIZABETH D. CRAWFORD

KING CROOKED-CHIN

A great King had a daughter who was very beautiful, but so
haughty that none of the suitors who came to ask her hand in
marriage were good enough for her; she only rejected them, and
made game of them.

One day the King held a great feast, to which he asked all her
lovers; and they sat in a row according to their rank – Kings, and
Princes, and Dukes, and Earls. Then the Princess came in and saw
them all, but she had something to say against every one. The first
was too fat. 'He's as round as a beerbarrel,' she said. The next was

189

too tall. 'What a maypole!' said she. The next was too short. 'What a dumpling!' said she. The fourth was too pale, and she called him 'White-face'. The fifth was too red, so she called him 'Coxcomb'. The sixth was not straight enough, so she said he was like a green stick that had been laid to dry over a baker's oven. And thus she had some joke to crack about every one; but she laughed more than all at a good King who was there, and whose chin was none of the handsomest. 'Look at him,' she said, 'he has a chin, and so has a thrush!' So the King got the nickname of Crooked-Chin.

But the old King was very angry when he saw that his daughter did nothing but laugh at all his guests and despise all the suitors that had been invited to the feast, and he vowed that she should marry the first beggar that came to the door.

Two days after there came by a travelling musician, who began to sing under the window, and to beg money; and when the King heard him, he said; 'Let him come in.' So they brought in a dirty-looking fellow; and when he had sung before the King and the Princess, he begged a boon. Then the King said:

'You have sung so well, that I will give you my daughter there for your wife.'

The Princess was horrified; but the King said: 'I have sworn to give you to the first beggar, and I will keep my word.'

So all entreaties were of no avail. The priest was sent for, and the marriage took place at once. When this was over, the King said:

'Now get ready to go; you must not stay in my palace any longer, but must travel on with your husband.'

Then the beggar departed, and took her with him, and they soon came to a great wood.

'Pray,' said she, 'whose is this wood?'

'It belongs to King Crooked-Chin,' answered he; 'had you taken him, all had been yours.'

'Ah! poor unhappy woman that I am!' sighed she, 'would that I had married King Crooked-Chin!'

Next they came to some fine meadows. 'Whose are these beautiful green meadows?' said she.

'They belong to King Crooked-Chin; had you taken him, they had all been yours.'

'Ah! poor unhappy woman that I am!' said she, 'would that I had married King Crooked-Chin!'

Then they came to a great city. 'Whose is this noble city?' said she.

'It belongs to King Crooked-Chin; had you taken him, it had all been yours.'

'Ah! poor unfortunate woman that I am!' sighed she, 'why did I not marry King Crooked-Chin?'

'That displeases me very much,' said the musician, 'that you should wish for another husband. Am I not good enough for you?'

At last they came to a small cottage. 'What a paltry place!' said she. 'To whom does that wretched little hole belong?'

Then the musician said: 'That is your house and mine, where we are to live.'

'Where are your servants?' cried she.

'Servants!' said he. 'You must serve yourself for whatever you want. Now make the fire, and put on water and cook my supper, for I am very tired.'

But the Princess did not know in the least how to make a fire or cook, and the beggar was forced to help her. When they had eaten a very poor supper, they went to bed; but the musician called her up very early in the morning to clean the house. Thus they lived in a miserable way for a few days; and when they had eaten up all their provisions, the man said:

'Wife, we can't go on thus, spending all and gaining nothing. You must learn to weave baskets.'

Then he went out and cut willows, and brought them home, and she began to weave; but they cut her delicate fingers.

'I see this work won't do,' said he; 'try to spin. Perhaps that will suit you better.'

So she sat down and tried to spin; but the tough threads cut her tender fingers till they bled again.

'See, now,' said the musician, 'you are fit for no work at all. What a bad bargain I have made! However, I'll try to set up business in the earthenware line, and you shall stand in the market and sell.'

'Alas!' thought she, 'when I stand in the market, and when any of my father's court pass by and see me there, how they will laugh at me!'

But it was of no use complaining; she must either work or starve. At first the trade went well, for many people, seeing such a beautiful woman, went to buy her wares out of compliment to her, and many even paid their money and left the dishes into the bargain. They lived on this as long as it lasted, and then her husband bought a fresh lot of ware, and she sat down with it all around her in a corner of the market; but a mad soldier soon came by, and rode his horse among her dishes, and broke them all into a thousand pieces. Then she began to cry, and knew not, in her grief, what to do.

'Ah, what will become of me!' said she. 'What will my husband say?' So she ran home and told him all.

'Who would have thought you would have been so silly,' said he, 'as to put earthenware in the corner of the market, where everybody passes? But let us have no more crying. I see you are not fit for any regular work, so I have been to the King's palace, and asked if they did not want a kitchen-maid, and they have engaged to take you for your food.'

Thus the Princess became a kitchen-maid, and helped the cook to do all the dirty work; but she was allowed to carry home in two

jars, one on each side, some of the food that was left, and on this she and her husband lived.

She had not been there long before she heard that the King's eldest son was passing by, on his way to be married; and she went to one of the doors and looked out, and seeing all the pomp and splendour, she thought with an aching heart of her own fate, and bitterly lamented the pride which had brought her to such poverty. And the servants gave her some of the rich meats, which she put into her jars to take home.

All at once the King's son appeared in golden clothes; and when he saw a beautiful woman at the door, he took her by the hand, and said she should be his partner in the dance; but she refused, and was afraid, for she saw that it was King Crooked-Chin, who had been one of her suitors, and whom she had repulsed with scorn. However, he kept fast hold and led her in, and the covers

of the jars fell off, so that the food in it was scattered about. Then everybody laughed and jeered at her when they saw this, and she was so ashamed that she wished herself a thousand miles deep in the earth. She sprang to the door to run away; but on the steps King Crooked-Chin overtook her, and brought her back, and said:

'Fear me not! I am the musician who lived with you in the poor hut; and it was because I loved you that I disguised myself like that. I am also the soldier who overset your crockery. I have done all this only to bring down your pride. Now all is over, and it is time to celebrate our wedding.'

Then the maids of honour came and brought her the richest dresses; and her father and his whole court came, and wished her all happiness on her marriage with King Crooked-Chin.

ANON.

ELIZABETH

'What do you want for Christmas?' asked Kate's mother.

'I want a red ball,' said Kate, 'and a new dress and a book and a doll. I want a doll with golden curls who walks and talks and turns somersaults.'

'Well,' said Kate's mother, 'we shall see what surprises Christmas brings.'

It seemed as though Christmas would never come, but of course Christmas came. Kate opened her presents under the tree. There was a red ball and a new dress and a book and other gifts. And underneath them all, in a long white box, there was a doll. It was a soft cloth doll with warm brown eyes and thick brown plaits like Kate's.

'What does it do?' asked Kate.

'Everything a doll's supposed to do,' her mother said.

Kate picked the doll up from its box. Its arms hung limply at its sides. Its weak legs flopped, and they couldn't hold it up. 'What's its name?' asked Kate.

'She doesn't have a name,' Kate's mother said. 'No one has a name until somebody loves her.'

Kate set the doll back in the box. 'Thank you,' she said to her mother politely. 'It's an ugly doll,' she said to herself inside. 'It's an ugly doll, and I hate it very much.'

There were no more presents under the tree.

Kate's cousin Agnes came for Christmas dinner. Agnes had a new doll whose name was Charlotte Louise. Charlotte Louise

could walk and talk. 'Where is your Christmas doll?' asked Agnes.

Kate showed her the cloth doll lying in the box.

'What does it do?' asked Agnes.

'It doesn't do anything,' Kate replied.

'What is its name?' asked Agnes.

'It doesn't have a name,' said Kate.

'It certainly is an ugly doll,' said Agnes. She set Charlotte Louise down on the floor, and Charlotte Louise turned a somersault.

'I hate you, Agnes,' Kate said, 'and I hate your ugly doll!'

Kate was sent upstairs to bed without any Christmas cake.

The next day was the day after Christmas. Kate's mother asked her to put away her presents. Kate put away her red ball and her new dress and her book and all her other gifts except the doll.

'I don't want this ugly doll,' she said to James the collie. 'You may have it if you like.'

James wagged his tail. He took the cloth doll in his mouth and carried it out to the snowy garden.

By lunchtime James hadn't come home, and Kate was sorry she had given her doll to him. She couldn't eat her sandwich or her cake. 'James will chew up that doll,' she said to herself. 'He'll chew and chew until there's nothing left but stuffing and some rags. He'll bury her somewhere in the snow.'

She put on her coat and mittens and boots and went out into the garden. James was nowhere to be seen. 'I'm sorry,' said Kate inside herself. 'I'm very, very sorry, and I want to find my doll.'

Kate looked all over the garden before she found her. The doll was lying under the cherry tree, half-buried in the snow, but except for being wet and cold, she seemed as good as new. Kate brushed her clean and cradled her in her arms. 'It's all right now, Elizabeth,' she said, 'because I love you after all.'

Elizabeth could do everything.

When Kate was happy, Elizabeth was happy.

When Kate was sad, Elizabeth understood.

When Kate was naughty and had to go upstairs, Elizabeth went with her.

Elizabeth didn't care for baths. 'She doesn't like water,' Kate explained, 'because of being buried in the snow.' Elizabeth sat on the edge of the bath and kept Kate company while she scrubbed.

Elizabeth loved to swing and slide and go round and round on the merry-go-round.

When Kate wanted to be the mother, Elizabeth was the baby.

When Kate wanted to be Cinderella, Elizabeth was a wicked stepsister and the fairy godmother too.

Sometimes Kate forgot about Elizabeth because she was playing with other friends.

Elizabeth waited patiently. When Kate came back, Elizabeth was always glad to see her.

In the spring, Elizabeth and Kate picked violets for Kate's mother's birthday and helped Kate's father fly a kite.

In the summer, everyone went to the seaside. Agnes was there too, but Agnes's doll, Charlotte Louise, was not.

'Where is Charlotte Louise?' Kate asked, holding Elizabeth in her arms.

'Charlotte Louise is broken,' Agnes said, 'We threw her in the dustbin. I shall have a new doll for Christmas.'

Agnes wouldn't go into the water. She was afraid. But Kate went in for a dip. She set Elizabeth on a towel to sleep safely in the sun. When she came out of the water, Elizabeth was gone.

'Help,' cried Kate, 'please, somebody help! Elizabeth is drowning!'

Everyone heard the word 'drowning', but nobody quite heard who. Grown-ups shouted and ran around pointing their fingers towards the sea.

> *Then out of nowhere*
> *Like a streak,*
> *Galloping, galloping,*
> *James the collie came.*

Out into the sea and back to shore he swam, Elizabeth hanging limply from his mouth.

After an hour in the sun, Elizabeth was as good as new.

Everyone except Agnes said that James was brave and good and a hero.

Kate didn't say that Agnes had thrown Elizabeth into the sea, but inside herself she thought that Agnes had.

In the autumn, Elizabeth helped Kate gather berries in the meadow for jams and jellies and berry pies.

Then Christmas came again. Of course there were presents under the tree. For Kate, there was a new sledge and a new dress and a book and other gifts. For Elizabeth, there was a woollen coat and hat, and two dresses, one of them velvet.

Agnes came for Christmas dinner. Agnes had a new doll whose name was Tina Marie.

'Tina Marie can sing songs,' said Agnes. 'She can blow bubbles too, and crawl along the floor.'

Kate held Elizabeth tightly in her arms. 'Well,' said Kate in a whisper, 'Tina Marie is the ugliest doll I ever saw. She is almost as ugly as you.'

Agnes kicked Kate sharply on the leg and said the most dreadful

things to Elizabeth, who was looking particularly nice in her velvet dress.

Agnes's mother was very cross with Agnes.

Agnes spent the rest of the day in disgrace and wasn't permitted any Christmas cake.

'Merry Christmas, Elizabeth,' said Kate as she tucked her into bed, 'and Happy Birthday too! You are the best and most beautiful doll in the world, and I wouldn't swop you for anyone else.'

LIESEL MOAK SKORPEN

HORRIBLE HARRY

This was the Davidson family's first taste of country life. Mr Carter, who had sold them the small farm and orchard, was leaving the district. As he climbed into his truck he heard Dad call out to him. Dad had noticed an old horse standing in the paddock.

'I thought you had sent all your horses to your new property, Mr Carter,' said Dad.

'All except old Harry,' said Mr Carter. 'I decided to leave him here.'

'I couldn't afford to buy a horse just now,' said Dad, frowning.

'I'm not asking you to buy him; I'm *giving* him to you.' Mr Carter looked at Dad slyly. 'He's lived here so long it would break his heart to leave, so I'd like him to stay here with you.'

Dad thanked him; then, back at the house, told Mum, Peter and Sue about Harry.

'How odd of him to *give* us a horse,' mused Mum. 'He seemed a very *mean* man. I really didn't like him at all. Well, I must have been mistaken.'

'Can we ride him?' Peter asked excitedly.

'I'd better have a good look at him first,' said Dad. 'Remember, you've never ridden before.' After a closer look at Harry, Dad admitted that it would be almost impossible for anyone to fall off his back; he was nearly as wide as he was long. 'Very low-slung too,' muttered Dad.

'What a funny-looking horse,' said Peter, feeling very disappointed.

'He's hardly what I'd call streamlined,' said Dad. 'Built a bit like an aircraft carrier, isn't he?' Harry swung round and gave Dad a very nasty look. He lifted his top lip and showed a row of large, yellow teeth. 'Don't go too near him,' said Dad. 'He looks a bit wild.'

'I think he's a nice old thing,' said Sue. 'Look, he's smiling!'

'I don't think it's a smile,' said Dad. 'I think it's a snarl.' He was beginning to wonder why Mr Carter had been so keen to leave Harry behind.

'Here boy! Here Harry!' said Peter, holding out his hand and walking slowly towards the horse. But for every step he went forward, Harry went back two. When Peter had him backed into a corner of the paddock he put his head down and butted the boy like a goat. Then he galloped off into the orchard where he began shaking branches with his teeth, snapping them and knocking fruit to the ground.

They found that Harry always went to the orchard if something greatly annoyed him. He would gallop in and do as much damage as he could, then stalk out again with a look on his face that seemed to say: '*That* will show *them*!' But if he was only slightly annoyed he would content himself with knocking down the clothes-prop and tearing washing off the line.

Next day he must have been feeling more friendly, because he let Peter climb on his back. Or perhaps he wasn't feeling more friendly – he could have had something else on his mind. He went round and round the paddock at a fast, erratic trot. Every few minutes he would do a sort of shuffle and change step, sending Peter lurching from one side of his broad back to the other. He made several attempts to bite Peter on the ankle and tried to scrape him off against the fence. When this failed, he headed towards a clump of blackberry bushes and Peter was scratched and sore by the time he had struggled out of it. He climbed on to Harry's back again, but this time Harry didn't fool around. He galloped straight to the dam, propped at the edge, and threw Peter over his head and into the muddy water. Wading out, a very muddy Peter decided never to try riding Harry again – and that, of course, was what Harry wanted.

On Monday the children started at their new school. Mum finished the unpacking, and Dad spent a busy morning in the orchard.

'I'll run the truck up to the front gate,' he told Mum at lunch time. 'The baker was to have left the bread in the mail box and the post should be here too. I'm expecting an important letter.'

When he reached the front gate, which was nearly a kilometre from the house, Harry was standing there with his head resting on the top rung. The mail box was empty.

'No bread and no mail. That's strange,' thought Dad. 'I'll ring the bakery and the post office from the house.'

'We can't deliver the bread unless you lock up Horrible,' said the baker firmly.

'Horrible?' asked Dad.

'Yes, Horrible the horse,' said the baker.

'The horse's name is Harry,' said Dad, not seeing what that had to do with bread deliveries.

'That's right,' said the baker. 'Horrible Harry. He bites anyone who goes near your front gate. I've had three men bitten by Harry and they won't deliver to your place unless he's locked up.'

The postmaster said the same thing. So, too, did the man who delivered fertilizer, and the TV repair-man, and even the doctor, as Dad discovered later.

'Lock him up! That's more easily said than done,' said Dad bitterly after he had wasted half an hour trying to coax Harry into the storage shed. 'All right then!' he spluttered, 'I'll go into town and pick up the bread and the mail myself!' He drove off in an angry cloud of dust, but looked back just in time to see Harry strolling into the storage shed all by himself, for an afternoon rest.

Returning with the bread and mail, Dad stopped the truck and climbed out to open the gate. Harry came galloping up and, as Dad reached for the latch, sank his teeth into Dad's hand.

'Ouch!' shouted Dad, jumping back. Harry lifted his top lip and leered. Each time Dad put his hand out, Harry snapped. Several minutes later Mr Timms from the next farm drove by. He pulled up when he saw Dad's plight.

'Old Horrible won't let you in unless you give him some carrots,' he explained. 'You'll always have to bribe him with carrots before he'll let you through the gate. Didn't Carter tell you about Harry before he left?'

'Carter didn't tell me *anything* about Harry,' Dad muttered darkly. He had to drive ten kilometres back into town to buy some carrots just to get through his own front gate.

'I'll sell him tomorrow,' he told Mum.

But the Stock Agent just laughed at him. 'Sell old Horrible? No one would buy him. You couldn't *give* him away around here!'

Peter *did* try to give him away at school, but everyone said they'd rather own a man-eating tiger than Harry. So the Davidsons just had to learn to live with him. They always made sure they had a carrot before going through the front gate, and they tried not to annoy him very much, especially on washing days.

As the fruit ripened and was almost ready for picking, the district was worried by a spate of robberies. Each night one or other of the farms would be robbed. A truck would be backed through the fence, the trees stripped of their fruit, and by morning only the bare trees were to be seen; the fruit was already on its way to the markets. Watch-dogs were doped and police patrols eluded.

'I hope they don't come here,' said Dad, looking worried. 'I can't afford to lose the crop in our first season.'

A few nights later they were awakened by weird snortings and wild shrieks. Dad raced out of the house and down to the bottom of the orchard. A man was half-way up one of the trees and Harry had his ankle firmly between his teeth, trying to haul him down.

A second man was trying to help the first, but every time he came close, Harry lashed out with his hind legs. Seeing Dad, he lifted his head and gave a fearsome neigh. The man in the tree, his ankle freed, jumped clear and the two men raced for their truck. Harry gave chase. From the way the men yelled, he must have managed a couple of good nips on the way. They scrambled into their truck and roared off with Harry tearing after them. He was neighing like a diesel train's horn.

'Well,' said Dad next morning as he repaired the fence the truck had smashed down, 'I don't think we'll have to worry about them coming back; not while we have Harry here.'

'I bet no one has *ever* heard of a horse like Harry before,' said Sue.

'I bet there's never *been* a *watch*-horse before,' said Peter, and they all laughed.

DIANA PETERSEN

THE PRACTICAL PRINCESS

Princess Bedelia was as lovely as the moon shining upon a lake full of waterlilies. She was as graceful as a cat leaping. And she was also extremely practical.

When she was born, three fairies had come to her cradle to give her gifts, as was usual in that country. The first fairy had given her beauty. The second had given her grace. But the third, who was a wise old creature, had said, 'I give her common sense.'

'I don't think much of that gift,' said King Ludwig, raising his eyebrows. 'What good is common sense to a Princess? All she needs is charm.'

Nevertheless, when Bedelia was eighteen years old, something happened which made the King change his mind.

A dragon moved into the neighbourhood. He settled in a dark cave on top of a mountain, and the first thing he did was to send a message to the King. 'I must have a Princess to devour,' the message said, 'or I shall breathe out my fiery breath and destroy the kingdom.'

Sadly, King Ludwig called together his counsellors and read them the message. 'Perhaps,' said the Prime Minister, 'we had better advertise for a knight to slay the dragon? That is what is generally done in these cases.'

'I'm afraid we haven't time,' answered the king. 'The dragon has only given us until tomorrow morning. There is no help for it. We shall have to send him the Princess.' Princess Bedelia had come to the meeting because, as she said, she liked to mind her own business and this was certainly her business.

'Rubbish!' she said. 'Dragons can't tell the difference between Princesses and anyone else. Use your common sense. He's just asking for me because he's a snob.'

'That may be so,' said her father, 'but if we don't send you along, he'll destroy the kingdom.'

'Right!' said Bedelia. 'I see I'll have to deal with this myself.' She left the council chamber. She got the largest and gaudiest of her state robes and stuffed it with straw, and tied it together with string. Into the centre of the bundle she packed about fifty kilos of gunpowder. She got two strong young men to carry it up the mountain for her. She stood in front of the dragon's cave, and called, 'Come out! Here's the Princess!'

The dragon came blinking and peering out of the darkness. Seeing the bright robe covered with gold and silver embroidery, and hearing Bedelia's voice, he opened his mouth wide.

At Bedelia's signal, the two young men swung the robe and gave it a good heave, right down the dragon's throat. Bedelia threw herself flat on the ground, and the two young men ran.

As the gunpowder met the flames inside the dragon, there was a tremendous explosion.

Bedelia got up, dusting herself off. 'Dragons,' she said, 'are not very bright.'

She left the two young men sweeping up the pieces, and she went back to the castle to have her geography lesson.

The lesson that morning was local geography. 'Our kingdom, Arapathia, is bounded on the north by Istven,' said the teacher. 'Lord Garp, the ruler of Istven, is old, crafty, rich and greedy.' At that very moment, Lord Garp of Istven was arriving at the castle. Word of Bedelia's destruction of the dragon had reached him. 'That girl,' said he, 'is just the wife for me.' And he had come with a hundred finely-dressed courtiers and many presents to ask King Ludwig for her hand.

The king sent for Bedelia. 'My dear,' he said, clearing his throat nervously, 'just see who is here.'

'I see. It's Lord Garp,' said Bedelia. She turned to go.

'He wants to marry you,' said the king.

Bedelia looked at Lord Garp. His face was like an old napkin, crumpled and wrinkled. It was covered with warts, as if someone had left crumbs on the napkin. He had only two teeth. Six long hairs grew from his chin, and none on his head. She felt like screaming.

However, she said, 'I'm very flattered. Thank you, Lord Garp.

207

Just let me talk to my father in private for a minute.' When they had retired to a small room behind the throne, Bedelia said to the king, 'What will Lord Garp do if I refuse to marry him?'

'He is rich, greedy and crafty,' said the king unhappily. 'He is also used to having his own way in everything. He will be insulted. He will probably declare war on us, and then there will be trouble.'

She returned to the throne room. Smiling sweetly at Lord Garp, she said, 'My lord, as you know, it is customary for a princess to set tasks for anyone who wishes to marry her. Surely you wouldn't like me to break the custom. And you are bold and powerful enough, I know, to perform any task.'

'That is true,' said Lord Garp smugly, stroking the six hairs on his chin. 'Name your task.'

'Bring me,' said Bedelia, 'a branch from the Jewel Tree of Paxis.'

Lord Garp bowed, and off he went. 'I think,' said Bedelia to her father, 'that we have seen the last of him. For Paxis is fifteen hundred kilometres away, and the Jewel Tree is guarded by lions, serpents and wolves.'

But in two weeks, Lord Garp was back. With him he bore a chest, and from the chest he took a wonderful twig. Its bark was of rough gold. The leaves that grew from it were of fine silver. The twig was covered with blossoms, and each blossom had petals of mother-of-pearl and centres of sapphires, the colour of the evening sky.

Bedelia's heart sank as she took the twig. But then she said to herself, 'Use your common sense, my girl! Lord Garp never travelled three thousand kilometres in two weeks, nor is he the man to fight his way through lions, serpents, and wolves.'

She looked carefully at the branch. Then she said, 'My lord, you know that the Jewel Tree of Paxis is a living tree, although it is all made of jewels.'

'Why, of course,' said Lord Garp. 'Everyone knows that.'

'Well,' said Bedelia, 'then why is it that these blossoms have no scent?'

Lord Garp turned red.

'I think,' Bedelia went on, 'that this branch was made by the jewellers of Istven, who are the best in the world. Not very nice of you, my lord. Some people might even call it cheating.'

Lord Garp shrugged. He was too old and rich to feel ashamed. But like many men used to having their own way, the more Bedelia refused him, the more he was determined to have her.

'Never mind all that,' he said. 'Set me another task. This time, I swear I will perform it.'

Bedelia sighed. 'Very well. Then bring me a cloak made from the skins of the salamanders who live in the Volcano of Scoria.'

Lord Garp bowed, and off he went. 'The Volcano of Scoria,' said Bedelia to her father, 'is covered with red-hot lava. It burns steadily with great flames, and pours out poisonous smoke so that no one can come within a metre of it.'

'You have certainly profited by your geography lessons,' said the King with admiration.

Nevertheless, in a week, Lord Garp was back. This time, he carried a cloak that shone and rippled like all the colours of fire. It was made of scaly skins, stitched together with golden wire as fine as a hair; and each scale was red and orange and blue, like a tiny flame.

Bedelia took the splendid cloak. She said to herself, 'Use your head, miss! Lord Garp never climbed the red-hot slopes of the Volcano of Scoria.'

209

A fire was burning in the fireplace of the throne room. Bedelia hurled the cloak into it. The skins blazed up in a flash, blackened, and fell to ashes.

Lord Garp's mouth fell open. Before he could speak, Bedelia said, 'That cloak was a fake, my lord. The skins of salamanders who can live in the Volcano of Scoria wouldn't burn in a little fire like that one.'

Lord Garp turned pale with anger. He hopped up and down, unable at first to do anything but splutter.

'Ub – ub – ub!' he cried. Then, controlling himself, he said, 'So be it. If I can't have you, no one shall!'

He pointed a long, skinny finger at her. On the finger was a magic ring. At once, a great wind arose. It blew through the throne room. It sent King Ludwig flying one way and his guards the other. It picked up Bedelia and whisked her off through the air. When she could catch her breath and look about her, she found herself in a room at the top of a tower.

Bedelia peered out of the window. About the tower stretched an empty, barren plain. As she watched, a speck appeared in the distance. A plume of dust rose behind it. It drew nearer and became Lord Garp on horseback.

He rode to the tower and looked up at Bedelia. 'Aha!' he croaked. 'So you are safe and snug, are you? And will you marry me now?'

'Never,' said Bedelia, firmly.

'Then stay there until never comes,' snarled Lord Garp.

Away he rode.

For the next two days, Bedelia felt very sorry for herself. She sat wistfully by the window, looking out at the empty plain. When she was hungry, food appeared on the table. When she was tired, she lay down on the narrow cot and slept. Each day, Lord Garp rode by and asked if she had changed her mind, and each day she refused him. Her only hope was that, as so often happens in old tales, a prince might come riding by who would rescue her.

But on the third day, she gave herself a shake.

'Now then, pull yourself together,' she said sternly. 'If you sit waiting for a prince to rescue you, you may sit here for ever. Be practical! If there's any rescuing to be done, you're going to have to do it yourself.'

She jumped up. There was something she had not yet done, and now she did it. She tried the door.

It opened.

Outside were three other doors. But there was no sign of a staircase, or any way down from the top of the tower.

She opened two of the doors and found that they led into cells just like hers, but empty.

Behind the fourth door, however, lay what appeared to be a haystack.

From beneath it came the sound of snores. And between snores, a voice said, 'Sixteen million and twelve ... *snore* ... sixteen million and thirteen ... *snore* ... sixteen million and fourteen ...'

Cautiously, she went closer. Then she saw that what she had taken for a haystack was in fact an immense pile of blond hair. Parting it, she found a young man, sound asleep.

As she stared, he opened his eyes. He blinked at her. 'Who – ?' he said. Then he said, 'Sixteen million and fifteen,' closed his eyes, and fell asleep again.

Bedelia took him by the shoulder and shook him hard. He awoke, yawning, and tried to sit up. But the mass of hair made this difficult.

'What on earth is the matter with you?' Bedelia asked. 'Who are you?'

'I am Prince Perian,' he replied, 'the rightful ruler of – oh dear! here I go again. Sixteen million and ...' His eyes began to close.

Bedelia shook him again. He made a violent effort and managed to wake up enough to continue, '– of Istven. But Lord Garp has put me under a spell. I have to count sheep jumping over a fence, and this puts me to slee – ee – ee –.'

He began to snore lightly.

'Dear me,' said Bedelia. 'I must do something.'

She thought hard. Then she pinched Perian's ear, and this woke him with a start. 'Listen,' she said. 'It's quite simple. It's all in your mind, you see. You are imagining the sheep jumping over the fence – no! don't go to sleep again!

'This is what you must do. Imagine them jumping backwards. As you do, *count* them backwards, and when you get to *one* you'll be wide awake.'

The prince's eyes snapped open. 'Marvellous!' he said. 'Will it work?'

'It's bound to,' said Bedelia. 'For if the sheep going one way will put you to sleep, their going back again will wake you up.'

Hastily, the prince began to count, 'Sixteen million and fourteen, sixteen million and thirteen, sixteen million and twelve ...'

'Oh, my goodness,' cried Bedelia, 'count by hundreds, or you'll never get there.'

He began to gabble as fast as he could, and with each moment that passed, his eyes sparkled more brightly, his face grew livelier, and he seemed a little stronger, until at last he shouted, 'Five, four, three, two, ONE!' and awoke completely.

He struggled to his feet, with a little help from Bedelia.

'Heavens!' he said. 'Look how my hair and beard have grown.

I've been here for years. Thank you, my dear. Who are you, and what are you doing here?'

Bedelia quickly explained.

Perian shook his head. 'One more crime of Lord Garp's,' he said. 'We must escape and see that he is punished.'

'Easier said than done,' Bedelia replied. 'There are no stairs in this tower, as far as I can tell, and the outside wall is much too smooth to climb.'

Perian frowned. 'This will take some thought,' he said. 'What we need is a long rope.'

'Use your common sense,' said Bedelia. 'We haven't any rope.'

Then her face brightened, and she clapped her hands. 'But we have your beard,' she laughed.

Perian understood at once, and chuckled. 'I'm sure it will reach almost to the ground,' he said. 'But we haven't any scissors to cut it off with.'

'That is so,' said Bedelia. 'Hang it out of the window and let me climb down. I'll search the tower and perhaps I can find a ladder, or a hidden staircase. If all else fails, I can go for help.'

She and the Prince gathered up great armfuls of the beard and staggered into Bedelia's room, which had the largest window. The prince's long hair trailed behind and nearly tripped him.

He threw the beard out of the window, and sure enough the end of it came to within a metre of the ground.

Perian braced himself, holding the beard with both hands to ease the pull on his chin. Bedelia climbed out of the window and slid down the beard. She dropped to the ground and sat for a moment, breathless.

And as she sat there, out of the wilderness came the drumming of hoofs, a cloud of dust, and then Lord Garp on his swift horse.

With one glance, he saw what was happening. He shook his fist up at Prince Perian.

'Meddlesome fool!' he shouted. 'I'll teach you to interfere.'

He leaped from the horse and grabbed the beard. He gave it a tremendous yank. Head first came Perian, out of the window. Down he fell, and, with a thump, he landed right on top of old Lord Garp.

This saved Perian, who was not hurt at all. But it was the end of Lord Garp.

Perian and Bedelia rode back to Istven on Lord Garp's horse.

In the great city, the Prince was greeted with cheers of joy – once everyone had recognized him after so many years and under so much hair.

And of course, since Bedelia had rescued him from captivity, she married him. First, however, she made him get a haircut and a shave so that she could see what he really looked like.

For she was always practical.

JAY WILLIAMS

THE WHITE DOVE

A long time ago, in a country by the sea, there lived a King and Queen who had two sons. And those two sons were reckless lads. One stormy day they put to sea in a little boat to go fishing. The wind howled, and they laughed. The waves dashed over the boat, and still they laughed. But when they were a long way from land, the wind tore their sail to ribbons, and the waves washed their oars overboard; and there they were, tossing about with the waves drenching them, while they clung to their seats to keep from being pitched out of the boat.

'Brother,' said one Prince, 'shall we ever reach home again?'

'No, brother,' said the other. 'It seems we shall not.'

Then they looked through the spray and saw the strangest vessel in the world come speeding towards them over the rolling billows. It was a kneading-trough, and in it sat an old witch, beating the waves with two long wooden ladles.

'Hey, my lads!' she yelled. 'What will you give me to send you safely home?'

'Anything we have!' shouted the Princes.

'Then give me your brother,' yelled the witch.

'We have no brother,' shouted the Princes.

'Aye, but you will have,' yelled the witch.

'Even so,' shouted the eldest Prince, 'should our mother bear another son, he will not belong to us.'

'So we can't give him away!' shouted the other Prince.

'Then you can rot in the salt sea, both of you!' yelled the witch. 'But I think your mother would rather keep the two sons she has than the one she hasn't yet got.' And she rowed off in her kneading-trough.

If the storm had been fierce before, it was now furious. The Princes' little boat was flung up high on the waves one moment, and the next sucked deep down, with the waves towering over it. It pitched and rolled and wallowed and filled with water.

'Brother,' said one Prince, 'we are going to drown.'

'Ah, how our mother will grieve!' said the other Prince.

'Brother,' said the first Prince, 'the old witch was right. Our mother would rather keep *us* than a son she may never have.'

So they shouted after the witch, and she turned her trough and came rowing back to them.

'Have you changed your minds?' she yelled.

'Yes,' shouted the Princes. 'If you will save us from drowning, we promise you the brother we may never have.'

Immediately the wind ceased howling and the sea grew flat. A current caught the boat and drove it swiftly over the calm water. The current brought the boat ashore just under the King's castle. The Princes sprang out, and ran into the castle. The Queen, who had been watching the storm from a window, flung her arms round them.

'Oh my sons!' cried the Queen. 'If you had been drowned I could not have lived!'

And one Prince whispered to the other, 'We did right to promise.'

But they said nothing to their mother about what they had promised, either then, or a year later, when a brother was born to them. The new little Prince was a beautiful child; and because he was so much younger than his brothers, the Queen did her best to spoil him. But it seemed he was unspoilable. He loved his brothers, and they loved him: and still they said nothing about their promise to give him to the witch. For some time, indeed, they

215

lived in dread lest the witch should come and claim him; but, as the years passed, and the little Prince grew up, and still the witch did not come, the two elder Princes almost succeeded in forgetting the promise they had made.

Now the youngest Prince was studious; and often, long after the rest of the household had gone to their beds, he would sit in a little room downstairs, reading and thinking. One night, as he so sat, the wind began to howl and the sea to roar, the stars disappeared behind mountainous black clouds, and the rain came down in torrents. The Prince lifted his head, listened for a moment, and went on reading. Then came three loud knocks on the door; and before the Prince could open it, in darted the witch, with her kneading-trough on her back.

'Come with me!' she said.

The Prince said, 'Why should I go with you?'

'Because you belong to me,' said the witch. And she told him all about that day on which his brothers came near to drowning, and how she had saved their lives, and what they had promised.

The young Prince closed his book and stood up. 'Since you saved my brothers' lives and they gave you their promise, I am ready to go with you,' he said

He followed the witch out of the castle and down to the sea. The witch launched her kneading-trough. They both got into it, and away they went, pitching and tossing over the raging waves, till they came to the witch's home.

'Now you are my servant,' said the witch, 'and everything I tell you to do, you must do. If you cannot do what I tell you to do, you are of no use to me. And when things are of no use to me, I throw them into the sea.'

'I will do my best,' said the young Prince.

The witch then took him to a barn which was piled high with feathers of different colours and sizes. 'Arrange these feathers in their heaps,' she said, 'and let the feathers in each heap be of the same colour and the same size. I am going out now, and when I come back in the evening I shall expect the task to be finished.'

'I will do my best,' said the Prince again.

Ho, ho! But will your best be good enough?' said she.

'That I cannot tell,' said he.

The witch went away then, and the Prince began his task. He worked very hard all day, and towards evening he had all the feathers except one goose quill arranged in their heaps – size to size and colour to colour. He was just going to place the goose quill on top of a heap of big white feathers, when there came a whirlwind that blew the feathers all about the barn. And when the whirlwind had passed and the feathers had settled, they were in worse confusion than they had been at first.

The Prince set to work again; but there was now only an hour left before the time the witch would return. 'I cannot possibly finish by then!' he said aloud. But still he went on with his task.

Then he heard a tapping at the window, and a little voice said:

Coo, coo, coo, please let me in,
If we work together, we'll always win.

It was a white dove, who was perched outside the glass, and was tapping on it with her beak.

The Prince opened the window, and the dove flew in. She set to work with her beak, he set to work with his hands; he worked swiftly, but she worked a hundred times more swiftly. By the time the hour was passed, all the feathers were neatly arranged in their heaps. The dove flew out of the window, and the witch came in at the door.

'So,' said she, 'I see Princes have neat fingers!'

'I have done my best,' said the Prince.

'And tomorrow you must do better,' said she. And she gave him some supper and sent him to bed.

In the morning she took him outside and showed him a great pile of firewood. 'Split this into small pieces for me,' she said. 'That is easy work, and will soon be done. But you must have it all ready by the time I come home.'

'I will do my best,' said the young Prince.

'If your best is not good enough, the sea is waiting,' said the witch. And off she went.

The Prince set to work with a will; he chipped and chopped till the sweat ran off him. But the more wood he chopped up, the more there seemed to be left unchopped. Yes, there was no doubt about it – the pile of unchopped firewood was growing and growing. He flung down his axe in despair. What could he do?

Then the white dove came flying, settled on the pile of wood, and said:

> Coo, coo, coo, take the axe by the head,
> And chop with the handle end instead.

The Prince took the axe by the head and began chopping with the handle; and the firewood flew into small pieces of its own accord. The Prince chopped, the dove took the little pieces in her beak and arranged them in a tidy pile. In no time at all, it seemed, the task was finished.

Then the dove flew up on to the prince's shoulder. And he stroked its soft feathers. 'How can I ever thank you?' he said. And he kissed its little red beak.

Immediately the dove vanished; and there, at the Prince's side, stood a beautiful maiden.

'How can I ever thank *you*,' said the maiden, 'for the kiss that has disenchanted me?'

She told him that she was a Princess, whom the witch had stolen and turned into a white dove.

'But the power of a grateful kiss is stronger than all the witch's enchantments,' said the maiden. 'And perhaps together we may find a way to escape her. That is, if you like me well enough?'

'I love you!' said the Prince. And truly, so he did.

'Then listen carefully to what I am going to tell you,' said the Princess. 'When the witch comes home ask her to grant you a wish, as a reward for having accomplished the tasks she has set you. If she agrees, ask her to give you the Princess who is flying about in the shape of a white dove. She will not want to do so; she will try to deceive you; but take this red silk thread and tie it round my little finger. Then you will recognize me, whatever shape she may turn me into.'

So the Prince tied the red silk thread round the Princess's little finger, and she turned into a dove again, and flew away. The Prince sat down by the pile of split firewood to wait until the witch came home. And very soon he saw her coming, with her kneading-trough on her back.

'Well, well, well!' said she. 'I see you are a clever fellow! I think I shall be pleased with you yet!'

'If you are pleased with me,' said the Prince, 'perhaps you will be willing to grant me a little pleasure also, and give me something I have taken a fancy to?'

'Well, well, that's only reasonable,' said the witch, who was in a very good temper. 'Tell me what it is you wish for, and if it is any little thing that is in my power to give you, I promise I will do so.'

'There is a Princess here, who flies about in the shape of a white dove,' said the Prince. 'It is that Princess I want.'

The witch screeched with laughter. 'What nonsense are you talking? As if Princesses ever flew around in the shape of white doves!'

'Nevertheless, I ask for that Princess,' said the Prince.

'Well, well, if you *will* have a Princess,' said the witch, 'you must take the only sort I have.' And she went away round the back of the house, and came again dragging by one long ear a shaggy little grey ass. 'Will you have this?' she said. 'You can't get any other kind of Princess here.'

The Prince looked at the little ass, and saw a thin thread of red silk round one of its hoofs. 'Yes, I will have it,' he said.

'It is too small for you to ride, and too old to draw a cart,' said the witch. 'Why should you have it? It is no use to you at all!' And she dragged the little ass away, and came back with a tottering, trembling old hag of a woman who was blind in one eye, and hadn't a tooth in her head.

'Here's a pretty Princess for you!' said the witch. 'What do you say, will you have her? She was born a Princess, and she's the only one I've got.'

'Yes, I will have her,' said the Prince, for he saw that the old hag had a thin thread of red silk bound about her little finger.

He took the old hag by the hand. Behold – there stood the Princess! The witch flew into such a terrible rage that she danced about and screamed and smashed everything within her reach, so that the splinters flew about the heads of the Prince and Princess. But she had promised the Prince that he should have his wish, and she had to keep her word. She said to herself, 'Yes, they shall be married. But when they *are* married, oh ho! let them look out!'

So the day of the wedding was fixed, and the Princess said to the Prince, 'At the wedding feast you may eat what you please, but you must not drink anything at all; for the witch will put a spell on both the water and the wine, and if you drink you will forget me.'

'How could I ever forget you?' said the Prince.

'Nevertheless, do not drink,' said the Princess.

A whole troop of witches came to the wedding feast. It was a hideous affair, and all the food was so highly seasoned that the Prince's throat was dry and burning. At last he could bear his thirst no longer, and he stretched out his hand for a cup of wine. But the Princess was keeping watch over him; she gave the Prince's arm a push with her elbow: all the wine was spilled over the tablecloth, and the cup rolled off the table and fell on the floor.

When the witch saw that she had been again foiled by the Princess, she flew once more into a terrible rage. She leaped up and laid about her among the plates and dishes, till the splinters flew about the room. The other witches howled with laughter, and joined in the fun, smashing everything they could lay hands on. But when the clamour was at its height, the Princess took the Prince by the hand, and whispered, 'Come!'

They ran up to the bridal chamber which had been got ready for them. And the Princess said, 'The witch had to keep her promise, and we are married. But it was sore against her will, and now she will seek to destroy us. We must escape while we may.'

From having lived so long with the witch, the Princess had learned some magic. Now she took two pieces of wood, spoke some whispered words to them, and laid them side by side in the bed.

'These will answer for us if the witch calls,' she said. 'Now take the flower pot from the ledge, and the bottle of water from the table, and help me down out of the window.'

The Prince picked up the flower pot and the water bottle, helped the Princess down out of the window, and scrambled out after her.

Then off they ran, hand in hand, through the dark night.

The nearest way to reach the Prince's home was across the sea. But they had no boat, so they had to run round the shore of a great bay. All night they were running. Meanwhile, at midnight, the witch went to the door of the bridal chamber, and called, 'Are you sleeping yet?'

And the two pieces of wood answered from the bed, 'No, we are waking.'

The witch went away. Before dawn she came again to the door of the bridal chamber, and called, 'Are you sleeping yet?'

And the two pieces of wood answered from the bed, 'We are waking still. But leave us now to sleep.'

The witch chuckled. 'Sleep soundly,' she muttered. 'You will not wake again in a hurry! For dawn brings a new day. Your wedding night will then be over. And what did I promise you? No more than that!'

She went to her window and watched impatiently for the rising of the new day. As soon as the rim of the sun appeared above the sea, she rushed to the bridal chamber again. But this time she did not stand at the door. She flung the door open, and bounded into the room.

'I have you now!' she screamed.

But what did she see? No Prince, no Princess: only two blocks of wood lying side by side in the bed.

'Ah, ah, ah!' she shrieked. She seized upon the blocks of wood and flung them to the floor so violently that they flew into hundreds of pieces. Then she rushed off after the runaways.

The Prince and Princess had run on through the night. They were still running now along the shore of the bay, with the first beams of the sun on their faces.

Said the Princess, 'Look round. Do you see anything behind us?'
Said the Prince, 'Yes, I see a dark cloud, far away.'
Said the Princess, 'Throw the flower pot over your head.'
The Prince threw the flower pot over his head, and a huge range

of hills rose up behind them. The witch came to the hills; she tried to climb them. But they were smooth and slippery as glass; every time she clambered up a little way, she slid down again. There was nothing for it but to run round the whole range, and that took her a very long time.

The Prince and Princess were still running along the shore of the bay. By and by the Princess said again, 'Look round. Do you see anything behind us?'

'Yes,' said the Prince, 'the big black cloud is there again.'

Said the Princess, 'Throw the bottle of water over your head.'

The Prince threw the bottle of water over his head, and a huge, turbulent lake spread out behind them. The witch came to the lake. It was so huge and so rough that she had to go all the way home again to fetch her kneading-trough before she could cross it.

By the time the witch had crossed the lake and was pelting on again, the Prince and Princess had rounded the bay and reached the castle which was the Prince's home. They climbed over the wall of the keep, and were just about to clamber into the castle through an open window, when the witch caught up with them.

'Ah! Ah! Ah! I have you now!' she screamed.

But the Princess turned and blew upon the witch. A great flock of white doves flew out of the Princess's mouth. They fluttered and flapped about the witch; she was completly hidden by their beating wings. And when the doves rose into the air and flew away, there was no witch. There was only a great grey stone standing outside the window.

The Prince led his Princess into his father's castle. 'I have come back to you,' he said to the King and Queen. 'And I have brought my bride with me.'

How they all rejoiced! The Prince's two elder brothers came and knelt at his feet and begged his forgiveness. 'You shall inherit the kingdom,' they said, 'and we will be for ever your faithful subjects.' And, in the course of time, when the old King died, that was what happened.

In the meantime, and ever afterwards, they lived in happiness.

RUTH MANNING-SANDERS

BABA YAGA*
AND THE LITTLE GIRL WITH
THE KIND HEART

Once upon a time there was a widowed old man who lived alone in a hut with his little daughter. Very merry they were together, and they used to smile at each other over a table just piled with bread and jam. Everything went well, until the old man took it into his head to marry again.

Yes, the old man became foolish in the years of his old age, and he took another wife. And so the poor little girl had a stepmother. And after that everything changed. There was no more bread and jam on the table, and no more playing bo-peep, first this side of the samovar and then that, as she sat with her father at tea. It was worse than that, for she never did sit at tea. The stepmother said that everything that went wrong was the little girl's fault.

*Baba Yaga is the traditional witch of Russian folklore.

And the old man believed his new wife, and so there were no more kind words for his little daughter. Day after day the stepmother used to say that the little girl was too naughty to sit at table. And then she would throw her a crust, and tell her to get out of the hut, and go and eat it somewhere else.

And the poor little girl used to go away by herself into the shed in the yard, and wet the dry crust with her tears, and eat it all alone. Ah me! she often wept for the old days, and she often wept at the thought of the days that were to come.

Mostly she wept because she was all alone, until one day she found a little friend in the shed. She was hunched up in a corner of the shed, eating her crust and crying bitterly, when she heard a little noise. It was like this: scratch, scratch. It was just that, a little grey mouse who lived in a hole.

Out he came, his little pointed nose and his long whiskers, his little round ears and his bright eyes. Out came his little humpy body and his long tail. And then he sat up on his hind-legs, and curled his tail twice round himself and looked at the little girl.

The little girl, who had a kind heart, forgot all her sorrows, and took a scrap of her crust and threw it to the little mouse. The mouseykin nibbled and nibbled, and there, it was gone, and he was looking for another. She gave him another bit, and presently that was gone, and another and another, until there was no crust left for the little girl. Well, she didn't mind that. You see, she was so happy seeing the little mouse nibbling and nibbling.

225

When the crust was done the mouseykin looks up at her with his little bright eyes, and 'Thank you,' he says, in a little squeaky voice. 'Thank you,' he says; 'you are a kind little girl, and I am only a mouse, and I've eaten all your crust. But there is one thing I can do for you, and that is to tell you to take care. The old woman in the hut (and that was the cruel stepmother) is own sister to Baba Yaga, the bony-legged, the witch. So if ever she sends you on a message to your aunt, you come and tell me. For Baba Yaga would eat you soon enough with her iron teeth if you did not know what to do.'

'Oh, thank you,' said the little girl; and just then she heard the stepmother calling to her to come in and clean up the tea things, and tidy the house, and brush out the floor, and clean everybody's boots.

So off she had to go.

When she went in she had a good look at her stepmother, and sure enough she had a long nose, and she was as bony as a fish with all the flesh picked off, and the little girl thought of Baba Yaga and shivered, though she did not feel so bad when she remembered the mouseykin out there in the shed in the yard.

The very next morning it happened. The old man went off to pay a visit to some friends of his in the next village. And as soon as the old man was out of sight the wicked stepmother called the little girl.

'You are to go today to your dear little aunt in the forest,' says she, 'and ask her for a needle and thread to mend a shirt.'

'But here is a needle and thread,' said the little girl.

'Hold your tongue,' says the stepmother, and she gnashes her teeth, and they make a noise like clattering tongs. 'Hold your tongue,' she says. 'Didn't I tell you you are to go today to your dear little aunt to ask for a needle and thread to mend a shirt?'

'How shall I find her?' says the little girl, nearly ready to cry, for she knew that her aunt was Baba Yaga, the bony-legged, the witch.

The stepmother took hold of the little girl's nose and pinched it.

'That is your nose,' she says. 'Can you feel it?'

'Yes,' says the poor little girl.

'You must go along the road into the forest till you come to a fallen tree; then you must turn left, and then follow your nose and you will find her,' says the stepmother. 'Now, be off with you, lazy one. Here is some food for you to eat by the way.' She gave the little girl a bundle wrapped up in a towel.

The little girl wanted to go into the shed to tell the mouseykin she was going to Baba Yaga, and to ask what she should do. But she looked back, and there was the stepmother at the door watching her. So she had to go straight on.

She walked along the road through the forest till she came to the fallen tree. Then she turned to the left. Her nose was still hurting where the stepmother had pinched it, so she knew she had to go straight ahead. She was just setting out when she heard a little noise under the fallen tree.

Scratch. Scratch.

And out jumped the little mouse, and sat up in the road in front of her.

'O mouseykin, mouseykin,' says the little girl, 'my stepmother has sent me to her sister. And that is Baba Yaga, the bony-legged, the witch, and I do not know what to do.'

'It will not be difficult,' says the little mouse, 'because of your kind heart. Take all the things you find in the road, and do with them what you like. Then you will escape from Baba Yaga, and everything will be well.'

'Are you hungry, mouseykin?' said the little girl.

'I could nibble, I think,' says the little mouse.

The little girl unfastened the towel, and there was nothing in it but stones. That was what the stepmother had given the little girl to eat by the way.

'Oh, I'm so sorry,' says the little girl. 'There's nothing for you to eat.'

'Isn't there?' said mouseykin, and as she looked at them the little girl saw the stones turn to bread and jam. The little girl sat down on the fallen tree, and the little mouse sat beside her, and they ate bread and jam until they were not hungry any more.

'Keep the towel,' says the little mouse; 'I think it will be useful. And remember what I said about the things you find on the way. And now good-bye,' says he.

'Good-bye,' says the little girl, and runs along.

As she was running along she found a nice new handkerchief lying in the road. She picked it up and took it with her. Then she found a little bottle of oil. She picked it up and took it with her. Then she found some scraps of meat.

'Perhaps I'd better take them too,' she said; and she took them.

Then she found a gay blue ribbon, and she took that. Then she found a little loaf of good bread, and she took that too.

'I dare say somebody will like it,' she said.

And then she came to the hut of Baba Yaga, the bony-legged, the witch. There was a high fence round it with big gates. When she pushed them open they squeaked miserably, as if it hurt them to move. The little girl was sorry for them.

'How lucky,' she says, 'that I picked up the bottle of oil.' And she poured the oil into the hinges of the gates.

Inside the railing was Baba Yaga's hut, and it stood on hen's legs and walked about the yard. And in the yard there was standing Baba Yaga's servant, and she was crying bitterly because of the tasks Baba Yaga set her to do. She was crying bitterly and wiping her eyes on her petticoat.

'How lucky,' says the little girl, 'that I picked up a handkerchief.' And she gave the handkerchief to Baba Yaga's servant, who wiped her eyes on it and smiled through her tears.

Close by the hut was a huge dog, very thin, gnawing a dry crust.

'How lucky,' says the little girl, 'that I picked up a loaf.' And she gave the loaf to the dog, and he gobbled it up and licked his lips.

The little girl went bravely up to the hut and knocked on the door.

'Come in,' says Baba Yaga.

The little girl went in, and there was Baba Yaga, the bony-legged, the witch, sitting weaving at a loom. In a corner of the hut was a thin black cat watching a mousehole.

'Good day to you, auntie,' says the little girl, trying not to tremble.

'Good day to you, niece,' says Baba Yaga.

'My stepmother has sent me to ask for a needle and thread to mend a shirt.'

'Very well,' says Baba Yaga, smiling, and showing her iron

teeth. 'You sit down here at the loom, and go on with my weaving, while I go and get you the needle and thread.'

The little girl sat down at the loom and began to weave.

Baba Yaga went out and called to her servant, 'Go, make the bath hot, and scrub my niece. Scrub her clean. I'll make a dainty meal of her.'

The servant came in for the jug. The little girl begged her, 'Be not too quick in making the fire, and carry the water in a sieve.' The servant smiled but said nothing, because she was afraid of Baba Yaga. But she took a very long time about getting the bath ready.

Baba Yaga came to the window and asked:

'Are you weaving, little niece? Are you weaving, my pretty?'

'I am weaving, auntie,' says the little girl.

When Baba Yaga went away from the window, the little girl spoke to the thin black cat who was watching the mousehole.

'What are you doing, thin black cat?'

'Watching for a mouse,' says the thin black cat. 'I haven't had any dinner for three days.'

'How lucky,' says the little girl, 'that I picked up the scraps of meat.' And she gave them to the thin black cat. The thin black cat gobbled them up, and said to the little girl:

'Little girl, do you want to get out of this?'

'Catkin dear,' says the little girl, 'I do want to get out of this, for Baba Yaga is going to eat me with her iron teeth.'

'Well,' says the cat, 'I will help you.'

Just then Baba Yaga came to the window.

'Are you weaving, little niece?' she asked. 'Are you weaving, my pretty?'

'I am weaving, auntie,' says the little girl, working away, while the loom went clickety clack, clickety clack.

Baba Yaga went away.

Says the thin black cat to the little girl: 'You have a comb in your hair, and you have a towel. Take them and run for it, while Baba Yaga is in the bath-house. When Baba Yaga chases after you, you must listen; and when she is close to you throw away the towel, and it will turn into a big, wide river. It will take her a little time to get over that. But when she does, you must listen; and as soon as she is close to you throw away the comb, and it will sprout up into such a forest that she will never get through it at all.'

'But she'll hear the loom stop,' says the little girl.

'I'll see to that,' says the thin black cat.

The cat took the little girl's place at the loom.

Clickety clack, clickety clack; the loom never stopped for a moment.

The little girl looked to see that Baba Yaga was in the bathhouse, and then she jumped down from the little hut on hen's legs, and ran to the gates as fast as her legs could flicker.

The big dog leapt up to tear her to pieces. Just as he was going to spring on her he saw who she was.

'Why, this is the little girl who gave me the loaf,' says he. 'A good journey to you, little girl,' and he lay down again with his head between his paws.

When she came to the gates they opened quietly, quietly, without making any noise at all, because of the oil she had poured into their hinges.

Outside the gates there was a little birch tree that beat her in the eyes so that she could not go by.

'How lucky,' says the little girl, 'that I picked up the ribbon.' And she tied up the birch tree with the pretty blue ribbon. And the birch tree was so pleased with the ribbon that it stood still, admiring itself, and let the little girl go by.

How she did run!

Meanwhile the thin black cat sat at the loom. Clickety clack, clickety clack, sang the loom; but you never saw such a tangle as the tangle made by the thin black cat.

And presently Baba Yaga came to the window.

'Are you weaving, little niece?' she asked. 'Are you weaving, my pretty?'

'I am weaving, auntie,' says the thin black cat, tangling and tangling, while the loom went clickety clack, clickety clack.

'That's not the voice of my little dinner,' says Baba Yaga, and she jumped into the hut, gnashing her iron teeth; and there was no little girl, but only the thin black cat, sitting at the loom, tangling and tangling the threads.

'Grr,' says Baba Yaga, and jumps for the cat, and begins banging it about. 'Why didn't you tear the little girl's eyes out?'

'In all the years I have served you,' says the cat, 'you have only given me one little bone; but the kind little girl gave me scraps of meat.'

Baba Yaga threw the cat into a corner, and went out into the yard.

'Why didn't you squeak when she opened you?' she asked the gates.

'Why didn't you tear her to pieces?' she asked the dog.

'Why didn't you beat her in the face, and not let her go by?' she asked the birch tree.

'Why were you so long in getting the bath ready? If you had

been quicker, she never would have got away,' said Baba Yaga to the servant.

And she rushed about the yard, beating them all, and scolding at the top of her voice.

'Ah!' said the gates, 'in all the years we have served you, you never eased us with water; but the kind little girl poured good oil into our hinges.'

'Ah!' said the dog, 'in all the years I've served you, you never threw me anything but burnt crusts; but the kind little girl gave me a good loaf.'

'Ah!' said the little birch tree, 'in all the years I've served you, you never tied me up, even with thread; but the kind little girl tied me up with a gay ribbon.'

'Ah!' said the servant, 'in all the years I've served you, you have never given me even a rag; but the kind little girl gave me a pretty handkerchief.'

Baba Yaga gnashed at them with her iron teeth. Then she jumped into the mortar and sat down. She drove it along with the pestle, and swept up her tracks with a besom, and flew off in pursuit of the little girl.

The little girl ran and ran. She put her ear to the ground and listened. Bang, bang, bangety bang! She could hear Baba Yaga beating the mortar with the pestle. Baba Yaga was quite close. There she was, beating with the pestle and sweeping with the besom, coming along the road.

As quickly as she could, the little girl took out the towel and threw it on the ground. And the towel grew bigger and bigger, and wetter and wetter, and there was a deep, broad river between Baba Yaga and the little girl.

The little girl turned and ran on. How she ran!

Baba Yaga came flying up in the mortar. But the mortar could not float in the river with Baba Yaga inside. She drove it in, but only got wet for her trouble. Tongs and pokers tumbling down a chimney are nothing to the noise she made as she gnashed her iron teeth. She turned home, and went flying back to the little hut on hen's legs. Then she got together all her cattle, and drove them to the river.

'Drink, drink!' she screamed at them; and the cattle drank up all the river to the last drop. And Baba Yaga, sitting in the mortar, drove it with the pestle, and swept up her tracks with the besom, and flew over the dry bed of the river in pursuit of the little girl.

The little girl put her ear to the ground and listened. Bang, bang, bangety bang! She could hear Baba Yaga beating the mortar with the pestle. Nearer and nearer came the noise, and there was Baba Yaga, beating with the pestle and sweeping with the besom, coming along the road close behind.

The little girl threw down the comb, and it grew bigger and bigger, and its teeth sprouted up into a thick forest, thicker than this forest where we live – so thick that not even Baba Yaga could force her way through. And Baba Yaga, gnashing her teeth and screaming with rage and disappointment, turned round and drove away home to her little hut on hen's legs.

233

The little girl ran on home. She was afraid to go in and see her stepmother, so she ran into the shed.

Scratch, scratch! Out came the little mouse.

'So you got away all right, my dear,' says the little mouse. 'Now run in. Don't be afraid. Your father is back, and you must tell him all about it.'

The little girl went into the house.

'Where have you been?' says her father, 'and why are you so out of breath?'

The stepmother turned yellow when she saw her, and her eyes glowed, and her teeth ground together until they broke.

But the little girl was not afraid, and she went to her father and climbed on his knee, and told him everything just as it had happened. And when the old man knew that the stepmother had sent his little daughter to be eaten by Baba Yaga, he was so angry that he drove her out of the hut, and ever afterwards lived alone with the little girl. Much better it was for both of them.

And the little mouse came and lived in the hut, and every day it used to sit up on the table and eat crumbs, and warm its paws on the little girl's glass of tea.

ARTHUR RANSOME

NUMBER TWELVE

Now this is a story of – *how many* people? . . . Well, this is the way *I* tell it.

One day, twelve people went fishing. All friends.

There was Mandy and Sandy, and Jimmy and Timmy. That makes four. There was Poll and Moll, and Ted and Ned. That makes eight. And Bobby and Robby is ten, and Lindy and Cindy is twelve . . . I *think*.

Hm, let me count them again. There was Lindy and Cindy and

234

Bobby and Robby. That makes four. And Poll and Moll and Ted and Ned. That makes eight. And Mandy and Timmy is ten, and Sandy and Jimmy is twelve ... I *think*.

Well anyway, they all went fishing. And the sun shone, and the water of the river winked and flashed in the sun. Oh it was a glorious day for fishing!

Mandy caught a piece of wood.

Timmy caught a sausage tin.

Jimmy caught a boot.

Moll caught Cindy.

Poll caught a tree.

Ned caught the other side.

Cindy caught a man in a boat.

Ted caught Sandy.

Bobby caught a fantastic hat.

Robby caught a pram wheel.

Lindy caught Sandy.

Sandy caught herself.

Everyone caught something, so they were all very happy.

They went home talking and shouting and singing.

'I caught a shark in the sea!'

'I caught a thousand sharks!'

'I caught a whale in the sea!'

'I caught a million whales!'

235

'An octopus strangled me!'

'I strangled an octopus!'

'I'm Superman!'

'I'm Superwoman!'

'I nearly drowned!'

'*I* nearly drowned!'

'*We* nearly drowned *millions* of times!'

'How do you know if someone has drowned?' said Lindy.

'You just count,' said Ned, 'and if you're one short, then you know someone has drowned.'

They thought they had better make sure that no one had drowned. So they all got in a long line, and Ned stood in front of them, and walked down the line, counting.

'Lindy is one, Cindy is two, Mandy is three, Sandy is four, Jimmy is five, Timmy is six, Robby is seven, Bobby is eight, Poll is nine, Moll is ten, Ted is eleven, and –'

There was no one else there! Only eleven people! But there were twelve when they went out to fish.

They began to run about, looking for Number Twelve.

'Where are you, Number Twelve? Where are you?' But nobody answered.

After a bit, Poll said, 'Make a line again. I'll count.'

So they made a line again, and Poll counted.

'Ned is one and Ted is two. Sandy is three and Mandy is four. Jimmy is five and Timmy is six. Lindy is seven and Cindy is eight. Bobby is nine and Robby is ten. Moll is eleven and . . .'

There was no one else to count. Number Twelve had gone!

They were really scared. They ran about looking for Number Twelve. Somebody else counted, and then somebody else. But whoever counted – and in the end, *everybody* had a turn at counting – it always came to the same, eleven. No Number Twelve. But they certainly had Number Twelve when they started out.

'Somebody's drowned!' they cried to each other. 'Somebody's drowned!'

And they all ran back to the river, and ran along the bank, looking and calling and looking and calling, and back the way they came, looking and calling again.

But not a sign did they see of Number Twelve. So they began to cry, all of them.

While they were sitting in a heap, crying, a man came along.

'Whatever's the matter?' he said.

'We've lost Number Twelve, poor Number Twelve! Number Twelve's drowned,' they wailed.

'Really? Why do you say that?'

'We counted. We all counted. But there's no Number Twelve any more.'

'Now calm down,' he said (for the noise was tremendous). 'Just count again for me.'

So Cindy counted. Everyone got in a line, and Cindy walked along it, counting. And it came to eleven.

'Yes, you're right,' said the man. 'I see. I shall have to think very hard about this. You're rather lucky I came along, you know. I *think*, I really do *think*, that I *might* be able to find Number Twelve for you. But what will you give me if I do?'

'Oh, everything we've got, everything!' And they turned out their pockets on the spot, and gave him everything that was in them. They did want to see dear Number Twelve again.

'Right!' said the man. 'Stand in a line, everyone.' And he took a stick, and counted each one of them, and tapped each head with the stick as he counted.

'There's one. There's two. There's three. There's four. There's five. There's six. There's seven. There's eight. There's nine. There's ten. There's eleven.'

And when he got to twelve – because of course there *were* twelve of them when they were all together in one line – he gave that one an extra hard bonk on the head.

'THERE'S NUMBER TWELVE!' he shouted.

They were so excited! So pleased! So thankful! They all rushed up to Number Twelve.

'You're back! How lovely to see you! We thought we'd never find you again! Let me give you a hug! Let me give you a kiss! Where have you *been*?' Then they all, all of them, shouted together, 'Yes, where have you *been*?'

And Number Twelve, who was still quite dazed from the thump, said, 'Me? I don't think I've been anywhere.'

237

'Don't be so silly. You *must* have been somewhere or we couldn't have found you,' they said. 'Wasn't it lucky we did?'

And they all went home, the twelve of them ... Or eleven ... Or was it thirteen? ... Hm.

> *Snip snap snover,*
> That *tale's over.*

LEILA BERG

DAD'S LORRY

Tom's Dad had a big lorry. It was green, with enormous wheels and fat black tyres. At the front of the lorry was the cab where Tom's Dad sat when he was driving. He was so high up that he could look down on the cars and small vans on the road.

The back of the lorry was open and it had a tail-board at the back which Tom's Dad let down every time he loaded or unloaded. Across the side of the lorry was written,

THOMAS BUCKTON. HAULAGE CONTRACTOR. PHONE 7618.

(because Tom's Dad was called Tom too!)

The lorry was kept in a yard at the side of Tom's house and he was very proud of it. He liked to watch his Dad drive in and park so cleverly in such a small space or reverse out of the narrow entrance without even bumping the gates.

'When I grow up I'm going to drive Dad's lorry,' he told his friends. 'I shall drive for miles and miles and miles.'

Tom's Dad often had phone calls.

'Can you take a load of bricks to the building site next week?' someone at the brick works would ask.

'I need a load of cement tomorrow,' said the builder.

'I've a rush order on. Can you pick up some kitchen cupboards from the factory?' asked the carpenter.

It seemed as if everyone depended on Dad and his lorry to move things from one place to another.

'Oh dear. Bother that phone,' grumbled Mum sometimes, just when she had Tom's baby sister to bath and feed. 'It is always ringing when I am busy.'

But Dad just laughed. 'It's a good thing so many people do need my lorry,' he said. 'That's how I earn enough money to look after us all.'

During the week Tom's Dad drove off every morning after break-fast in the lorry. But on Saturdays he stayed at home. Tom thought it was the best day of the week. He always helped Dad to clean the lorry. They swept out the back and Tom loved it when he was lifted up there. It was like being up in an aeroplane because he could see over the fences into other people's gardens and into the street where the traffic went by.

After they had washed the lorry with a hose-pipe it looked really smart.

Now every Saturday afternoon Dad put on his best trousers and sweater and Mum put the baby in the push chair and they all went off into town to do their shopping. They bought groceries, meat, vegetables, bread and fruit from the supermarket, and if they had enough money left they went to a café and had hamburgers or sausage and chips.

Saturday was a SUPER day.

But one weekend Tom was looking forward especially to their shopping trip. It was the first weekend in December and Mum had promised him they would go to town and do some Christmas shopping. Their next-door neighbour had offered to look after the baby. 'With all those parcels to carry and crowds of Christmas shoppers,' she said, 'it will be no place for a pram and a baby.'

'It is going to be a lovely Christmas this year,' said Mum, with a dreamy look in her eye. 'It will be baby's first Christmas and Grandma and Grandad are coming from London to stay with us.'

'And I'll buy their Christmas presents with my pocket money,' said Tom, 'and something for the baby.'

However, just when they were all sitting down to breakfast on Saturday morning the phone rang.

'Oh dear,' they heard Dad say. 'Yes. I'll be very pleased to help you out. Yes. Yes I'll be sure and have my lorry there by one o'clock.'

He put the phone down.

'Sorry. I shan't be able to come Christmas shopping with you after all,' he said. 'I've an emergency job on. A very special job.'

Mum looked surprised. She knew Dad never worked on Saturdays. It sounded as if someone was in trouble and needed the lorry.

Tom was upset. 'But it won't be the same without you, Dad,' he said crossly. He couldn't understand it at all. Dad didn't even look disappointed. In fact he was almost smiling, and Tom pushed his toast round and round the plate instead of eating it.

'Why did someone have to want Dad's lorry just on this particular Saturday?' he muttered to himself.

Dad drove off in his lorry at midday, waving and calling cheerily, 'Have a good time in town, Tom. There'll be lots of traffic about so look after Mum, won't you?'

Tom nodded gloomily and went off to fetch his pocket money ready to buy Christmas presents for Grandma and Grandad and his baby sister. But he didn't feel happy at all.

The shops were crowded with people all doing their Christmas shopping and Mum was very glad to have Tom's help to carry a big plastic bag. Crackers, decorations for the Christmas cake, nuts, mincemeat, a packet of stuffing for the turkey and silver balls to hang on the tree – they all went into the plastic bag.

Tom began to feel excited. Christmas would soon be here. He found a mobile to hang in his little sister's room with shiny silver stars on it. She would love that for a present, and a pen for Grandad and pink handkerchiefs for Grandma were just the very thing.

'Oh dear!' Mum looked very tired. 'That is as much shopping as I can do today.' She looked at her watch. 'Half past three. Time for a special treat now, Tom. Come along. We'll go over to Barclay's Store across the road. Father Christmas is due to arrive there at four o'clock.'

'Father Christmas!' cried Tom. 'You didn't tell me he was coming this afternoon.'

Mum laughed. 'He is coming to open the "Fairy Grotto" and I

wanted it to be a surprise for you,' she said. 'A nice ending to our Christmas shopping trip '

When they arrived outside the store there was no doubt something very exciting was about to happen. The police had stopped all the traffic and the pavements were crowded with people. But Tom and his Mum were lucky and found a place to stand just near the main entrance where Father Christmas would be entering the store.

'You stand here in front of us,' said a friendly old gentleman and his wife. 'You'll be able to see everything here,' and moving up close together they made a space for Tom and his Mum.

It was all very exciting. People were laughing and talking and the children were waving and jumping about and looking up the road to see if Father Christmas was coming. One kind policeman leaned over and put a tiny girl on his shoulders so she would be able to see better.

Tom did wish his Dad was there because he loved treats like this. The Christmas lights which decorated the shops and which were strung across the road shone and twinkled in the early winter dusk, and two big Christmas trees stood on either side of the entrance to the store. They were covered with tinsel and fairy lights. The street looked really wonderful.

One lady pointed to the big clock outside the store. 'Four o'clock. He'll soon be here,' she said. And just then, away in the distance Tom could hear music.

Rudolph the red-nosed reindeer,
Had a very shiny nose.

'He's coming Mum,' he cried. 'Father Christmas. Look!'

Everyone began to cheer and shout. The policemen were busy keeping the road clear for Father Christmas and along came a

lorry. It was strung all over with fairy lights and decorated with holly and branches of greenery. Two big flood lights on the sides lit up a tall red chimney, and there, standing beside the chimney, was jolly Father Christmas, with a flowing white beard, a red hood and cloak and carrying an enormous sack on his shoulder.

He was waving to the children as the music played,

Jingle bells. Jingle bells.

BUT TOM WAS NOT EVEN LOOKING AT FATHER CHRISTMAS.

'Mum,' he shouted above the noise. 'It's Dad's lorry ... and it's DAD DRIVING!'

By this time Mum was getting as excited as Tom. 'It is. It's Dad in his lorry and he is driving Father Christmas. So *that's* the special job he had to do, and he kept it a secret so we could have a wonderful surprise.'

Tom shouted to the old lady and gentleman who had helped them to find such a good place to stand.

'It's my Dad. Look, he's driving Father Christmas in his lorry.'

By this time the lorry had stopped – just outside the entrance to the store where Tom and his Mum were and Dad peeped out of the cab and winked at them.

'How's that then?' he called. 'You didn't expect to see *me* with Father Christmas, did you?'

Tom had never felt so proud in his life. Whatever would his friends at school say when he told them?

The manager of the store, looking very important, was waiting to help Father Christmas down from the back of the lorry.

'We are very pleased to welcome you to our store today, Father Christmas,' he said. 'Will you please come and open our Fairy Grotto?'

Father Christmas waved to everyone. 'Happy Christmas, children,' he called. 'Come and see me in the Fairy Grotto. I shall be waiting there with some presents for you all.'

Then ... just as he was about to go in through the big entrance door, he turned and hurried back to the lorry. Reaching up he shook Tom's Dad by the hand and said, so loudly that all the people standing round could hear, 'My lorry broke down this morning and I was very worried about how I should get here. I

don't know what I should have done without your lorry. Thank you for all your help.'

'It was a pleasure, Father Christmas,' said Tom's Dad, looking very pleased with himself indeed.

Mum and Tom decided they would come back another day when there were not so many people around and see the Fairy Grotto then. They were so excited that all they really wanted to do was hurry home as fast as they could and hear all that Dad had to tell them about his adventure.

They carried all the shopping home, talking all the time, and just had time to get the tea ready when they heard a 'Honk, honk,' and Dad came driving into the yard, lights blazing and pieces of holly still hanging on the sides of the lorry.

Tom and his Mum hugged Dad. 'Who's got an early Christmas present?' he said, laughing and handing Tom a parcel all wrapped up in Christmas paper. 'And one for the baby too,' he said. 'Father Christmas gave them to me.'

'This really must be the most exciting Saturday ever,' Tom thought when he opened his parcel and saw a police car – just what he wanted to add to his collection of small cars. The baby had a plastic ball with a bell inside which tinkled as it rolled along. She would love that.

It didn't seem possible that anything else exciting could happen to add to the wonderful day. But do you know, there was one more surprise before Tom went to bed!

Tom's Dad turned on the television to get the News and there – right on their own television set – was a picture of Tom's Dad driving his lorry down the main street of the town, lights blazing, music playing and Father Christmas waving to all the people. And when Tom looked very carefully, there standing by the main entrance to the store, he could just see Mum and HIMSELF, jumping up and down and pointing to Dad.

'Everyone seems to need Dad's lorry,' thought Tom, as he went off to sleep that night, 'even Father Christmas.'

PHYLLIS PEARCE

GOAT COMES TO THE CHRISTMAS PARTY

'Hurry! Hurry! Hurry!' said Gran'ma to Araminta. 'It's time to go to the party.'

'Hurry! Hurry! Hurry!' said Araminta to Jerome Anthony. 'It's time to go to the party.'

Christmas had come to the country, and there was going to be a party at the schoolhouse. Everybody was going, so Araminta and Jerome Anthony and Gran'ma had to hurry, else they'd be late and miss something.

'I wish Goat could go to the party,' said Araminta, shaking her head sadly. 'It seems a shame that Goat can't have any Christmas at all.'

'Goats don't have Christmas,' laughed Jerome Anthony. 'What ever would Goat do at a party?'

'Hurry! Hurry! Hurry!' said Gran'ma, looking at her watch.

So they put on their hats and coats and mittens. They tied their scarves under their chins, and they started out. It was cold, so

244

they walked fast and it didn't take any time to get to the schoolhouse. If they hadn't hurried they might have been late, for the party was just about to begin.

Everyone was there sitting on the school benches that were pushed back against the wall of the room. The beautiful paper chains and popcorn strings were there on the Christmas tree just where they belonged. And over in one corner was a table filled with cakes and lemonade and candy, for of course a party isn't a party without good things to eat.

'Where is Gran'pa?' asked Jerome Anthony, turning around in his seat. 'I'm afraid Gran'pa is going to be late.'

'Don't you worry,' said Gran'ma, smiling. 'Gran'pa will get here. He has a surprise for you.'

'Surprise!' whispered Araminta, very excited. Then her face was sad. 'Oh dear, I do wish Goat could be here for the surprise.'

Just then there was a little noise at the back door and everyone turned around. Well, you can't imagine what they saw! Santa

245

Claus! There he was in a red suit with white trimmings, and a red cap with a white tassel. And he had the reddest face you've ever seen, with a long white beard at the bottom of it.

'Oh! Oh!' yelled everybody.

'Shh-h-h!' whispered everybody.

For Santa Claus had somebody with him. This somebody was black and white with long floppy ears and a short stumpy tail. This somebody had long curly horns that looked very much like the branches of a tree. This somebody was hitched to a new green wagon. Yes, you've guessed it, Santa Claus had a reindeer with him, and this reindeer was pulling a wagon full of toys!

'Oh! Oh! Oh!' yelled everybody.

'Shh-h-h-h!' whispered everybody.

For Santa Claus and the reindeer were starting up the aisle towards the Christmas tree. They walked along steadily until they came to a bench where Jerome Anthony and Araminta were sitting, and then something very queer happened. That reindeer lifted his stumpy tail; he shook his head and his ears went flip-flop.

'GOAT!' yelled Araminta, jumping up and down. 'Goat has come to the party!'

We can't be sure whether it was Araminta yelling or the sight of the Christmas tree, but anyway, just then Santa Claus's

reindeer stopped acting like a reindeer and began acting like a goat instead. He butted Santa Claus out of the way. He broke loose from his wagon. He began *eating* the Christmas tree!

'Hey! Watch out!' said Santa Claus, falling against one of the benches. When he got up, that red face with the long white beard had fallen off.

'Gran'pa!' yelled Jerome Anthony. 'Gran'pa got here after all!'

We can't be sure whether it was Jerome Anthony yelling or the sight of that goat eating the Christmas tree, but anyway, Santa Claus stopped acting like Santa Claus and began to act like Gran'pa instead. He grabbed hold of Goat. But every time he tried to stop Goat eating the popcorn off the tree, Goat reared up and butted him against the benches again.

'Let me help,' said Araminta, jumping up. 'I can manage that Goat.'

She grabbed Goat by his bridle and started to lead him away before he ruined the tree. But just then Goat caught sight of the table full of cakes and candy and lemonade, and he pulled towards that.

Now when goats see something that they want to eat, you know how hard it is to keep them away from it. Araminta pulled and pulled, but it didn't do any good. Goat kept on getting closer and closer to that table of good food.

'Oh! Oh! Oh!' everybody yelled. They didn't want all their party refreshments to be eaten up.

'Shh-h-h!' everybody whispered, because it looked as if Jerome Anthony was going to do something about it.

He took two pieces of chocolate cake from the table and he held them out to Goat.

'Here, Goat!' he said.

Goat looked at the cake held out for him to eat; he reared up on his hind legs and shook those pretend reindeer horns off his short horns; then he ran after Jerome Anthony! Jerome Anthony ran down the middle of the schoolhouse, holding that cake so Goat could see it. Goat ran after him.

'Humph!' said Araminta, taking a deep breath, 'I shouldn't have worried about Goat not having any Christmas. He had more than anybody else.'

Gran'pa put on his red face with the white whiskers and there he was – a Santa Claus again. 'Merry Christmas!' he laughed as he began to give out the toys. 'Merry Christmas!' yelled everybody.

'Maa-aa! Maa-a-a!' came Goat's voice from the schoolhouse yard.

But nobody opened the door to let him in.

EVA KNOX EVANS

COLD FEET

Once upon a time, there were a King and Queen. Most of the time, they were very happy. The only trouble was that the King was terribly untidy – he would keep leaving his clothes all over the palace.

'If you leave ANY more clothes lying around,' said the Queen one morning, as she picked up a jumper, some hats and a coat off the bedroom floor, 'or lose your socks again – I'll – I'll – I won't make any more special fruit cake for tea!' And she stormed out.

'Oh dear,' said the King to himself, 'I'd better not tell her I've lost my crown and my socks. I couldn't go without my fruit cake. I wonder where the crown can be?'

And he sat down on his throne, to have a think.

'Ow!' The King leapt up again – and looked at his throne. There was his crown.

'Well, at least I've found *that*!' He put the crown on his head, and sat back on the throne. 'Now where have I left my socks?'

He thought and thought. It was no good. He couldn't even think where he'd left one sock.

He hunted all round the royal bedroom – under the bed, inside

the chest, on top of the wardrobe, even all through his dirty clothes. Not one sock to be found.

'Dear oh dear!' said the King. 'I dare not tell the Queen I've lost them. I shall have to think of a reason for not wearing them, that's all.'

Then he had an idea. 'I know! I'll issue a proclamation – that's what kings do when they're in a spot of trouble.'

Next day, all over the palace there were large notices, proclaiming: 'NO SOCKS TO BE WORN IN THIS PALACE FOR A WEEK. SIGNED – THE KING.'

People were rather surprised, but if the King told them to take off their socks, then take them off they must. So, for a week, everyone in the palace, and everyone who came to the palace, went barefoot.

At the end of the week, the King, very pleased with his idea, was getting ready to write out a new proclamation to carry on for another week, when the Queen came in looking tearful over a large bundle of assorted socks.

'Something the matter, dear?' asked the King, as he signed his name with a flourish.

'It's all these socks,' said the Queen, shaking her head. 'Everybody who's come to visit the palace this week – the milkman, the postman, the baker, the King of Belgravia and his son – they've all had to take their socks off, and leave them in a pile on the doorstep. But the socks always get mixed up, and they all look alike – nobody can find their own! So they keep going home barefoot.'

'Never mind, my dear,' said the King, 'at least the sock-maker in town will have a lot of work making new socks for everyone ... Now I'll just go and get this new proclamation printed ...'

But at that moment, there was a knock at the palace door.

'I'll get it,' said the Queen. 'I expect it's the postman.'

She came back in a few moments with a letter and a large parcel. 'They're for you,' she said handing them to the King.

'I'll leave the parcel till last,' he said, opening the letter. 'Well, well, well! What a surprise! It's from Fred Bonker – Maker of Best Quality Socks!'

'Is he pleased with the work he's been getting?' asked the Queen.

'Well, he says: "Your Majesty, I have been making socks night and day for the last week and I am VERY TIRED. Please will you cancel your proclamation, and let everyone keep their socks on again, because I need a rest." Signed, "Fred Bonker, Sock Maker." '

'Poor man,' said the Queen. 'You will cancel the proclamation, won't you?'

'No, no!' said the King hurriedly. 'I couldn't possibly.' And he quickly opened the parcel. He couldn't believe his eyes. It was a box full of socks – different colours, different patterns, some short and some long.

'By jove!' said the King. 'These are rather nice – much nicer than any of the ones I lost – I mean, than any of the ones I'm not wearing at the moment.'

'They're from Fred Bonker,' said the Queen, reading the note which was inside. 'He hopes you'll like them so much, you'll want to keep them on your feet and cancel the proclamation.'

'Splendid!' said the King, beaming from ear to ear. 'I'll wear this pair today, and that pair tomorrow ...'

'But what about the proclamation?'

'Oh, cancel the proclamation!' said the King.

'Hurray!' said the Queen. 'I'll make some fruit cake for tea to celebrate.' And she rushed off to the kitchen.

The King tried on a pair of his new socks. 'Wonderful!' he exclaimed, wiggling his toes. 'It's going to take me a very long time to lose all these!' And he tore up his proclamation and went off to the kitchen to wait for the fruit cake.

SUSAN EAMES

THE CLOWN PRINCE

Once there was a Prince who was very unhappy; nothing ever made him laugh or smile. No matter how many clowns or minstrels the King brought to the palace, the Prince just sat sadly sighing.

They tried everything to brighten him up: circuses from far-off places, acrobats, parties and dances, but the Prince's face remained sad and glum. The King and the court all loved the Prince, and as he became more unhappy, so did they.

The people of the country also grew sad when they heard how unhappy their Prince was. Soon the whole country was very quiet and sad. No one sang or danced, and the children forgot how to play.

When the Prince saw he was making everyone unhappy, he decided to go away, so one day he rode off. Across the land,

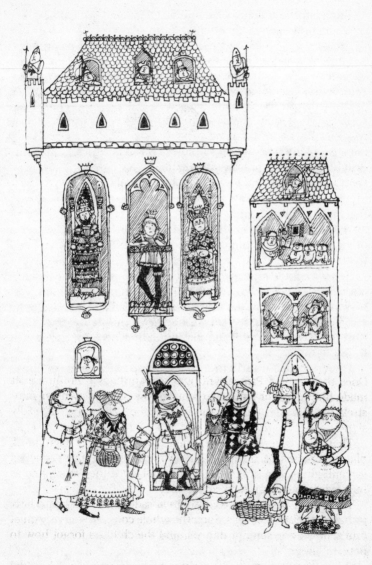

253

through cities and villages he travelled, looking for happiness, but he found only sadness in the land.

Finally he came to a dark forest. 'This place looks as unhappy as I am,' he thought as he rode through it. Soon he came upon a very old man sitting by a statue of a girl. The old man told the Prince that the statue was really his daughter, who had long ago been turned into stone by a wicked witch and could only come alive again when everyone in the land smiled and was happy.

When the Prince saw how beautiful the stone girl was his heart sank. 'Everyone is unhappy in the land,' he sighed, 'and it is all because of me. How can people find happiness?'

'That is no secret,' said the old man. 'To be happy yourself you must make others happy.'

The Prince had never thought of this because he had expected other people to make him happy, so he decided to try it, there and then.

He took off his princely robes and tried to make the careworn old man smile. The Prince looked so odd, tumbling around with his long, sad face that the old man soon smiled and laughed as he had not done for many years. Glancing at the statue, the Prince saw tiny cracks around the girl's mouth where the stone was trying to smile.

The Prince felt a thrill in his heart. 'I see how to make others happy,' he said. 'I will go through the land until all the people smile, but I shall never be happy until your daughter is real again, because I love her.'

The Prince went off, telling the old man he would return when he had broken the spell. On his journey he charmed the animals of the forest with his antics, and sang such tunes that long after he had gone the animals were still singing them and playing in the sun.

The Prince went into villages full of sad people; with his tricks and antics and his long, sad face, he looked so strange that soon everyone was laughing at him, and when they had remembered how to laugh, the Prince played such games and sung such wonderful songs that the people became happy again and laughed whenever they thought of him.

The Prince loved to see the people happy, but he did not feel the same thrill as when the statue had tried to smile.

As he went through the country his fame spread. Whole towns came to see him and went away singing and dancing. He wore strange clothes and taught others how to clown and jest, but no one could look as funny as the Prince with his long, sad face.

So the country became the happiest place in the world. When everyone was happy and smiling the Clown Prince thought, 'Now the statue will be real.'

He went back to the forest and found the old man still sitting by the statue.

'Why is she still stone?' asked the Prince.

The old man shook his head and said, 'There must be one person in the land who is still unhappy.'

The Prince went searching for the unhappy person. He travelled far and wide, but found only happiness; then he received a summons to the palace, to make the King laugh.

When he arrived he realized it was the King who was keeping the spell from being broken, because he was sad. Yet no amount of the clown's antics could cheer him up.

'Why are you so sad, King?' he asked.

'Because my son the unhappy Prince has never returned,' the King told the clown. Then the Clown Prince took off his hood and the make-up from his face, and showed the King who he really was; that made the King very happy. So the Prince went back again to the forest. He found the old man, and the statue. But the beautiful girl was still locked in stone.

'Why is she still a statue?' the Prince cried to the old man. 'I've made everyone in the kingdom smile.'

'There must still be one who isn't smiling,' the old man said.

The Prince wandered through the forest. 'Who can he be?' he thought, and sat by a lake to think. The Prince then saw his own reflection in the water: his solemn, sad face stared at him.

'It's me,' he cried. 'I am the only one who has never smiled, because I couldn't be happy until the spell was broken.'

So the Prince laughed at himself and broke the spell. Rushing back, he found the statue cracking and becoming a real girl.

The Prince took her and her father home. The King married them and they lived in the happiest land in the world.

If ever anyone was sad, the Prince would put on his clown's clothes and his long face, and soon had them laughing again. So he became known as the Clown Prince.

MALCOLM CARRICK

ELEPHANT BIG AND ELEPHANT LITTLE

Elephant Big was always boasting.

'I'm bigger and better than you,' he told Elephant Little. 'I can run faster, and shoot water higher out of my trunk, and eat more, and . . .'

'No, you can't!' said Elephant Little.

Elephant Big was surprised. Elephant Big was *always* right. Then he curled up his trunk and laughed and laughed.

'What's more, I'll show you,' said Elephant Little. 'Let's have a running race, and a shooting-water-out-of-our-trunks race, and an eating race. We'll soon see who wins.'

'I shall, of course,' boasted Elephant Big. 'Lion shall be judge.'

'The running race first!' Lion said. 'Run two miles there and two miles back. One of you runs in the field, the other one runs in the forest. Elephant Big shall choose.'

Elephant Big thought and thought, and Elephant Little pretended to talk to himself: 'I hope he chooses to run in the field, because *I* want to run in the forest.'

When Elephant Big heard this, he thought: 'If Elephant Little wants very much to run in the forest, that means the forest is best.' Aloud he said: 'I choose the forest.'

'Very well,' said Lion. 'One, two, three, go!'

Elephant Little had short legs, but they ran very fast on the springy smooth grass of the field. Elephant Big had long, strong legs, but they could not carry him quickly along through the forest. Broken branches lay in his way; thorns tore at him; tangled grass caught at his feet. By the time he stumbled, tired and panting, back to the winning post, Elephant Little had run his four miles, and was standing talking to Lion.

'What ages you've been!' said Elephant Little. 'We thought you were lost.'

'Elephant Little wins,' said Lion.

Elephant Little smiled to himself.

'But I'll win the next race,' said Elephant Big. 'I can shoot water much higher than you can.'

'All right!' said Lion. 'One of you fills his trunk from the river, the other fills his trunk from the lake. Elephant Big shall choose.'

Elephant Big thought and thought, and Elephant Little pretended to talk to himself: 'I hope he chooses the river, because I want to fill my trunk from the lake.'

When Elephant Big heard this, he thought: 'If Elephant Little wants very much to fill his trunk from the lake, that means the lake is best.' Aloud he said: 'I choose the lake.'

'Very well!' said Lion. 'One, two, three, go!'

Elephant Little ran to the river and filled his trunk with clear, sparkling water. His trunk was small, but he spouted the water as high as a tree.

Elephant Big ran to the lake, and filled his long, strong trunk with water. But the lake water was heavy with mud, and full of slippery, tickly fishes. When Elephant Big spouted it out, it rose only as high as a middle-sized thorn bush. He lifted his trunk and tried harder than ever. A cold little fish slipped down his throat, and Elephant Big spluttered and choked.

'Elephant Little wins,' said Lion.

Elephant Little smiled to himself.

When Elephant Big stopped coughing, he said: 'But I'll win the next race, see if I don't. I can eat much more than you can.'

'Very well!' said Lion. 'Eat where you like and how you like.'

Elephant Big thought and thought, and Elephant Little pretended to talk to himself: 'I must eat and eat as fast as I can, and I mustn't stop; not for a minute.'

Elephant Big thought to himself: 'Then I must do exactly the same. I must eat and eat as fast as I can, and I mustn't stop; not for a minute.'

'Are you ready?' asked Lion. 'One, two, three, go!'

Elephant Big bit and swallowed, and bit and swallowed, as fast as he could, without stopping. Before very long, he began to feel full up inside.

Elephant Little bit and swallowed, and bit and swallowed. Then

he stopped eating and ran round a thorn bush three times. He felt perfectly well inside.

Elephant Big went on biting and swallowing, biting and swallowing, without stopping. He began to feel very, very funny inside.

Elephant Little bit and swallowed, and bit and swallowed. Then again he stopped eating, and ran round a thorn bush six times. He felt perfectly well inside.

Elephant Big bit and swallowed, and bit and swallowed, as fast as he could, without stopping once, until he felt so dreadfully ill inside that he had to sit down.

Elephant Little had just finished running around a thorn bush nine times, and he still felt perfectly well inside. When he saw Elephant Big on the ground, holding his tummy and groaning horribly, Elephant Little smiled to himself.

'Oh, I do like eating, don't you?' he said. 'I've only just started. I could eat and eat and eat and eat.'

'Oh, oh, oh!' groaned Elephant Big.

'Why, what's the matter?' asked Elephant Little. 'You look queer. Sort of green! When are you going to start eating again?'

'Not a single leaf more!' groaned Elephant Big. 'Not a blade of grass, not a twig can I eat!'

'Elephant Little wins,' said Lion.

Elephant Big felt too ill to speak.

After that day, if Elephant Big began to boast, Elephant Little smiled, and said: 'Shall we have a running race? Shall we spout water? Or shall we just eat and eat and eat?'

Then Elephant Big would remember. Before very long, he was one of the nicest, most friendly elephants ever to take a mud bath.

ANITA HEWETT

ALPHA BETA
AND GRANDMA DELTA

Do you want to know what made big, handsome Alpha Beta, dog-with-a-bark-that-could-be-heard-in-the-next-street, angrier than anything?

Grandma Delta, old Grandma Delta cat, with twenty-three children and one hundred and twenty-one grandchildren, could leap up and over the garden fence, could leap any fence she met and *go wherever she liked*. Alpha Beta walked around the garden. Fence at the end, fence at each side, house and gate to the front, lawn in the middle, with one tree. He knew it all. There was

no way out for a dog. Same grass, same plants and same tree, every day.

Alpha Beta looked up at Grandma Delta lying relaxed along the branch of a tree. He growled. Grandma Delta flicked her tail. 'How dare that cat sit in the tree?' thought Alpha Beta. There was no chance of reaching her. And she looked comfortable.

Grandma Delta was bored with the tree. She sprang down, ran along the path, leapt on to the top of the fence, balanced – then with one long leap she reached the upstairs window-sill at the side of the house. The window-sill was warm in the sun. Grandma Delta curled up and went to sleep.

Alpha Beta growled with rage. How dare that cat! He ran around the garden and back. Round the tree. *Bark! Bark!* He ran the other way round the tree. What was the use? Alpha Beta lay down, not looking at Grandma Delta, and pretended to sleep. Grandma Delta had not moved. High up on the window-sill she could see about three gardens at once, if she wanted to.

Alpha Beta sighed. What was on the other side of the fence? He could not see through the fence, nor over it. He could only hear noises, and smell the smells. Alpha Beta dozed in the sun.

A sudden click woke him. Grandma Delta had padded past without him noticing and leapt up the fence. She paused, and was gone.

Alpha Beta put his nose in the air and howled with despair.

Something touched him on the paw. Alpha Beta looked through his howls and saw the most beautiful Fairy Dog.

'Oh, Alpha Beta,' said the Fairy Dog. 'I have come to grant you your wish.'

'Let me do what that cat can do,' breathed Alpha Beta.

'I will grant you your wish,' said the Fairy Dog. 'But you can only un-wish it three times.'

And she was gone.

Alpha Beta stood still. Thank goodness the Fairy Dog had not changed him into a cat! That would be terrible. But could he really do what a cat can do? Did he dare?

Alpha Beta looked up at the tree. He rushed at the trunk and threw his paws at it. A miracle! They held to the bark. He clambered up – up – to the branch where Grandma Delta always sat. It worked.

He felt dizzy with joy. Then he looked down. No, don't do that. Alpha Beta lay along the branch of the tree. The branch moved with the wind. Alpha Beta clung on tighter. The branch swayed, the light jigged between the leaves, and the ground looked a long way down. 'I'm doing it, I'm doing it,' chanted Alpha Beta to himself. 'Just let Grandma Delta come back and she will see that I am here instead of her.'

He held on a little tighter. 'But I think that is probably enough for the first day and I'll get down now.'

How? Suddenly Alpha Beta could not remember how Grandma Delta got down out of the tree. Front first? Not possible! Jump? It was too far. He edged himself along the branch towards the trunk. Perhaps the back legs first? But he didn't feel like letting go. The branch seemed very narrow and thin. 'Oh, help!' cried Alpha Beta. 'I wish I was back on the ground.'

And he was.

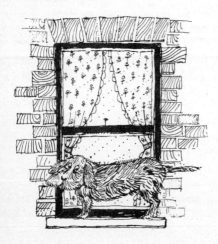

That was much better. Good old ground. It did not sway about. 'Just lack of practice,' said Alpha Beta to himself. 'That is the only problem, but I don't think I will go back up into the tree at the moment. I know,' thought Alpha Beta, 'the window-sill! That can't move. It will be much better. I should have tried it first.'

As soon as he got up on the window-sill Alpha

Beta knew it was a mistake. The sill was far too narrow. It was terrible. 'Help!' called Alpha Beta, forgetting everything except how frightened he was. 'Get me *down*.'

And he was.

'Never, never, never again,' said Alpha Beta.

But how silly he was being. The really important thing was the fence. Now he could get out. At long last he, Alpha Beta dog, could get over the fence and see what lay beyond.

Alpha Beta stood back. Then he ran a few steps forwards, leapt, clung briefly half-way up the fence – another leap up – balance on the top – and he was over.

The first thing Alpha Beta noticed was another fence. It looked like the one he had just come over. In fact everything looked rather the same. He was in another garden. There was a fence at the bottom, a fence at each side, grass, a tree. Alpha Beta was just going to inspect the bottom of the garden when there was a most awful noise.

'There's a dog! A dog in the garden! That dog from next door has got into our garden. Get him out!'

The shouts came louder, closer. Things were being thrown at him.

'Oh, get me out of here!' cried Alpha Beta. 'I wish I was back home.' And he was.

Alpha Beta dog lay on the grass. He supposed the Fairy Dog meant it when she said, 'You can only un-wish your wish three times.' But he did not mind. He did not want to even try and see if he could do what a cat can do. Grandma Delta could dance on the roof for all he cared. She could swing upside down from the top of the tree, or walk backwards along every fence. He was staying where he was.

But Grandma Delta had not seen one of the awful things that had happened. And that was all that mattered.

MEREDITH HOOPER

DID I EVER TELL YOU ABOUT THE TIME WHEN I BIT A BOY CALLED DANNY PAYNE?

When I first started school we all sat at little desks. There were six children in each row. We kept our books and crayons in cardboard boxes which the teacher called Tidy Boxes.

One of the children who sat by my desk was a boy called Danny Payne. He stole the best crayons from our Tidy Boxes. He made dirty smudges on our work. The worst thing Danny Payne did was to pinch us.

Whenever Miss White, the teacher, wasn't looking he pinched us on our arms, our hands, our chests and our backs. When Miss White was looking Danny Payne would stick his horrible dirty hands under the desk and pinch us on our thighs.

In the playground Danny Payne was just as bad. He kicked and punched and tripped children over. We all tried to keep away from him.

Nobody wanted to sit next to him in the classroom. We all waited until Danny Payne sat down. Then we would rush to sit as far away from him as possible. The last two children shoved their chairs as far away as possible.

Even when we sat as far away as possible from Danny Payne, his arms would reach under the desk to pinch us. He was an expert pincher. In the playground we would show each other the little black bruises Danny Payne had made.

One day Danny Payne kept pinching my friend Margaret. Her legs were covered in black bruises. Margaret went to the front of the classroom to tell Miss White. But Miss White didn't listen. She told Margaret to sit down and get on with her writing.

Graham, Susie and I put our heads together. We decided we

would all go to tell Miss White about Danny Payne and about the bruises all over Margaret's legs.

Miss White looked up from her desk. She said a really stupid thing. 'If it's a tale, go and tie a knot in it.' Of course she meant 'tale' like a story, not 'tail' like an animal has. So we all sat down again. You can't tie knots in stories.

Then Danny Payne started pinching us for trying to tell tales about him. He pinched me on my arm. He pinched Graham on his neck and he pinched Susie a mighty pinch right on her bottom.

Danny Payne was impossible! I grabbed his arm and buried my teeth into the back of his wrist. I kept on biting until he screamed.

Miss White had to take notice this time. Danny Payne threw himself down on the floor. He screamed and screamed and screamed. When Miss White picked him up he sobbed and sobbed. 'Poor Danny,' said Miss White.

Miss White took us both to the headmistress, Mrs Musselbrook. 'Poor Danny,' said Mrs Musselbrook when she saw my teethmarks in his wrist, 'you're a wicked, cruel girl,' she squawked.

Then she gave me a horrible punishment. Mrs Musselbrook went into the cloakroom and came back with a bar of soggy soap. She made me bite the soap to teach me not to bite poor little boys like Danny Payne.

This story has a happy ending. I was nearly sick from biting the

bar of soap, but Danny Payne never pinched anyone again, even though he still punched and kicked and tripped over children in the playground. I was glad I bit him.

IRIS GRENDER

MY NAUGHTY LITTLE SISTER AT THE PARTY

You wouldn't think there could be another child as naughty as my naughty little sister, would you? But there was. There was a thoroughly bad boy who was my naughty little sister's best boy-friend, and this boy's name was Harry.

This Bad Harry and my naughty little sister used to play together quite a lot in Harry's garden, or in our garden, and got up to dreadful mischief between them, picking all the baby gooseberries,

268

and the green blackcurrants, and throwing sand on the flower-beds, and digging up the runner-bean seeds, and all the naughty sorts of things you never, never do in the garden.

Now, one day this Bad Harry's birthday was near, and Bad Harry's mother said he could have a birthday-party and invite lots of children to tea. So Bad Harry came round to our house with a pretty card in an envelope for my naughty little sister, and this card was an invitation asking my naughty little sister to come to the birthday-party.

Bad Harry told my naughty little sister that there would be a lovely tea with jellies and sandwiches and birthday-cake, and my naughty little sister said, 'Jolly good.'

And every time she thought about the party she said, 'Nice tea and birthday-cake.' Wasn't she greedy? And when the party day came she didn't make any fuss when my mother dressed her in her new green party-dress, and her green party-shoes and her green hair-ribbon, and she didn't fidget and she didn't wriggle her head about when she was having her hair combed, she kept as still as still, because she was so pleased to think about the party, and when my mother said, 'Now, what must you say at the party?' my naughty little sister said, 'I must say, "nice tea".'

But my mother said, 'No, no, that would be a greedy thing to say. You must say "please" and "thank you" like a good polite child at tea-time, and say, "thank you very much for having me," when the party is over.'

And my naughty little sister said, 'All right, Mother, I promise.'

So my mother took my naughty little sister to the party, and what do you think the silly little girl did as soon as she got there? She went up to Bad Harry's mother and said very quickly, 'Please-and-thank-you, and-thank-you-very-much for-having-me,' all at once – just like that, before she forgot to be polite, and then she said, 'Now, may I have a lovely tea?'

Wasn't that rude and greedy? Bad Harry's mother said, 'I'm afraid you will have to wait until all the other children are here, but Harry shall show you the tea-table if you like.'

Bad Harry looked very smart in a blue party-suit, with white socks and shoes and a *real man's haircut*, and he said, 'Come on, I'll show you.'

So they went into the tea-room and there was the birthday-tea spread out on the table. Bad Harry's mother had made red jellies and yellow jellies, and blancmanges and biscuits and sandwiches and cakes-with-cherries-on, and a big birthday-cake with white icing on it and candles and 'Happy Birthday Harry' written on it.

My naughty little sister's eyes grew bigger and bigger, and Bad Harry said, 'There's something else in the larder. It's going to be a surprise treat, but you shall see it because you are my best girl-friend.'

So Bad Harry took my naughty little sister out into the kitchen and they took chairs and climbed up to the larder shelf – which is a dangerous thing to do, and it would have been their own faults if they had fallen down – and Bad Harry showed my naughty little sister a lovely spongy trifle, covered with creamy stuff and with silver balls and jelly-sweets on the top. And my naughty little sister stared more than ever because she liked spongy trifle better than jellies or blancmanges or biscuits or sandwiches or cakes-with-cherries-on, or even birthday-cake, so she said, 'For me.'

Bad Harry said, 'For me too,' because he liked spongy trifle best as well.

Then Bad Harry's mother called to them and said, 'Come along, the other children are arriving.'

So they went to say, 'How do you do?' to the other children, and then Bad Harry's mother said, 'I think we will have a few games now before tea – just until everyone has arrived.'

All the other children stood in a ring and Bad Harry's mother said, 'Ring O'Roses first, I think.' And all the nice party children said, 'Oh, we'd like that.'

But my naughty little sister said, 'No Ring O'Roses – nasty Ring O'Roses' – just like that, because she didn't like Ring O'Roses very much, and Bad Harry said, 'Silly game.' So Bad Harry and my naughty little sister stood and watched the others. The other children sang beautifully too. They sang:

> Ring o'ring o'roses,
> A pocket full of posies –
> A-tishoo, a-tishoo, we all fall down.

And they all fell down and laughed, but Harry and my naughty little sister didn't laugh. They got tired of watching and they went for a little walk. Do you know where they went to?

Yes. To the larder. To take another look at the spongy trifle. They climbed up on to the chairs to look at it really properly. It was very pretty.

'Ring o'ring o'roses' sang the good party children.

'Nice jelly-sweets,' said my naughty little sister. 'Nice silver balls,' and she looked at that terribly Bad Harry and he looked at her.

'Take one,' said that naughty boy, and my naughty little sister did take one, she took a red jelly-sweet from the top of the trifle;

and then Bad Harry took a green jelly-sweet; and then my naughty little sister took a yellow jelly-sweet and a silver ball, and then Bad Harry took three jelly-sweets, red, green and yellow, and six silver balls. One, two, three, four, five, six, and put them all in his mouth at once.

Now some of the creamy stuff had come off upon Bad Harry's fingers and he liked it very much, so he put his finger into the creamy stuff on the trifle, and took some of it off and ate it, and my naughty little sister ate some too. I'm sorry to have to tell you this, because I feel so ashamed of them, and expect you feel ashamed of them too.

I hope you aren't too shocked to hear any more? Because, do you know, those two bad children forgot all about the party and the nice children all singing 'Ring O'Roses'. They took a spoon each and scraped off the creamy stuff and ate it, and then they began to eat the nice spongy inside.

Bad Harry said, 'Now we've made the trifle look so untidy, no one else will want any, so we may as well eat it all up.' So they dug away into the spongy inside of the trifle and found lots of nice fruity bits inside. It was a very big trifle, but those greedy children ate and ate.

Then, just as they had nearly finished the whole big trifle, the 'Ring O'Roses'-ing stopped, and Bad Harry's mother called, 'Where are you two? We are ready for tea.'

Then my naughty little sister was very frightened. Because she knew she had been very naughty, and she looked at Bad Harry and *he* knew *he* had been very naughty, and they both felt terrible. Bad Harry had a creamy mess of trifle all over his face, and even in his real man's haircut, and my naughty little sister had made her new green party-dress all trifly – you know how it happens if you eat too quickly and greedily.

'It's tea-time,' said Bad Harry, and he looked at my naughty little sister, and my naughty little sister thought of the jellies and the cakes and the sandwiches, and all the other things, and she felt very full of trifle, and she said, 'Don't want any.'

And do you know what she did? Just as Bad Harry's mother came into the kitchen, my naughty little sister slipped out of the door, and ran and ran all the way home. It was a good thing our home was only down the street and no roads to cross, or I don't know what would have happened to her.

Bad Harry's mother was so cross when she saw the trifle, that she sent Bad Harry straight to bed, and he had to stay there and hear all the nice children enjoying themselves. I don't know what happened to him in the night, but I know that my naughty little sister wasn't at all a well girl, from having eaten so much trifle – and I also know that she doesn't like spongy trifle any more.

DOROTHY EDWARDS

PAUL'S TALE

' "Ho! Ho!" said the King, slapping his fat thighs. "Methinks this youth shows promise." But at that moment the Court Magician stepped forward ... What is the matter, Paul? Don't you like this story?'

'Yes, I like it.'

'Then lie quiet, dear, and listen.'

'It was just a sort of stalk of a feather pushing itself up through the eiderdown.'

'Well, don't help it, dear, it's destructive. Where were we?' Aunt Isobel's short-sighted eyes searched down the page of the book; she looked comfortable and pink, rocking there in the firelight '... stepped forward ... You see the Court Magician knew that the witch had taken the magic music-box, and that Colin ... Paul, you aren't listening!'

'Yes, I am. I can hear.'

'Of course you can't hear – right under the bedclothes. What are you doing, dear?'

'I'm seeing what a hot-water bottle feels like.'

'Don't you know what a hot-water bottle feels like?'

'I know what it feels like to me. I don't know what it feels like to itself.'

'Well, shall I go on or not?'

273

'Yes, go on,' said Paul. He emerged from the bedclothes, his hair ruffled.

Aunt Isobel looked at him curiously. He was her godson; he had a bad feverish cold; his mother had gone to London. 'Does it tire you, dear, to be read to?' she said at last.

'No. But I like told stories better than read stories.'

Aunt Isobel got up and put some more coal on the fire. Then she looked at the clock. She sighed. 'Well, dear,' she said brightly, as she sat down once more on the rocking-chair. 'What sort of story would you like?' She unfolded her knitting.

'I'd like a real story.'

'How do you mean, dear?' Aunt Isobel began to cast on. The cord of her pince-nez, anchored to her bosom, rose and fell in gentle undulations.

Paul flung round on his back, staring at the ceiling. 'You know,' he said, 'quite real – so you know it must have happened.'

'Shall I tell you about Grace Darling?'

'No, tell me about a little man.'

'What sort of a little man?'

'A little man just as high – ' Paul's eyes searched the room '– as that candlestick on the mantelshelf, but without the candle.'

'But that's a very small candlestick. It's only about six inches.'

'Well, about that big.'

Aunt Isobel began knitting a few stitches. She was disappointed about the fairy story. She had been reading with so much expression, making a deep voice for the king, and a wicked oily voice for the Court Magician, and a fine cheerful boyish voice for Colin, the swineherd. A little man – what could she say about a little man? 'Ah!' she exclaimed suddenly, and laid down her knitting, smiling at Paul. 'Little men ... of course ...

'Well,' said Aunt Isobel, drawing in her breath. 'Once upon a time, there was a little, tiny man, and he was no bigger than that candlestick – there on the mantelshelf.'

Paul settled down, his cheek on his crook'd arm, his eyes on Aunt Isobel's face. The firelight flickered softly on the walls and ceiling.

'He was the sweetest little man you ever saw, and he wore a

little red jerkin and a dear little cap made out of a foxglove. His
boots ...'

'He didn't have any,' said Paul.

Aunt Isobel looked startled. 'Yes,' she exclaimed. 'He had boots –
little, pointed –'

'He didn't have any clothes,' contradicted Paul. 'He was bare.'

Aunt Isobel looked perturbed. 'But he would have been cold,'
she pointed out.

'He had thick skin,' explained Paul. 'Like a twig.'

'Like a twig?'

'Yes. You know that sort of wrinkly, nubbly skin on a twig.'

Aunt Isobel knitted in silence for a second or two. She didn't
like the little naked man nearly as much as the little clothed man:
she was trying to get used to him. After a while she went on.

'He lived in a bluebell wood, among the roots of a dear old tree.

He had a dear little house, tunnelled out of the soft, loamy earth, with a bright blue front door.'

'Why didn't he live in it?' asked Paul.

'He did live in it, dear,' explained Aunt Isobel patiently.

'I thought he lived in the potting-shed.'

'In the potting-shed?'

'Well, perhaps he had two houses. Some people do. I wish I'd seen the one with the blue front door.'

'Did you see the one in the potting-shed?' asked Aunt Isobel, after a moment's silence.

'Not inside. Right inside. I'm too big. I just sort of saw into it with a flashlight.'

'And what was it like?' asked Aunt Isobel, in spite of herself.

'Well, it was clean – in a potting-shed sort of way. He'd made the furniture himself. The floor was just earth, but he'd trodden it down so that it was hard. It took him years.'

'Well, dear, you seem to know more about this little man than I do.'

Paul snuggled his head more comfortably against his elbow. He half closed his eyes. 'Go on,' he said dreamily.

Aunt Isobel glanced at him hesitatingly. How beautiful he looked, she thought, lying there in the firelight with one curled hand lying lightly on the counterpane. 'Well,' she went on, 'this little man had a little pipe made of straw.' She paused, rather pleased with this idea. 'A little hollow straw, through which he played jiggity little tunes. And to which he danced.' She hesitated. 'Among the bluebells,' she added. Really this was quite a pretty story. She knitted hard for a few seconds, breathing heavily, before the next bit would come. 'Now,' she continued brightly, in a changed, higher and more conversational voice, 'up in the tree, there lived a fairy.'

'In the tree?' asked Paul, incredulously.

'Yes,' said Aunt Isobel, 'in the tree.'

Paul raised his head. 'Do you know that for certain?'

'Well, Paul,' began Aunt Isobel. Then she added playfully, 'Well, I suppose I do.'

'Go on,' said Paul.

'Well, this fairy . . .'

Paul raised his head again. 'Couldn't you go on about the little man?'

'But, dear, we've done the little man – how he lived in the roots, and played a pipe, and all that.'

'You didn't say about his hands and feet.'

'His hands and feet!'

'How sort of big his hands and feet looked, and how he could scuttle along. Like a rat,' Paul added.

'Like a rat!' exclaimed Aunt Isobel.

'And his voice. You didn't say anything about his voice.'

'What sort of a voice,' Aunt Isobel looked almost scared, 'did he have?'

'A croaky sort of voice. Like a frog. And he says "Will 'ee" and "Do 'ee".'

'Willy and Dooey . . .' repeated Aunt Isobel.

'Instead of "Will you" and "Do you". You know.'

'Has he – got a Sussex accent?'

'Sort of. He isn't used to talking. He is the last one. He's been all alone, for years and years.'

'Did he –' Aunt Isobel swallowed. 'Did he tell you that?'

'Yes. He had an aunt and she died about fifteen years ago. But even when she was alive, he never spoke to her.'

'Why?' asked Aunt Isobel.

'He didn't like her,' said Paul.

There was silence. Paul stared dreamily into the fire. Aunt Isobel sat as if turned to stone, her hands idle in her lap. After a while, she cleared her throat.

'When did you first see this little man, Paul?'

'Oh, ages and ages ago. When did you?'

'I – Where did you find him?'

'Under the chicken house.'

'Did you – did you speak to him?'

Paul made a little snort. 'No. I just popped a tin over him.'

'You caught him!'

'Yes. There was an old, rusty chicken-food tin near. I just popped it over him.' Paul laughed. 'He scrabbled away inside. Then I popped an old kitchen plate that was there on top of the tin.'

Aunt Isobel sat staring at Paul. 'What – what did you do with him then?'

'I put him in a cake-tin, and made holes in the lid. I gave him a bit of bread and milk.'

'Didn't he – say anything?'

'Well, he was sort of croaking.'

'And then?'

'Well, I sort of forgot I had him.'

'You forgot!'

'I went fishing, you see. Then it was bedtime. And next day I didn't remember him. Then when I went to look for him, he was lying curled up at the bottom of the tin. He'd gone all soft. He just hung over my finger. All soft.'

Aunt Isobel's eyes protruded dully.

'What did you do then?'

'I gave him some cherry cordial in a fountain-pen filler.'

'That revived him?'

'Yes, that's when he began to talk. And he told me all about his aunt and everything. I harnessed him up, then, with a bit of string.'

'Oh, Paul,' exclaimed Aunt Isobel, 'how cruel.'

'Well, he'd have got away. It didn't hurt him. Then I tamed him.'

'How did you tame him?'

'Oh, how do you tame anything? With food mostly. Chips of gelatine and raw sago he liked best. Cheese, he liked. I'd take him out and let him go down rabbit holes and things, on the string. Then he would come back and tell me what was going on. I put him down all kinds of holes in trees and things.'

'Whatever for?'

'Just to know what was going on. I have all kinds of uses for him.'

'Why,' stammered Aunt Isobel, half rising from her chair, 'you haven't still got him, have you?'

Paul sat up on his elbows. 'Yes. I've got him. I'm going to keep him till I go to school. I'll need him at school like anything.'

'But it isn't – You wouldn't be allowed –' Aunt Isobel suddenly became extremely grave. 'Where is he now?'

'In the cake-tin.'

'Where is the cake-tin?'

'Over there. In the toy cupboard.'

Aunt Isobel looked fearfully across the shadowed room. She stood up. 'I am going to put the light on, and I shall take that cake-tin out into the garden.'

'It's raining,' Paul reminded her.

'I can't help that,' said Aunt Isobel. 'It is wrong and wicked to keep a little thing like that shut up in a cake-tin. I shall take it out on to the back porch and open the lid.'

'He can hear you,' said Paul.

'I don't care if he can hear me.' Aunt Isobel walked towards the door. 'I'm thinking of his good, as much as of anyone else's.' She switched on the light. 'Now, which was the cupboard?'

'That one, near the fireplace.'

The door was ajar. Timidly Aunt Isobel pulled it open with one finger. There stood the cake-tin amid a medley of torn cardboard, playing cards, pieces of jig-saw puzzle and an open paint box.

'What a mess, Paul!'

Nervously Aunt Isobel stared at the cake-tin and, falsely innocent, the British Royal Family stared back at her, painted brightly

on a background of Allied flags. The holes in the lid were narrow and wedge-shaped, made, no doubt, by the big blade of the best cutting-out scissors. Aunt Isobel drew in her breath sharply. 'If you weren't ill, I'd make you do this. I'd make you carry the tin out and watch you open the lid –' She hesitated as if unnerved by the stillness of the rain-darkened room and the sinister quiet within the cake-tin.

Then, bravely, she put out a hand. Paul watched her, absorbed, as she stretched forward the other one and, very gingerly, picked up the cake-tin. His eyes were dark and deep. He saw the lid was not quite on. He saw the corner, in contact with that ample bosom, rise. He saw the sharp edge catch the cord of Aunt Isobel's pince-nez and, fearing for her rimless glasses, he sat up in bed.

Aunt Isobel felt the tension, the pressure of the pince-nez on the bridge of her nose. A pull it was, a little steady pull as if a small dark claw, as wrinkled as a twig, had caught the hanging cord ...

'Look out!' cried Paul.

Loudly she shrieked and dropped the box. It bounced away and then lay still, gaping emptily on its side. In the horrid hush, they heard the measured planking of the lid as it trundled off beneath the bed.

Paul broke the silence with a croupy cough.

'Did you see him?' he asked, hoarse but interested.

'No,' stammered Aunt Isobel, almost with a sob. 'I didn't. I didn't see him.'

'But you nearly did.'

Aunt Isobel sat down limply in the upholstered chair. Her hand wavered vaguely round her brow and her cheeks looked white and pendulous, as if deflated. 'Yes,' she

muttered, shivering slightly, 'Heaven help me – I nearly did.'

Paul gazed at her a moment longer. 'That's what I mean,' he said.

'What?' asked Aunt Isobel weakly, but as if she did not really care.

Paul lay down again. Gently, sleepily, he pressed his face into the pillow.

'About stories. Being real . . .'

MARY NORTON

THE STORIES CLASSIFIED

STORIES FOR THE VERY YOUNG

CREATURES

PALACES

PEOPLE

COUNTRY

MAGICAL

AT HOME

DRAGONS AND MONSTERS

CHRISTMAS

SCARY STORIES

SCHOOL STORIES

FUNNY STORIES

INDEX OF TITLES

Index of Authors

INDEX OF AUTHORS

ACKNOWLEDGEMENTS

The editor and publishers gratefully acknowledge permission to reproduce copyright material in this book:

'The Old Woman Who Lived in a Cola Can' by Bernard Ashley, reprinted by permission of the author; 'Benny Tries the Magic' from *A Box for Benny* by Leila Berg, reprinted by permission of the author and of Hodder and Stoughton Ltd; 'Number Twelve' from *Tales for Telling* by Leila Berg, reprinted by permission of the author and Methuen Children's Books; 'Mother Mouse' by Paul Biegel, reprinted by permission of the author and of Patricia Crampton, the translator; 'The Limp Little Donkey' by Judy Bond, reprinted by permission of the author; 'The City Boy and the Country Horse' by Charlotte Brookman, reprinted by permission of the author; 'Goose Feathers' by Emma L. Brock, reprinted by permission of Thomas Crowell Inc.; 'The Clown Prince' by Malcolm Carrick, reprinted by permission of the author; 'The Awful Baby', and 'Sally's Christmas Eve' by Jean Chapman, reprinted by permission of the author; 'The Baddest Witch in the World' from *Ramona the Pest* by Beverly Cleary, reprinted by permission of Hamish Hamilton Ltd; 'Tailor Green and the Grand Collection' by Meryl Doney, reprinted by permission of the author; 'Cold Feet' by Susan Eames, reprinted by permission of the author; 'My Naughty Little Sister at the Party' from *My Naughty Little Sister* by Dorothy Edwards, reprinted by permission of Methuen Children's Books; 'Louise' by René Goscinny, reprinted by permission of Les Editions Denoël Gonthier Planete and of Blackie and Son Ltd; 'Did I ever tell you about the time when I bit a boy called Danny Payne?' by Iris Grender, reprinted by permission of Century Hutchinson Ltd; 'The Harum-Scarum Boys' by Kathleen Hersom from *The Second Read-to-Me Story Book*, reprinted by permission of Methuen Children's Books; 'Elephant Big and Elephant Little' from *The Anita Hewett Animal Story Book* by Anita Hewett, reprinted by permission of The Bodley Head; 'Alpha Beta and Grandma Delta' by Meredith Hooper, reprinted by permission of the author; 'Naughty Little Thursday' by Barbara Ireson, reprinted by permission of the author; 'The Kidnapping of Lord Cockerel' by Jean Kenward, reprinted by permission of the author; 'Irritating Irma' and 'J. Roodie' copyright © Robin Klein, 1984, reprinted by permission of Curtis Brown Ltd, London; 'Silly Billy' by Gladys Lees, reprinted by permission of the author; 'The Fish Angel' from *The Witch of Fourth Street and Other Stories* by Myron Levy, reprinted by permission of Harper & Row; 'The Flying Rabbit' by Kenneth McLeish, reprinted by permission of the author; 'Trouble in the Supermarket' from *Nonstop Nonsense* by Margaret Mahy, reprinted by permission of the author and J. M. Dent & Sons Ltd; 'The Blackstairs Mountain' and 'The White Dove' from *A Book of Witches* by Ruth Manning-Sanders, reprinted by permission of Methuen Children's Books; 'The One that Got Away' by Jan Mark, reprinted by permission of the author; 'A Tree for Miss Jenny Miller' by Lilian Moore, reprinted by permission of the author; 'Paul's Tale' by Mary Norton, reprinted by permission of the author; 'The Terribly Plain Princess' from *The Terribly Plain Princess* by Pamela Oldfield, reprinted by permission of Hodder & Stoughton Ltd; 'Dad's Lorry' by Phyllis Pearce, reprinted by permission of the author; 'Horrible Harry' by Diana Petersen, reprinted by permission of the author; 'The Runaway Shoes' by Edna Preston, reprinted by permission of Parents Magazine Press; 'Baba Yaga and the Little Girl with the Kind Heart' from *Old Peter's Russian Tales* by Arthur Ransome, reprinted by permission of the Arthur Ransome Estate and Jonathan Cape Ltd; 'The Discontented King' by James Reeves, reprinted by permission of the James Reeves Estate; 'The Christmas Roast' by Margret Rettich from *The Silver Touch and Other Family Christmas Stories*, reprinted by permission of William Morrow & Co. Inc.; 'Young Hedgehog Has a Good Friend' by Vera Rushbrooke, reprinted by permission of the author; 'Elizabeth' from *The Silent Playmate* by Liesel Moak Skorpen, reprinted by permission of World's Work Ltd; 'Thomas and the Monster' by Marjorie

Stannard, reprinted by permission of the author; 'The Practical Princess' from *The Practical Princess and Other Liberating Fairy Tales* by Jay Williams. Copyright © 1978 by Jay Williams. Reprinted by permission of Scholastic Inc.; 'The Fig-Tree Beggar and the Wilful Princess' retold by Diana Wolkstein in *Lazy Stories*, reprinted by permission of Clarion Books.

Every effort has been made to trace copyright holders, but in a few cases this has proved impossible. The editor and publishers apologize for these unwilling cases of copyright transgression and would like to hear from any copyright holders not acknowledged.

THE WILD RIDE AND OTHER SCOTTISH STORIES
ed. Gordon Jarvie

A spirited anthology of modern short stories from Scotland, ranging widely through ghost stories, adventure, drama and humour.

GUARDIAN ANGELS
ed. Stephanie Nettell

An anthology of stories specially written to commemorate the prestigious Guardian Children's Book Award's 20th anniversary.

TALES FOR THE TELLING
Edna O'Brien

A collection of heroic Irish tales to stir the imagination.

THE GNOME FACTORY AND OTHER STORIES
James Reeves

The imagination of James Reeves's stories and the wit of Edward Ardizzone's drawings combine to make this an enchanting collection.

GHOSTS AT LARGE
Susan Price

Beautiful retellings of traditional ghostly folk tales, legends and fairy tales.

CHOCOLATE PORRIDGE AND OTHER STORIES
Margaret Mahy

Here is a collection of twenty-one stories, full of fun and surprises, that will captivate every reader.

DON'T COUNT YOUR CHICKENS
AND OTHER FABULOUS FABLES
Mark Cohen

Always fun, and often funny, this is a wide-ranging collection of fables from all around the world, for both children and adults to enjoy.

NEVER MEDDLE WITH MAGIC
AND OTHER STORIES
Chosen by Barbara Ireson

Fifty fabulous stories full of magic and mischief, fun and fantasy. Stories short and long, funny stories, sad stories, 'once upon a time' stories, fairy tales and ghost stories, birthday stories and Christmas stories – there's something for everyone in this enticing collection.

A THIEF IN THE VILLAGE
AND OTHER STORIES
James Berry

Wonderfully atmospheric, rich and moving, these very contemporary narratives bring alive the setting and culture highly relevant to today's multi-ethnic Britain.

THE PUFFIN BOOK OF PET STORIES
Sara and Stephen Corrin

This wonderful collection of pet stories features pets for every possible taste and will appeal to anyone who ever wanted to have a pet of their own.

MR CORBETT'S GHOST AND OTHER STORIES
Leon Garfield

Three chilling stories for those who like a shivery thrill.

SWEETS FROM A STRANGER
AND OTHER STRANGE TALES
Nicholas Fisk

A collection of imaginative and macabre science fiction stories.

MESSAGES
Marjorie Darke

A collection of shivery tales which you'd better not read alone . . .

IMAGINE THAT!
Sara and Stephen Corrin

Fifteen fantastic tales, mostly traditional, from all over the world, including China and Asia.

THE GHOSTS COMPANION
ed. Peter Haining

Thrilling ghost stories by well-known writers – and the incidents which first gave them the idea.